RAGE

BENSON SECURITY 3

JANET ELIZABETH HENDERSON

Copyright © 2019 by Janet Elizabeth Henderson

All rights reserved.

No part of this book may be reproduced in any form or by any electronic or mechanical means, including information storage and retrieval systems, without written permission from the author, except for the use of brief quotations in a book review.

ISBN: 9781074440886

Cover design by Janet Elizabeth Henderson

Editing by Liz Dempsey

❀ Created with Vellum

ACKNOWLEDGMENTS

I want to thank the Blatchford Group. An amazing company in the UK that works with amputees to make sure they get the best prosthetic limbs to suit their needs. Their Blatchford's Linx system was awarded the Gold Medal Award in Rehabilitation and Assistive Technology Products category, and the Best in Show Award at the Medical Design Excellence Awards in 2017. Not only that, they took time out of their important work to answer the many questions of a completely ignorant writer. And for that I am eternally grateful. Their information was invaluable to me in writing this book. Any mistakes, or liberties I've taken for the purposes of the story, are completely on me and not due to anything they told me. If you're interested in their work, you can find them here at blatchford.co.uk

ALSO BY JANET ELIZABETH HENDERSON

Lingerie Wars
Goody Two Shoes
Magenta Mine
Calamity Jena
Bad Boy
Here Comes The Rainne Again
Caught

Reckless
Relentless
Rage
Ransom

Can't Tie Me Down
Can't Stop The Feeling
Can't Buy Me Love

CHAPTER 1

FOUR MONTHS EARLIER, LONDON

Callum McKay sat on the floor with his back to the wall and looked at the wreckage he'd wrought. His TV was shattered, spreading glass across the room. His books were in shreds. There was a KA-BAR knife sticking out of what was left of his leather sofa. And every piece of wooden furniture in the room had been smashed.

Feeling no regret, Callum clasped the neck of a bottle of Glenfiddich. He brought the whisky to his lips and drained what was left. One swallow emptied it, and he tossed it into the mess in front of him, watching with some satisfaction as the bottle smashed.

He was done.

Totally.

Absolutely.

Fucking done.

He wanted to burn the place down. Let the flames take it all. And him along with it. But he'd need to find his damn legs if he wanted to get up and finish the job. His blurred gaze caught sight of the prosthetics he'd thrown across the room after he'd collapsed against the wall.

A dry laugh erupted from him. He'd have to drag himself over broken glass to get to his legs—if he wanted to get up. Which he didn't. Because he was done.

Totally fucking done.

He was done pretending he was useful. Done pretending he was normal. Done acting as though his life was the same as it'd been before his legs were blown off in Afghanistan. Before he'd become half a man. Before he'd become a liability to his team.

His head landed back against the wall, with a thump he barely registered, and his eyes focused on the ceiling. The pristine white ceiling. It was perfect. And that was wrong. He didn't want anything around him that was perfect. Unblemished. Unspoiled. Whole. He should have trashed the ceiling along with the rest of the room.

A loud thumping disturbed his thoughts, and it took a minute to register it was coming from the door and not from inside his head. Callum ignored it, as he'd been ignoring every well-meaning visit from his team for days. No. Not *his* team. Not anymore. Because he was done.

The banging got louder, and Callum frowned in the direction of his front door. They'd get fed up and leave. They always did. No one wanted to risk facing his wrath. That thought caused another mirthless laugh. He was a bloody cliché. A grumpy-arsed Scot who terrified women and children. He reached for his whisky before remembering he'd finished the bottle.

"Open the door." The shouted order snagged Callum's dulled attention. He almost jumped to comply—before he remembered that he'd need his legs to do it, and that Lake Benson was no longer his SAS commander, or his business partner. Because Callum was done—he just hadn't told anyone yet.

"Callum," Lake snapped. "Open the door."

"Go to hell," Callum roared.

He heard muttered voices and scraping. Bloody stubborn Englishman was picking the lock. Callum didn't care enough to try to stop him. Anyway, what could he do? Nothing. That was what. Because he was fucking useless.

The heavy door swung open and the room was suddenly flooded with light. Callum squinted against the glare. He could just make out the solid shape of Lake filling the doorway.

"It's time for this to end," Lake said.

"Get the hell out of here and leave me be," Callum said.

"Too many people have been leaving you be." Lake strode into the room, glass crunching underfoot. He crouched beside Callum, his forearms resting on his knees. "You're a mess."

That struck Callum as particularly funny, and he started giggling like a schoolgirl.

"And drunk," Lake said in disgust.

Callum's attention was snagged by the sound of movement in the debris that used to be his home. The women. Elle and Julia. Members of his team who smothered him with their pity.

"I've got his legs." Elle waved something in the air, but all Callum could see was her shocking blue hair.

"Don't touch those! Get out of my house!" Callum reached for something to throw at her.

A strong hand stayed him.

"Give the legs to me," Lake said.

They were ignoring him. As if he wasn't a person anymore. For a minute, he forgot where he was exactly. In his head, he was back in hospital being poked and prodded by the team fitting his prosthetics. A team that was more interested in the tech than the person who'd wear it. He'd felt invisible. A project. A pathetic problem to be fixed.

"Get out, get out, get out, get out!" His rage made him dizzy, and he tilted, slipping down the wall.

Strong hands pulled him upright again.

"Leave us," Lake ordered, and the room cleared.

Of course they listened to Lake. He was whole. He wasn't an invalid. He wasn't half a man. Callum stared down at what remained of his legs, hating the sight of them. Hating that there was nothing but stumps where his knees used to be. Hating that he couldn't see his feet, but could damn well feel them. That constant searing pain that never went away. That constant reminder of who he used to be.

"You get out too," Callum spat.

"You might be able to intimidate the civilians with your bad attitude, but all it does is piss me off. Now put these legs on so I can help you get out of this mess." Lake cocked an eyebrow. "Unless you want me to carry you."

"Fuck off."

Lake stared at him in reply.

The stubborn bastard would sit there until he got his way. With a snarl, Callum snatched a prosthetic from his *former* friend and tried to line the cup up with his stump. It wasn't possible. Everything kept moving. His stump kept slipping out. His hands wouldn't work properly. And his rage grew again. He lifted the leg, ready to throw it across the room. Lake snatched it from his grasp.

"You're too drunk to do it." He looked behind him and yelled, "Joe. Get in here."

"No!" Callum shoved Lake. He rocked back but didn't topple.

Callum wished he'd remembered to bring a weapon home. He could have shot the bastard.

"And we're all grateful you aren't armed," Lake said as he stood, making Callum realise he'd been thinking out loud.

"I should shoot you, you interfering bastard. You dragged me into this mess. This *team*. You should have known I'd be no use to them. I'm a fucking liability. I almost got them killed in Peru."

"Almost doesn't count." Joe stood beside Lake. "You're talking garbage. Which figures, because that's what you smell like."

"Fuck off," Callum said again, and the American paid about as much attention to him as Lake had.

"It's going to take the two of us to get him into bed," Lake said to Joe. "He might need to be restrained. He's a violent dickhead when he's drunk."

"Get out!" Callum roared. "I don't want you here. I don't want your help. Or your pity. Leave me alone."

The two men ignored him as, between them, they scooped Callum up. They carried him in a sitting position, their arms under his thighs and around his shoulders—as if he were a child or an old invalid.

Hell no.

Callum swung his fist and managed to connect with Lake's jaw.

"You hit me again and I'm going to hit back. You got it?"

Like Callum gave a crap. "Bring it on, English."

An arm clamped across his forearms, holding them in place.

"Hurry," Joe said. "He's strong."

Callum shouted obscenities until he felt the veins in his neck bulge and his head grew light. Suddenly, the cool cotton sheets of his bed were at his back.

"Get his legs," Lake said. "Put them on the chest. I'll put the wheelchair beside his bed. He's less likely to throw the wheelchair at us. If he wants his legs, he can roll over and get them."

Callum grabbed his alarm clock and lobbed it at Lake's

head. His aim was off and the clock hit the wall and shattered.

Cold eyes caught his. "I *will* knock you out." Lake's voice was icy calm.

"Bring it on." Callum made a fist and waved it. "I can take you. You arrogant English bastard."

Joe shook his head and left the room. Callum could hear voices coming from the other room. All of his damn team were there. All of them. He'd locked himself away from them. And they were there anyway.

"I don't want them in here," he told Lake.

"What the hell *do* you want?" Lake folded his arms and glared down at Callum.

The question knocked the wind out of him. He sagged back into his bed and stared at the ceiling. But he didn't see it. He saw his past. The part of his life that was never coming back. The part where he knew who he was and what he could do. The part where he'd felt invincible.

"I want out," he said. "I'm done being part of Benson Security. I want to go home."

To Scotland. To die.

Because.

He.

Was.

Done.

CHAPTER 2

PRESENT DAY, THE VILLAGE OF ARNESS, SCOTLAND

Isobel Sinclair should have contacted the authorities the first time she saw the boat sneaking into the cove. But she didn't. She should have called when there was a storm during the boat's third visit, and the crew lost some of their baggage on the rocky path up to Arness. But she didn't. Instead, she'd gathered their lost cargo, called it her own and sold it to help pay off her ex-husband's debts.

Which made her a thief, just like him.

And her thieving was the reason she still didn't call in the authorities the time the boat turned up in the dead of night, and there was shouting in the darkness. Or the time she'd seen evidence that someone had dragged something heavy over the beach.

No, she'd never called the authorities. Not once. Even though she knew the boat brought nothing but trouble each time it snuck into shore.

But she should have called, because the boat had come back.

And this time, they'd left a body behind.

"What are we going to do with him?" Isobel's youngest sister, Mairi, stared down at the man.

The dead man.

"I suppose we could bury him," Agnes, one of their middle sisters, said.

"We can't bury him here." Isobel gestured to the rock-strewn beach. "Even if we do manage to dig a hole, the tide will unearth him in a day or two."

Mairi looked up at the steep, rocky path behind them, the only route down from the bluff where the tiny town of Arness sat. "We'll never get him back up there. He looks like he weighs a ton."

"And he's wet." Agnes nodded. "That makes you heavier."

"Aye," Mairi said. "Water retention."

Isobel and Agnes stared at their sister.

"What?" Mairi said.

With shakes of their heads, Agnes and Isobel turned their attention back to the body.

"How do you think he died?" Agnes said.

"I suppose we should look him over and see if we can tell." Isobel didn't like the thought of touching the man, let alone examining him for clues as to his cause of death.

"Does it really matter how he died?" Mairi said. "I mean, it isn't going to change the fact that he's dead. Or that he was left here by the boat people."

"The boat people?" Agnes looked towards heaven and seemed to be counting to ten. Again.

Mairi shrugged, her long red hair shifting with the movement. "What else are we to call them? And he *was* left here by the boat crew. Isobel saw them while she was spying."

Isobel adopted her patented "haughty eldest sister" look—it helped take her mind off her shaking hands and the fear gnawing at her stomach. "I wasn't spying. I was looking out of my window and saw them carry him off the boat and dump him here."

"You were looking out of your window with the aid of binoculars," Mairi reminded her.

She had a point. "What I don't get is if these *boat people* are so keen on going unnoticed, then why are they dumping bodies on the beach?" Isobel said. "I mean, they only come in the dead of night. And we know they're up to no good."

"Smuggling," Mairi said with a decisive nod.

Agnes walked around the prone man and looked back out at the choppy waters behind them, then up at the hill leading to town. "Do you think they meant for him to be swept out to sea? Or to be eaten by the crabs?"

"If they wanted him to be swept out to sea, why not dump him out there in the first place?" Isobel said. "And I don't think half a dozen crabs are enough to eat a full-grown body. At least not fast enough to get rid of the evidence."

"Even then," Mairi said, "there would still be the bones."

They nodded in agreement, and Isobel couldn't help but notice that her sisters were struggling to hide their shaking hands, just as she was doing.

"I think we should call the police." Seeing as Agnes wasn't the most law-abiding member of the family, it said a lot that she was the one to suggest calling them in.

"I can't." Isobel tugged at the sleeves of her oversized purple cardigan and wrapped her arms around herself. "They'll find out that I sold the stuff I found, rather than reporting it to them in the first place."

"I told you, you shouldn't have gone to the pawn shop in Campbeltown," Mairi said. "Too many people know us there."

"I wanted rid of it fast."

Plus, she'd needed the money to pay off the loan shark who was hounding her over her ex-husband's debt. Seeing as the man couldn't find Robert, he'd decided to make Isobel pay in his stead, with cash or her body, making it clear that her family would suffer if she didn't comply. That was the reason Isobel's moral judgment had been silenced when she'd found the stolen goods on the path—the thought of handing over her body to pay her ex-husband's debt made her ill. But she'd do it if she had to. She'd do just about anything to make sure her kids were safe.

"Enough of this." Agnes crouched down and turned the body over.

He flopped onto his back, and the cause of death was instantly clear. There was a wide, gaping slit where his throat used to be.

"I think I'm going to be sick." Mairi covered her mouth and turned her back on the body, making gagging sounds as she did so.

"Don't," Agnes ordered. "You know I'm a sympathetic puker. If you start vomiting, we'll both be doing it."

Isobel ignored her sisters as she stared at the body. It was the most horrifying thing she'd ever seen. She swallowed hard. "You can't accidentally slit your own throat, can you?"

"No," Agnes said firmly.

Aye, that would have been too much to hope for.

There was a scrambling noise from the bluff behind them. The women yelped and spun, to see their remaining sister coming down the rocky path.

Isobel put her hand to her chest. Her heart was racing hard. "You nearly gave me a heart attack," she told her sister.

Donna rushed up to them, her blonde hair flying out behind her. "Sorry. What's so urgent we had to meet in the dark on the beach? Did you find more bounty?"

It was then she saw the body. The colour drained from her face, she turned and promptly vomited. Which, in turn, made Agnes vomit.

Mairi started making gagging noises. "I'm okay, I'm okay." She held one hand up, pressing the other to her stomach. "I can hold it."

"What a relief," Isobel told her.

Mairi shot her an irritated look. "I told you not to call Donna. She's vegetarian."

"I didn't expect her to eat him." Isobel glared back at her.

"That's just gross," Mairi said, and gagged again.

Isobel threw her hands up in disgust. "Why did I bother calling any of you? You're no use at all. We have a situation here and all you're doing is being sick."

"It's not like we can help it," Agnes said, looking decidedly green.

"Some warning would have been good." Donna swayed in place. Her eyes were on the water instead of the man.

"I did warn you when I called," Isobel said through gritted teeth. "I said, come quick, there's a dead body on the beach."

"I thought you were joking," Donna said.

"About a dead body?" Isobel practically shrieked.

"Right." Agnes held up her hands. "Everybody calm down. This isn't helping. It's getting light, and we need to deal with the body. It's not like people use this beach, but if someone did come down here, they'd call the police." She looked at Isobel. "And seeing as your house is the closest, you'd be first on their list to interview."

"That wouldn't go well," Mairi said. "Your whole face goes red when you lie, and you start stuttering."

"Then you just blab the truth and apologise for trying to lie," Donna added.

"Which means you'd get arrested for fencing stolen goods." Agnes nodded. "Something we're trying to avoid."

"Are you all about done?" Isobel put her hands on her hips and glared at them. Was this really the time to bring up every single one of her flaws? "The kids will be awake soon. We need to deal with this now."

They all stared at the man.

"I've never seen a dead body before," Mairi said. "They look so lifeless."

"Idiot." Agnes smacked Mairi on the back of the head.

"What was that for?" Mairi rubbed her head.

"For being an idiot," Agnes said. "Now focus. Do we leave him here? Cover him and come back later to bury him? Bury him now? Or move him somewhere else while we think things over?"

"I think we need to move him. It would be too hard to bury him here, and we couldn't guarantee the tide wouldn't unearth him later." Isobel felt weary. She was sick of the stress in her life. Sick of dealing with other people's messes. Sick of struggling every single day just to survive. "Whatever we do, we need to do it fast, before the kids wake up. Either way, I want him off the beach. Jack sometimes comes down here with his friends after school, and I wouldn't want them to find the body."

"You could put him in the freezer in your garage," Donna said. "It still works, doesn't it?"

"Aye, but it's old, full of rust and smelly," Isobel said.

"I don't think he'll care," Donna said.

"What do we do with him once he's in the freezer? We can't leave him there forever." Isobel gnawed at her bottom lip and wondered how her life had come to this point.

She was a single mother of two, with two failed relationships behind her, a mountain of debt she hadn't personally accumulated, a minimum-wage job in the village shop and an ever-growing list of crimes under her belt. It was not how she'd imagined life would be at the grand old age of thirty-two.

"We need advice. We need someone who knows what to do with a dead body," Agnes said. "We need an expert."

"I'm not calling the police," Isobel said adamantly. She was the only stability her kids had. She couldn't even think of risking it.

"I wasn't thinking of the police," Agnes said. "I was thinking of an outlaw."

"Yes!" Mairi clapped her hands and grinned. "Great idea, Aggie."

"No." Isobel shook her head. "No. Just no."

Donna placed her hand on Isobel's arm. "Don't dismiss this idea just because you fancy the man. He used to be in the army. He's bound to have seen dead bodies during conflict. He must have an idea what to do with them."

"I-I don't f-fancy him," Isobel protested, but nobody was listening. No, she just dreamed about him every blooming night. What was it with her and bad boys? Hadn't she learned her lesson by now? Why couldn't she find a nice six-stone weakling of an accountant to fall in love with?

"It's well known he's dangerous," Agnes said. "Old man McKay used to tell everyone that his grandson was deadly. He was in the Special Forces. He knows about dead bodies."

"Plus," Mairi said, "there's a security company watching him *covertly*." She whispered the last word as though it had special powers. "That must mean he's on the other side of the law now, which means he won't report us to the cops."

"I didn't know he was being watched." Donna's eyes went wide. "Maybe talking to him isn't such a good idea."

"I spoke to the woman who was setting up cameras," Isobel said. Of course she was going to grill a stranger who was setting up CCTV in the street, in the dark. "She showed me her ID and said he wasn't dangerous to the town. He isn't a criminal. She said he's only dangerous to bad guys." And then the blue-haired woman had laughed. It wasn't reassuring. Neither was the fact she was wearing a Wonder Woman T-shirt and a pair of pink, glittery Doc Marten boots. "She gave me her business card, in case I was ever worried about anything."

"Maybe we should call the security company instead?" Mairi said. "We can ask them what to do."

Agnes groaned. "I can just imagine that conversation—'Hello, we have the body of a stranger in our freezer and we're looking for suggestions on what to do with it.' Aye, that would go well."

"It was only an idea." Mairi frowned at Agnes.

"Whatever," Agnes said. "I think our best bet is the outlaw. You said he's huge and there are weapons lying around in his house. He's obviously used to dangerous situations. I bet he'd know what to do with the body. You need to ask him for help."

"No."

Isobel had been delivering groceries to Callum McKay's house for almost four months, and she'd only seen the man three times. All three times, he'd scared the life out of her. Rage covered him like a shroud. But there was also something about him that made her heart ache. Maybe it was the utter desolation in his eyes, or the fact that the only people she'd seen near him had been from a security company that was hiding in the dark. She'd never met someone so completely alone. And so brutally raw. He was the embodiment of her own personal weakness—the tortured bad boy, with muscles like Thor. She didn't have to be massively self-aware to realise that he was the *last* person she should approach for help. No, for the sake of her sanity, it was best to keep far, far away from the man.

"Honey," Agnes said, "we don't have a lot of options here. Either you get help from someone who knows what to do with a body, or you keep the guy frozen in your old chest freezer for the foreseeable future."

"Aye," Donna said. "And what if this is just the beginning? What if the boat people dump more bodies? We need a plan. We need advice."

"Or we need to start our own crematorium business," Mairi said.

"Think of your kids," Agnes said. "This is getting worse every month. We're in way over our heads. We need help. If this guy can help, then great. If not, we'll try something else."

Isobel's heart sank. Agnes was right. They were out of options. Staying away from Callum McKay had become a luxury she couldn't afford. And it wasn't as if she wanted to start a relationship with him. No, she just wanted advice on what to do with the dead stranger who'd been dumped on her beach.

"You can do it," Donna said softly. "We have your back."

Isobel blinked back tears, as love for her sisters overwhelmed her. She didn't know how she'd survive without them. She needed to talk to Callum for their sakes. This situation with the mysterious boat was well past the point of being dangerous, and they were getting in deeper every month. No, *they* weren't —*she* was. And she was dragging her sisters down with her.

"Okay, I'll talk to him."

"You'll be okay, honey," Agnes said.

"Just keep your hands off him," Mairi said. "Maybe you could call him instead of talking to him face to face."

That caused Agnes to smack her again. "She isn't going to jump the man, idiot."

There was a pause as all three sisters gave her speculative looks. Isobel threw up her hands in disgust. "So I have a type. So what? It's not like I'm going to throw myself at him and offer to sleep with him in return for his help."

There was a shuffling of feet as her sisters cast sideward glances at each other.

"Thanks a lot," Isobel said. "Good to know you have so much faith in me."

"You tend to get physical without thinking it through," Donna said gently.

"I only did that once," Isobel protested. And ended up pregnant and alone at sixteen because of it.

Her sisters stared at her.

"Fine. Twice." And she had the ex-husband from hell to show for that little slip in self-control.

"If it's any consolation," Mairi said, "I've totally learned from your mistakes."

"No. It's no consolation. Now do you three think you could stop analysing my past mistakes long enough to help me get this body off the beach?" She looked at the sliver of light on the horizon. "Sun's coming. We need to get him to the garage and into the freezer before the kids wake up."

"This is going to be gross," Mairi said. "I'll need to burn my clothes after this."

"I might vomit again," Donna said.

"Get a grip," Agnes snapped, "and take an arm or a leg each."

With each of them clutching a limb, the four sisters carried the dead man up the hill to Isobel's house. Donna and Agnes were only sick twice.

CHAPTER 3

Callum McKay had found hope in an unlikely saviour—eighty-nine-year-old Betty McLeod. The cuboid-shaped woman, with her signature hairnet, but no hair, and tartan tent dresses, was the scourge of the Highlands. She had the personality of a rabid hyena and the moral compass of a campaigning politician. But for some reason, in spite of her failings, or maybe because of them, Lake Benson had practically adopted her. He called her his pet Hobbit; she called him son. As far as Callum knew, Lake had been the only person on the planet Betty wasn't out to mess with—until him.

Callum wasn't sure what he'd done to acquire her interest in his life, but it seemed there was no getting rid of her. And heaven knew he'd tried. She'd come with Lake on one of the days he'd visited to check up on Callum, when he'd first moved into his grandfather's old house in Scotland. She'd barrelled through the door, cackling like a witch when he told her to go to hell. Then she'd taken a look around, and said, "Son, it looks like I'm already there. This place is a pigsty. Make me a cup of tea. Lake's got the cake. Then tell me why you're trying to kill yourself and what I can do to help." From the evil glint in her eye, Callum was pretty sure she meant help to end his life and not help to stop him.

For some reason, Callum had made the tea. He now had weekly phone calls from Betty, where she told him he was being an arse and discussed euthanasia methods with him. As far as therapy went, it was probably enough to get them both committed.

"Why the hell didn't you answer the phone earlier?" Betty said by way of hello when Callum picked it up this time.

"I was busy." For once, he hadn't been busy staring at his gun and wondering if this was the day he was going to put the barrel in his mouth and pull the trigger.

"Doing what?" Her aged croak of a voice was like sandpaper on his eardrums.

"None of your bloody business."

She laughed, and Callum shook his head.

"Did it involve some self-pleasure?" she said. "If it did, film it next time and send it to me. I need to make the most of the years I have left."

"I think I'm going to be sick."

"Pansy arse."

"What do you want?"

Callum caught sight of movement through the kitchen window. Someone was coming down his drive. A very familiar someone. His heart began to beat faster at the sight of Isobel Sinclair. She'd been delivering his groceries for months now, but he'd rarely seen her. It had been a deliberate move on his part, forced by self-preservation. Everything about Isobel called to him, making him want to drag the curvy woman into his lair and spend a few hours forgetting his life with her body. And that was something he couldn't let happen. He'd learned the hard way that he was better off alone.

"I'm phoning to see if you're dead," Betty said, dragging his attention back to her. "Still with us, I see."

"Why do you sound disappointed?"

"We've already established that I think you're a big pansy arse for even thinking about offing yourself. I've been through a helluva lot more in my lifetime than you have, and I'm still standing. You need to suck it up and get on with the life you've been given."

Aye, so she'd told him. On numerous occasions. Callum wondered yet again why he bothered to pick up the phone when she called. "What have you endured that's worse than having both your legs blown off?" He should have kept his mouth shut. It was an amateur mistake. One he'd only made because he was distracted by the woman walking towards his house.

"You don't know loss and agony until you've had a hysterectomy, son. Don't even get me started on what a double mastectomy feels like."

"No," Callum said. "Let's not get you started."

He was still dazed from the visit when she'd offered to flash her boobless chest at him, in order to show him it was still possible to live a good life with missing body parts. Or as she had said, "So you'll see that you can still be sexy when there's stuff missing. Being boobless hasn't slowed me down any. Ask the vicar." Then she'd given him a toothless grin because she'd lost her teeth in Lake's car. It had taken the two men working together to get her under control. Callum was still traumatised just thinking about it.

"I need to go," Callum said, his eyes on Isobel as she let herself through his gate. There were no groceries in her hands. This wasn't a delivery. Immediately, every instinct he had went on alert and he noted every detail about her.

She was paler than usual, and her dark hair, tied in a twist, was nowhere as neat as she normally kept it. She looked around furtively, as though afraid someone was watching.

Or she was afraid of him.

"Are you going to shoot yourself? Is that why you need to go?" Betty asked.

"Not today, Satan, not today."

"Good. Then can you finish that bowl you're making and send it to me, so I can give it to Kirsty? I need something to bribe her with."

That was enough to pull his attention away from Isobel. Just. How the hell did Betty know he was woodturning? His eyes scanned the room and he cursed under his breath. There was a tiny camera fixed in the corner of the room near the ceiling. Bloody Elle, she'd bugged him. Of course she had. He'd bet there were cameras all over the damn property, watching every damn move he made. The staff of Benson Security had no concept of personal boundaries.

"I'm going to kill them," Callum muttered. Right after he found every bloody surveillance toy on his property.

"Can you do it after you've finished the bowl?"

"I can't believe you lot have been watching me. What have you been doing? Sitting around, eating popcorn and monitoring the sad sack in Arness?"

"Don't get your knickers in a twist. There's no camera in the bathroom. I argued for one, but everybody kept saying that was an abuse of your privacy. They wouldn't let me watch the night-time feed, either." Betty's voice turned wicked. "Is it true you sleep in the nude?"

Callum shuddered. He couldn't even think of anything to say to that. As soon as the call ended, he was going to remove every damn camera and shove them up…

"Kirsty would like it," Betty said, pulling his attention away from his plans. "She likes all that arty-farty crap. And she's banned me from the security office, so I need to bribe my way back in. Can you send it to me this weekend? Before you kill yourself?"

Callum didn't have the energy to follow Betty's logic. Isobel was at his door, and his house was full of cameras, so that his *ex*-colleagues could spy on him. He sure as hell didn't have the time to ask Betty what she'd done that was bad enough to get her banned from Benson Security's Invertary office—she practically lived in her armchair in the corner of the reception area.

"I'm hanging up now," Callum said as Isobel rang his doorbell.

"Don't die before you finish the bowl," Betty shouted, "and put a bow on it. Make it fancy before you send it. Kirsty's in a foul mood, and a bow would definitely help."

With a shake of his head, Callum ended the call. He had more on his mind than Betty's pathetic attempt to pay off Lake Benson's wife. It wasn't going to work, anyway. Kirsty had grown up in Invertary. A deep distrust of Betty had been bred into her from birth.

Callum stared at the door as Isobel rang the bell again. If he opened it, he'd be opening himself up to whatever problem she obviously had. He didn't do that anymore. He didn't get involved with other people's problems. And he sure as hell wasn't someone who could help her.

Through the frosted glass, he saw her shift in place before she rapped the door with her knuckles. Callum broke out in a cold sweat. Part of him itched to pull open the door and offer his help. The rest of him knew that what little help he could offer wouldn't be of much use.

Isobel knocked the door again, and this time, it was a much more timid tap, as though she was losing her confidence. Callum's heart pounded. She would soon get fed up and go, taking her problems along with her. That was what he wanted. He rubbed his sweaty palms on his jeans.

Aye, he definitely wanted her to take her problems elsewhere.

Through the window, he watched her step back, look at the door and chew at her bottom lip. She wrung her hands in front of her. All colour had gone from her face. Her usually pink cheeks were pale. Slowly, her eyes closed, and she nodded and turned, heading back down the path.

And just like that, something inside Callum, something he'd thought long dead, snapped into action.

"Damn it to hell!"

He shot a one-fingered salute at the camera and then lunged for the door.

Isobel turned away from the old house, torn between feeling relief and disappointment that the Arness Outlaw wasn't home. It was probably for the best. She'd been going over what to say all the way to his house, which was a fair walk along the bluff from her place, and she still hadn't come up with a way to *casually* mention the dead man in her freezer.

"What do you want?"

The sudden, terse words made Isobel squeak and trip over her own feet. She righted herself fast, and spun to find Callum McKay standing in his open doorway. And just like that, her mind emptied of all rational thought.

"Well?" The word rumbled out of him in a menacing growl.

Isobel looked up. And up. She almost had to crane her neck to look him in the eye. At just over five foot, Isobel was used to looking up at people. What she wasn't used to, was feeling so incredibly vulnerable while she did it.

With his arms folded over his tight grey T-shirt, making his already oversized shoulders bulge, Callum looked like everything the villagers whispered about him—outlaw, bad boy, marauder, stealer of virtue…

"You going to talk, or just stare at me?" Even his voice was pure, rough whisky.

Isobel blinked a couple of times, trying to pull herself out of the daze he'd put her in. The cloak of danger hung heavily on him. He was a man who was used to being the strongest, meanest threat around. Isobel wasn't sure if knowing that made her want to run from him or to him.

She licked her very dry lips and forced out some words. "You're Callum McKay."

She fought the urge to cringe. For an opening line, it wasn't that impressive. But what else could she say? *You're the sexiest, most terrifying man I've ever met and I think I just ovulated from being in your presence. Oh, and by the way, there's a dead man in my freezer.*

His eyes narrowed, drawing her attention to the harsh planes of his face. He'd been chiselled out of granite, and the sculptor had been too intimidated by the result to polish him. Callum was all rough edges and solid power. And he was waiting for her to say something else.

"I'm Isobel Sinclair."

He frowned. "I know that. What I don't know is what you want."

To be naked and at your mercy?

Isobel smacked her palm over her mouth, before she realised she hadn't said the words aloud. Her face began to burn, and she actually considered running from Callum and taking her chances with the police.

She peeled her fingers from her mouth one at a time and tried to smile. She was pretty sure it only made her look more manic. *Casual*, she told herself, *be casual. You can do this.*

"So, I hear you were in the army?"

Oh, that was not the right thing to say. If Callum was

scary before, he was downright terrifying now. Every muscle in his body turned to steel and his eyes became glacial.

"Where did you hear that?"

Isobel swallowed hard. "A-around."

"And what's it to you?"

Isobel took a step back and felt a bush poke into her rear. It hurt, but she didn't step forward again. "J-just being friendly. Neighbourly. You've been here a few months and I-I thought I should welcome you…s-seeing as you're here alone…and you…you know…don't go out much." Her face was burning up now, and with every tiny lie she told, her stutter got worse. In desperation, she reached for something to say that was truth. "I live along the bluff." She pointed in the direction of her house. "On a clear day, I can see Ireland from my house."

Kill me now!

Callum stared at her as though he was trying to figure out a puzzle. Isobel started to back up again before she remembered she was already in the bush. The silence became so heavy that it was hard to breathe.

"Did you see any conflict?" she blurted. "In the army, I mean. Y-you must have seen some interesting things. I've a-always been really i-interested in guns and other a-army stuff. Tanks! T-tanks are especially c-cool. And big. Tanks are big. And don't have any w-windows. I-I've always w-wondered how the s-soldier could see to drive…w-without windows…in a tank…with tank-sized g-guns. You must know a lot about g-guns. A-and tanks. A-and…" she cast around for anything at all she could remember about the army. *Anything!* "And c-camouflage…" Honestly, it took all her self-control not to groan loudly and run away as fast as her legs could carry her.

Callum didn't move, didn't speak—he only watched her as she dug her hole deeper with every word.

"I-I hear there are d-different types of camouflage f-for different environments."

He stared at her with that blank expression.

Isobel swallowed hard. "I-I had a pink camouflage dress o-once."

Still blank.

"Not m-much use for p-pink in the army, though…" She forced a laugh, and it morphed into something quite hysterical that she had to work hard to stop. "So." She cleared her throat. "I thought, maybe, y-you'd like to c-come to my house and h-have tea and talk about army s-stuff." She looked at him hopefully. Desperately.

Callum's chin jerked upwards as though she'd struck him. His cheeks coloured with what she knew was rage.

"You're one of *those* women, then," he said. "The kind that thinks combat is sexy. Do you get hot hearing battle stories? Are you hoping I'll show you my scars? You're out of luck, lady. I don't sleep with army groupies. You want to get off with a soldier, look elsewhere."

Isobel felt like she'd been slapped. "What? No!"

Callum shook his head. "Clear out before I lose my temper." He turned his back on her.

Isobel rushed forward, but her top snagged in the bush, holding her back.

"It's not like that. That's not why I'm here."

He strode into the house, ignoring her.

Isobel panicked and did what she always did under pressure: she blurted the truth.

"There's a dead body in my freezer and I don't know what to do with it!"

CHAPTER 4

Callum stopped dead in his tracks and slowly turned to face Isobel. She was frozen in place, her cheeks a deep red and her green eyes so wide that they almost took over her face. She looked as though she'd been caught naked on stage, with the spotlight firmly on her. In three long strides, Callum was at her side. She tensed, ready to run. He reached out, wrapped his fingers around her wrist and held her in place. Firmly, but gently.

"Explain." He used the same tone he'd used when he'd been in charge of an SAS operation. It demanded nothing but compliance.

"Um…" She blinked up at him, as the colour started to drain from her face.

He could almost read her thoughts. They were scrolling over her incredibly expressive face. He watched intently as he saw regret—presumably at blurting out her secret—fear, probably over the worry that he would use it against her, and desperation—most likely to disappear and forget their encounter had ever happened. Well, it was too late for that. Isobel Sinclair was neck-deep in a situation that Callum couldn't ignore. A situation she obviously wasn't equipped to handle.

"Talk, Isobel."

Her name was smooth on his tongue. It was almost as though he could taste her. He clenched his jaw and forced his thoughts from places they shouldn't go—not with this woman. Isobel had the words *permanent relationship* written all over her. She wasn't the kind of woman Callum could take to bed without repercussions. And standing close enough to breathe her in, Callum could admit that he very much wanted to take her to bed.

"Why is there a body in your freezer? What happened to it?" His voice dropped an octave. "Did you kill him?"

He didn't believe for one second she was capable of killing a man, but possibilities were racing through his head. An accident? Self-defence? He studied her wide eyes and saw only panic. He knew he was looming over her, but there was nothing he could do about his size or his intense personality. She'd come to him with her crazy confession and she'd just have to deal with him.

"Breathe," he ordered. Her lips were beginning to turn blue, and she was shaking so hard her teeth were chattering. "You're going to pass out if you don't take in some air. You need to breathe. Damn it, woman, I'm not going to hurt you. I just want some information. Take a breath and talk. Do as I tell you!"

She didn't do as she was told.

Callum tightened his hold on her wrist. "Breathe. Now."

Her eyes became wider and began to lose focus. She was going to faint. Callum felt a surge of panic at the thought. Give him a terrorist armed with a bomb over a fainting woman any day.

"Snap out of it, woman, take a breath!" He felt her knees begin to crumple and quickly wrapped an arm around her waist to keep her upright. Her eyes held his. Her mouth opened and closed like a fish on dry land. But nothing happened. Callum cursed and did the only thing he could think of to shock her out of her panicked state without harming her.

He kissed her.

It was a mistake.

As soon as Callum's lips touched hers, he knew there was no going back. The only thing that mattered was the desperate, overwhelming need for more.

A gasp.

A moan.

Fingers in his hair, pulling him closer, demanding more. Her body undulated against him in time with her lips. She tasted of cinnamon and chocolate, and a desperation that inflamed his own. They burned together, each of them acting as fuel for the other's flame.

Tongues duelled. Lips caressed. Teeth nipped. He poured himself into her and she demanded even more. He stroked down her body, across her hips to her thighs, and lifted her. Automatically, her legs wrapped around his waist and they were face to face. The perfect height. They were mouth to mouth. Hard to soft.

There was no rational thought. Only brutal, raw, desperate need. Isobel's teeth nipped at Callum's bottom lip, and the noise that escaped him was base. He was functioning on pure, unadulterated instinct. He needed this woman. He needed to be inside her. He needed it now.

Callum broke the kiss, searching for a surface to press her against. He wanted to wedge her between the hard wall and his even harder body. He needed access for his hands, and teeth, and tongue. Isobel squirmed, and moaned her protest at losing his lips. Her head lowered and she sucked on his neck before biting hard enough to leave a mark. Callum tightened his hand in her hair, and strode through his already open door.

He slammed her against the wall, letting his hips and the pressure of his body hold her in place. Hands went under shirts in a frantic exploration. Her nipples were hard against his palms, her teeth rough against his ear. There was panting. Loud. Desperate. Uncivilised.

With a desperate rip, he tugged her shirt over her head and tossed it to the floor. Her bra was a wisp of lace that hid nothing. Perfect pink nipples made his mouth water, and with a growl, he lowered his head to capture one through the lace. He sucked it deep into his mouth.

"Yes!" Isobel threw her head back and pressed her flesh into his eager mouth, her hands clasping at his head, tugging his hair to keep him in place.

He licked and sucked and bit her ripe, hard nipple as he slid her skirt up to her waist. Satin-soft skin. Warm, wet heat.

He had to get inside her.

He had to.

His body had broken out in a sweat with desperation to be inside this woman. With one hand helping to support her against the wall, Callum reached for the buttons on his jeans to free himself.

His cock was desperately hard and ready for her. He pushed her underwear aside and caressed her slick, wet heat. Gasps filled his ears. The sound he made in reply was one he didn't recognise. In that moment, he was more animal than man. All he could think about, all he could feel, was Isobel. Their chemistry was a fog around him, wiping out the rest of the world, blanketing his past and his worries and his fears.

He positioned his aching shaft at her entrance and focused on her face. Her head was back against the wall, lips swollen and parted, eyes closed. Her cheeks were flushed and her hair was wild. She was clinging to him, panting hard, just as lost and desperate as he was.

"Isobel," he barked. "Look at me."

Slowly, languorously, Isobel opened her beautiful green eyes. She was dazed, her eyelids heavy with desire. He'd never seen a more sensual sight.

"Say yes," he demanded.

She pressed her hips towards him, making the head of his cock rub against her sensitive flesh. She moaned and her eyes drifted closed. She was lost to sensation. Lost in him. The feeling of power her reaction caused made Callum heady. He had done this. Barely keeping hold of the tenuous awareness of reality that he'd managed to grasp, he needed her answer.

"Isobel, say yes." He flexed his hips and pressed against her.

She undulated as she forced her eyes open. Her tongue swept across her lips as she stared into him. Not *at* him. *Into him.* She grasped the hair on either side of his head and yanked his face forward until there was nothing to see but the desperation in each other's eyes.

"Get. Inside. Me. Now!"

He captured her mouth in a punishing kiss as he thrust his length inside her. Warm, grasping flesh enveloped him, and he swallowed her moans as he ground his hips against her. Nails raked his shoulder. Her thighs tightened on his hips.

"Yes, yes, yes…" she chanted.

Callum buried his face in the crook of her neck and licked at her skin. Cinnamon and fire. His addiction. Something deeply primitive within him reared its head. He clamped his mouth over the muscle where her shoulder met her throat. He sucked hard, wanting to mark her. Wanting to leave his brand on her porcelain skin. Wanting the world to know that she was his. There was no logic in his reasoning.

No thought of the future or what his need meant. All that existed was instinct.

"Come for me, Isobel," he said against her ear.

It was enough to send her over. With one desperate cry, she arched. Her skin flushed and her body shuddered. Callum felt her clench around him and his muscles locked in place. He rushed over with her, roaring his release. They were in the centre of a tornado, the world replaced by spiralling winds and the ferocious force of nature.

Slowly.

Gradually.

The winds died and reality returned.

He felt Isobel tense against him and knew that she too was coming back to the world. Callum's sex-addled brain sputtered back to life and he silently cursed. He'd only meant to make her breathe. He didn't know what had happened. Never had it been like that before. Never.

It was a huge mistake.

Isobel was a woman made for relationships. And Callum was damaged goods. Useless to everyone around him.

"Oh no," Isobel whispered, bringing him out of his own head. "I've done it again." She shoved at his shoulders. "Put me down."

There was nothing else he could do but comply. With a wince, he slid from her body and then lowered her to the ground in front of him. He didn't step back, but kept her between him and the wall. Her top was gone, ripped and tossed to the floor. Apart from that, she was still wearing everything she'd arrived in.

Everything she'd worn to his house to ask him for help.

"Fuck," he muttered.

"Aye." Isobel looked at him with a mixture of horror and flushed satiation. "I don't suppose you've had a vasectomy?"

As her words registered, it was Callum's turn to feel faint.

CHAPTER 5

"We probably shouldn't have watched that," Elle Roberts said as she shut her laptop.

As tech expert for Benson Security, she'd been the one to install the cameras in Callum's house. She was also the one who'd written the program that would make alarms go off in both Benson Security offices if Callum mentioned any key words or phrases—like "kill myself", "end it all", "dead", and "I need my gun". To say they were worried about his state of mind was putting it mildly.

"I think this is a sign he's getting over his depression," Megan Raast said as she fanned her burning face. Her smile was supermodel wide. "Who knew Callum was that hot?"

"You won't be thinking that when he kills you after he finds out we watched him having sex."

"Baby? You watching porn again?" Dimitri, Megan's husband and fellow security specialist, sauntered into the computer room. "We talked about that. No watching porn without me."

Megan launched herself into Dimitri's arms. "I don't watch porn. Trust me, women don't find porn sexy. It's an objectification of their bodies and it's really icky. But I have watched erotic female cinema."

"Lady porn," Dimitri scoffed, but it was ruined by the smile that lit up his eyes. The one that said his wife could do no wrong.

"I can live with it being called that." Megan pulled him in for a kiss. One that lasted until they were both panting.

"I'm sitting right here," Elle snapped at them. "I just watched one colleague have sex. I don't need a repeat right in front of my face."

Dimitri tore his mouth from his wife, and his eyebrows shot up his forehead. "Callum had sex? Who with? Did you record it?" He looked behind him at the open door and shouted, "Joe, Ryan, Callum had sex."

Elle groaned and smacked her palm to her forehead. "We were trying to be discreet, for Callum's sake."

"No we weren't," the blonde traitor, who was wrapped around Dimitri like a clip-on monkey, said. "If we'd been thinking of Callum's privacy, we wouldn't have watched in the first place. Mainly, we were thinking that it's hot the way he goes all caveman when he does it."

Elle scowled at Megan, but as usual, she shrugged it off.

"Callum had sex?" Ryan, the most laid-back member of their team, strode into the room. "Who with? Where? What position? Did you tape it?"

"You lot are sick." Elle was aware she should be wearing a T-shirt with the word *Hypocrite* emblazoned across it instead of one that said *I Own a Deathstar*.

"He had sex with the woman who delivers his shopping," Megan said, still clinging to Dimitri. "He threw her up against the hall wall. They didn't even get as far as taking off their clothes. It was hot." She leaned in and whispered something in her husband's ear that made his eyes turn dark and his cheeks flush.

Elle pointed at them. "Whatever you're planning, keep it out of the office. We don't want to be your audience."

Megan pouted, but there was pure mischief in her eyes. "I can't help that I have an exhibitionist streak. It's genetic."

Dimitri looked towards heaven and clamped a hand over Megan's mouth. "Pretend you didn't hear that."

Ryan snorted. "Like we didn't already know."

"What's this about Callum and a woman?" Joe Barone, ex-US marine and team trainer, frowned as he came up beside Elle. "He didn't hurt her, did he?" he asked her quietly.

Elle gasped. "He wouldn't do that. You know he wouldn't."

"He hasn't been himself for months. I'm worried about him."

"We all are. But he'd never hurt a woman. You know that, Joe." Elle glared at him. "That was out of order."

"I know, I know." The American ran a hand through his short brown hair, making it stand on end. "But he trashed his house, Elle. You were there. He hit Lake and would have knocked him out if he hadn't been drunk off his ass. I'm not sure what he's capable of anymore. He hasn't even spoken to any of the team for months."

Elle cast a glance at Dimitri to make sure he wasn't listening when she brought up his sister. Although Katrina was doing well now, living and working in a shelter for abused women in Invertary, the memory of what had happened to her was still very fresh for all of them.

"You saw how Callum reacted after we rescued Katrina from the bastard who was holding her as his sex slave," Elle whispered. "He would never force himself on someone. Never."

Joe's eyes went hard. "I didn't say that. I asked if he was too rough. I wanted to know if he was in control."

"Well, hell, Joe, why didn't you just say that?" She turned

back to her laptop, wishing she was dealing with code instead of people. There was never any chance of misunderstanding computer code. "I've been worried about him."

Joe nodded, placed a hand on her shoulder and gave it a squeeze. "We all are."

"Why are you all in here?" Rachel Ford-Talbot's voice cut through the room like a buzzsaw on glass. "We're meeting in the conference room." She made a show of looking at her Rolex. "Five minutes ago."

Ryan caught Elle's gaze and rolled his eyes. They were all desperate for Callum to come back to work, because that meant Rachel would no longer be their only on-site boss. Being in charge was going to Rachel's head, and it was only a matter of time before someone locked her in one of the basement interrogation rooms and "forgot" she was there.

"We're monitoring Callum," Elle told Rachel. "He seems to be doing better. I think it's time he came back."

"I miss Callum," Megan said. "I miss the way he'd come in, shout at us, grumble about having to work with a bunch of amateurs and then lock himself in his office for hours planning military manoeuvres, in case we needed them."

"Good times," Joe agreed.

"Elle's right: we need to make more of an effort to get him back," Megan said.

"How exactly should we do that?" Dimitri said. "He won't even talk to any of us. If he knew about the surveillance we have on him, he'd lose his mind."

"I thought he'd notice it months ago," Elle said. "But he hasn't been his usual paranoid self. He shows no interest in anything. The only person he talks to is Betty, and those conversations are seriously disturbing."

Megan made the sign of the cross. "Betty McLeod is Invertary's answer to Satan. She's probably whispering ways he could off himself into his ear." She stopped suddenly, her eyes going wide. "Could he be brainwashed?"

"Don't be daft," Ryan said.

"No, seriously," Megan said. "Think about it. He was perfectly fine until Peru. Maybe Betty was in contact with him earlier than we think."

"I don't think Betty has the skills to brainwash anyone," Joe said of the eighty-nine-year-old. "Half the time she can't even find her own teeth. Brainwashing seems beyond her abilities."

"Don't underestimate her," Megan warned. "That's where people usually go wrong. It's best to assume she can do whatever you suspect her of doing."

"I've been monitoring his cell since he came on board with Benson Security," Elle said. "I would know if he'd been talking to Betty."

Everyone gaped at her.

"What?" She held up her hands.

Joe frowned at her. "Do you monitor our cell phones too?"

The tension in the room amped up. Elle wasn't threatened. She was doing it for their own good. "Sure I do. I have GPS tracking on all of you. If there's a problem, I'm going to know about it. And after Megan's run-in with the psycho who kept texting her, I also record all your messages and calls."

The glares were uniform, so Elle didn't bother telling them that she had tracking devices planted in their belongings, and monitoring software on all of their devices. If someone was going to be threatened, or go missing, on her watch, she was prepared to deal with it.

"It's not like I listen to your calls," she told them. "I have a program that monitors for keywords, and alerts me if they come up."

"Keywords such as?" Megan folded her arms over her black leather biker jacket and tapped her toe.

"Like 'ransom', 'death', stuff like that. Get a grip. I'm looking out for you the best way I know how."

"Without our knowledge or permission," Dimitri said.

"And in a way that is obviously illegal," Rachel said.

"What she said." Megan pointed at Rachel. "Plus it's icky. You're like a mastermind stalker."

Rachel's pointed a talon at Elle. "I'm ordering you to stop it. Immediately."

"You didn't wave your magic wand," Ryan said. "It only counts when you wave the wand."

They glared at each other.

"Whatever," Elle muttered as an alert came from her laptop.

"What is it?" Joe stepped up behind her.

"Some keywords triggered my alert program." Elle's fingers flew over the keyboard.

"What keywords?" Dimitri asked as the rest of them crowded behind Elle.

Her fingers froze when the answer came up. "Dead body," she said.

As one, they leaned towards the laptop while Elle brought up the sound bite that had triggered her program. A female voice rang out through the room: "I came here for help with the dead body!"

"What the hell?" Joe said. "Bring up the live feed. We need to see what's going on. If Callum's found trouble, he's going to need our help."

"Thank God," Ryan said towards heaven. "It's about time."

"I'll start packing," Megan said. "How long will it take us to get there?"

"Couple of hours," Dimitri said.

"Stop right there," Rachel ordered.

As one, the team turned to look at her. She folded her arms, blood-red fingernails spread out against the dark wool of her designer suit. "Nobody is rushing to help Callum. Not until he asks for it."

"But Rachel…" Elle said.

"No." Rachel held up a hand. "He walked out on us. He can damn well walk back in. I'm tired of pandering to his childish tantrums. So he lost limbs. Boohoo. It's time for him to man up and get past it. Until then, we focus on the work we do have, from the people who actually want us to help them. Am I clear?"

There was muttering, shuffling feet and dejected nods.

Rachel straightened her shoulders and flicked back her poker-straight hair. "Now. Meeting in the conference room. Five minutes."

With that, she turned and swept out of the room.

"I hate it when she's right," Megan said. "It goes against the laws of nature."

"I want Callum back," Elle said.

"We all do," Ryan said, watching the door which Rachel had just sailed through. "Hopefully before one of us kills Rachel and buries her body in the basement." He looked at the others. "Which could be pretty damn soon."

There was nothing to do with that, except agree.

CHAPTER 6

"I can't believe I did this again," Isobel wailed, as she scooped her shirt from the floor. It was ripped down the front. "I can't wear this. Where are your shirts?"

Callum didn't answer. In fact, he didn't even seem to register she was still there. He'd turned into a statue that blocked his front door. His *open* front door. Yeah, she'd had sex with a virtual stranger, in full view of the world. She was just oozing with class.

"Fine! I'll find them myself." She strode away from him, into the house. She also needed to find a bathroom and get cleaned up.

Because she'd had unprotected sex.

Again!

Had she learned from her teenage mistake, the way any other reasonable adult woman did? No. Because here she was at thirty-two, jumping the local bad boy without even sparing a thought for the consequences. She had no one to blame but herself. He'd stopped to make sure she wanted to carry on. And what had she said? *Get in me now!* Because she'd been thinking with her hoo-ha and not with her brain.

If she'd been thinking with her brain, she might have remembered that she already had two kids and didn't need a third.

She slammed open doors until she found the main bedroom. There was hardly any sign that Callum actually lived in the house. The furnishings were sparse and there were no personal knick-knacks anywhere. She yanked open drawers until she found a shirt. One of many identical grey Henleys. What the hell was that? Only a serial killer dressed in the same thing every damn day. She froze for a second. Had she had sex with a serial killer? Up against the wall. Without any protection.

She spun around and saw the perfectly made bed, which irritated her even more. Only someone with a deeply disturbed mind could be that neat. It was a bad sign. One of many she should have picked up *before* she jumped the man. Furious, Isobel bounced on the bed until it was a mess.

Better. She felt much better.

There was still no sign of Callum when Isobel strode into the bathroom. She turned the shower on to warm up as she surveyed the mess she'd made of herself. Her skirt was tucked in on itself and she'd been flashing her backside at Callum as she stormed through the house. Not that it mattered. Because really, was there any way she could add to her humiliation? She'd had sex with someone who was practically a stranger. In his hallway. In broad daylight. With the door open.

As steam filled the room, Isobel stripped and threw her trashed underwear in the bin. She stepped into the shower and let the heat take her away for a second, before her hand covered her abdomen. She did the math and figured out that it wasn't the best time to fall pregnant. It was still possible, but it wasn't probable. She clung to that hope with the smidgeon of sanity she had left.

"You aren't on the pill."

The rough voice startled Isobel, and she screamed.

"Are you insane?" She glared through the glass at Callum, who was standing, legs apart and arms folded, glaring back at her. "You nearly gave me a heart attack."

"You aren't on the pill," he said again. "And we didn't use protection."

She could have sworn he paled under his tan.

"No. We didn't. But don't worry. I-I'm sure I'm n-not pregnant." Okay, so that was an outright lie, but still, what else was she supposed to say? *If I am pregnant, there's a good chance I'll put my head in the oven and leave all three kids to you.* Yeah, she didn't think that'd go over well.

His eyes narrowed. "You stutter when you lie."

It wasn't a question, so she ignored him. Instead, she shut off the water, grabbed a perfectly folded towel from the rack and wrapped herself in it. Even his towels were equidistant from each other. Another thing that irritated her.

"Do you have OCD?" she asked.

His eyes went wide before they narrowed again. "No. But I'm beginning to think you might suffer from attention deficit disorder. Focus. We didn't use protection." For one second his calm demeanour cracked and he looked harried. "That's never happened to me. I always use protection. Always."

"Not this time, you didn't. Guess I'm just special that way."

His eyes hardened at her flippancy. "You could be pregnant."

"No." She shook her head. "No. I won't allow it." She couldn't be pregnant. She just couldn't.

The temperature in the room seemed to drop about forty degrees. Callum stepped right into the small bathroom, taking up all the space, and his hand wrapped around her bicep.

"Do you plan to abort my baby?" His tone was death.

She blinked up at him as the words sank in, and then she yanked her arm from his grip. "What? No! I plan to not be pregnant in the first place. I can't be. It can't happen. Not again."

She pushed past him, holding what clothes she had left tight against her chest, and strode into his bedroom. Callum didn't seem to have any problem watching her dress.

"A little privacy, if you don't mind?" she snapped at him.

He cocked an eyebrow at her as though she was daft to ask. Which, quite possibly, she was. He blocked the door, so Isobel had no choice but to turn her back on him and pretend he wasn't there. She dropped the towel and pulled on his shirt.

"I can't believe this is happening again. I must be an idiot." She stopped dead in the middle of pulling the shirt over her head as a horrible thought occurred to her. "I'm not an idiot. I'm one of those women who turn up on Jerry Springer. The kind who has four million kids by four million fathers and is still having an affair with her sister's husband and her best friend's boyfriend—at the same time. I'm a white-trash cliché!"

"What the hell are you talking about?"

Isobel barely registered that he was talking, as she carried on tugging on her clothes. "The first time I ever slept with a boy, I got pregnant. I was fifteen. I could be forgiven for being naïve and in love. I even thought we'd get married and live happily ever after. But no. As soon as I told him he was going to be a father, he ran. I haven't seen him since. So I got wise." She yanked on her skirt. "The next guy I slept with had to marry me first, so that I could do things in the right order for once. So that I would be certain he wouldn't run out on me after we had sex." She spun on Callum. "And do you know what happened?"

He stared at her as though she was losing her mind. And, quite possibly, she might be.

"I'll tell you what happened. We had a beautiful little girl together and he said he was going to Glasgow for a job interview. A promotion. A step up the ladder in his career." She snorted. "It was rubbish. He ran and he never came back! The next I heard from him was divorce papers in the mail."

She stomped past Callum and headed for his kitchen. He followed behind her, not saying a word when she started opening and shutting cupboard doors looking for junk food.

Isobel slammed the pantry door shut and glared at him. "There is no chocolate in your house."

"No. But there appears to be an irrational woman in my kitchen."

She clenched her fists and glared at him, wondering if she would have to jump to hit him in the jaw. He was so damn tall. For a second, she swore she could see amusement in his eyes before they became flat and hard again.

"I want to know the minute you find out if you're pregnant or not."

"I am not pregnant!" she shouted at the top of her lungs, hoping volume would make it so.

He just stared at her.

"I can't cope with this right now," Isobel told him. "I have a mountain of bad debt my ex-husband left in my name. A loan shark after me for payments. And a dead body in my freezer. I need to make a list. I need to prioritise. I need a plan. I need chocolate!" she wailed.

Callum cursed loudly, and then she felt his hands on her shoulders and realised he was moving her towards the table in the corner of the kitchen. "Sit." He pushed her down into a wooden chair. He pointed at her. "Stay. I'll make tea."

"I am not a dog!" She was shouting again.

She wasn't too proud to admit that she might have

become a little hysterical. But, to be fair, she was having a helluva day. She sat fuming, her mind racing over her many, many problems, as Callum went about making tea. Every movement he made was efficient and controlled. Which made it all the stranger that he'd lost that control with her earlier. Her face burned at the memory. Although the dull ache throughout her body wasn't going to let her forget what they'd done anytime soon.

"Here." He placed a mug and spoon on the table in front of her then reached into the cupboard behind him and produced a jar of honey. "Add this. It will help."

Isobel fell on the honey like Winnie the Pooh. She ignored the tea and spooned some into her mouth instead. Sugar. Better. She closed her eyes and sighed. It wasn't chocolate, but maybe if she finished the whole jar she'd get the same high?

"I wish I drank," she said wistfully. "Now would be a good time to develop a taste for whisky."

"It wouldn't make any difference. I don't keep any alcohol in the house."

Her eyes shot to his. "Why not?"

"I don't like who I am when I drink."

"Oh. I just don't like the taste." She ate another spoonful of honey while she thought about it. "But then, I never needed to be drunk to make ill-advised decisions. Seems I'm capable of doing that stone-cold sober."

They sat in silence for a minute, while she ate her way through the honey and Callum dealt with being one of her ill-advised decisions.

"Tell me about the body," he said.

"Do you only speak in demands? Are you capable of asking a polite question? Like, 'Isobel, would you like to have sex with me?' Or 'Isobel, why is there a dead man in your freezer?'"

His eyes narrowed. "I asked if you wanted to have sex. If I remember right, you moaned your answer in my ear. Again. And again. And again."

She felt her stomach lurch. "There's no need to be a bastard about it."

"There's never any need for my being a bastard. It happens naturally." He leaned forward, into her space. "Now tell me about the body."

The words hit her hard and her stomach clenched even tighter. There was a body. In her freezer. Suddenly it was hard to breathe.

"Don't you dare," Callum snapped. "You freaking out and forgetting how to breathe is how we got into this mess in the first place." He lifted the warm mug of tea and pressed it into her hands. "Drink. Then talk."

For once, Isobel did as she was told. The hot tea was soothing. It would have been better if he'd put milk in it, but you couldn't have everything. As she drank, she studied the man she'd had sex with. He'd been starring in her dreams for months, with his brooding good looks and his dangerous persona. Everything about him simultaneously warned her off and attracted her to him. From his broad shoulders and bulging arms, to the lines around his eyes that spoke of experience. His nose had been broken at some point, and there was a scar on his chin that had whitened with age. Even the planes of his face were sharp and brutal. But it was all softened by the lush fullness of his lips. She blushed just thinking about those lips and the parts of her body that had already experienced the feel of them.

Callum's eyes darkened as though he could read her mind, and the air between them crackled. He shifted in his seat, drawing her attention to the fact that his jeans had become too tight again. A secret part of her was pleased by the effect she had on him. She shook her head to clear it.

What was she thinking? She had enough to deal with without adding the Arness Outlaw to the mix.

She put her mug on the table. Folded her hands in her lap and looked at him. "My sisters and I found a dead man on the beach this morning."

There was silence for a minute. "And you thought it would be a good idea to freeze him?"

Wouldn't you know that the first question he asked her would be a sarcastic one?

She scowled at him. "We put him in the freezer because I can't call the police and I don't know who he is. We were going to bury him, but the beach is hard and rocky and we were worried we wouldn't be able to dig a hole deep enough to stop the waves from unearthing him when the tide came in. I came here to see if, maybe, you had some idea what to do with the body." She remembered their conversation and looked away. "I lied. I'm sorry. I have absolutely no interest in tanks or camouflage. I just didn't know how to bring up the topic of the dead body. I thought if I got you talking about the army, it would lead to talking about wars and stuff, and then you might mention some dead people you've seen and I could casually say, 'Speaking of dead people, there happens to be one in my freezer.' It didn't go as planned."

He had a look of pure incredulity on his face. "I can see why it didn't go as planned," he said dryly. "But let's back up some. Why can't you call the cops?"

"Oh." Isobel blinked several times while she tried to work out whether it was worth trying to lie again. In the end, she figured it wasn't. "I kind of did something illegal that I really wouldn't like them to know about."

Callum stared at her. It was impossible to read his expression. "Was this thing more, or less, illegal than stuffing a body in your freezer?"

"How would I know?"

With a sigh, he got to his feet, towering over her even more. "Show me the body. We'll talk about this while we're there."

"But you won't call the cops?" She affected the same pleading face her three-year-old used on her that worked without fail. "He came off a boat that sneaks into the cove now and again. I don't think they're doing legal stuff, but I don't want the police around asking questions."

This story just kept getting better and better.

"We'll see." He reached for her hand and tugged her to her feet.

"I don't like that answer. That's what I say to the kids when I mean no." She tried to pull her hand from Callum's but he wouldn't let go. "Do you think I'm going to run? You know where I live. I'm easy to find."

"Who knows what you're going to do," he muttered. "And 'we'll see' means we'll see. Nothing else."

"This day is not going as planned," Isobel said as she let him drag her back up the road towards her house.

"No kidding," Callum muttered.

CHAPTER 7

There was indeed a body in the freezer in Isobel's garage.

"We think his throat was slit." Isobel stood behind Callum as he leaned in to get a better look at the man.

"What gave it away?" Callum couldn't stop the sarcasm. He took out his phone and started snapping pictures.

Isobel muttered something he couldn't catch, and started pacing. She'd changed out of his shirt, and, for some reason, that irritated Callum. It was as though she wanted to distance herself from him, and what had happened, as fast as she could. He didn't like that idea at all, and was irritated with himself that it bothered him.

He tuned Isobel out and lifted the dead guy's left hand. There was a tattoo on the webbing between his thumb and forefinger.

"He's been in prison."

If he'd been in prison, he'd be in a database somewhere. It would make searching for an identity that much easier. And an identity would help Callum figure out how the guy had ended up in Arness cove with his throat slit.

"Prison? How do you know that?" Isobel was behind him

in an instant, trying to peer over his shoulder. Which, considering she was a full head shorter than he was, wasn't going to work. He moved to the side to make space for her, and pointed at the five dots on the man's hand.

"Four dots forming a square, like walls of a building. One dot in the middle to show he'd been locked inside." Callum reached for the man's right hand, already knowing what he would find. He pointed at the letters above the knuckles of each finger. "ACAB—'all cops are bastards'."

Isobel's eyes were wide again. "He's a criminal?"

"Woman, he came off a boat that skulks into shore in the middle of the night. Did you think he was a tourist?"

"Is sarcasm your default setting?"

"Aye." He turned back to the body.

The man looked to have been in his thirties, and there was evidence that he'd lived a rough life. His nose had been broken at least once. There was a patch of hair missing on the side of his head where an old scar was. And he had two teeth missing. Callum snapped photos of the face, making sure to get the front angle and the profile.

He shifted the body to get into the man's pockets and spotted more of that telltale jail-black ink peeking out from under his shirt, along his hip. He lifted the material to get a look at the tattoo, and stilled when he saw it. Things had just gotten a whole lot worse.

"We need to call in the police." He kept his voice even.

"We can't. You promised. I can't go to jail. I have two kids to look after. I can't leave my kids." Isobel was pacing again, wringing her hands and looking as though she might flee at any moment.

"He's Russian mob." Callum kept his eyes on her as he dropped that information. "The cops need to deal with this guy."

She stopped and stared at him. "If he's Russian, why is he here?"

"The Russian mob are everywhere. And you do not mess with them. Whatever is happening in your cove is way bigger than you thought it was." Callum didn't like this one bit. Every instinct he had said to call in the authorities and get Isobel and her family as far from this as possible.

He felt a gentle hand on his arm. The heat from it seared right through him. "I can't, Callum. Please, don't make me. There has to be another way to deal with this. Please."

Callum sighed. He was an idiot. A complete and utter idiot. He should walk away while he still could. He cast a glance at Isobel's belly, to remind himself that the time for running had passed.

"If the mob is involved," he said, "this is no amateur operation. These guys know exactly what they're doing. They wouldn't have dumped the body on the beach without having a reason. A warning, maybe?" Callum stilled as his heart skipped a beat. He looked at Isobel. "They had to know you'd seen them. How would they know that? Have you had contact with anyone who's come off that boat?"

Isobel started to shake. She reached behind her, dragged an old wooden chair closer and sat down.

"No." Her voice was as shaky as her hands. "Maybe the dead-body message was for someone else."

"Maybe." But he didn't think so. Callum's brain was firing fast, connecting the dots of sketchy information Isobel had provided. He didn't like the picture that was forming. "Isobel, have you had anything at all to do with these men?"

Her lush bottom lip disappeared between her teeth. It was almost enough to distract him. Almost. She looked up at him through thick black lashes.

"Last month…" She cleared her throat, and Callum didn't dare move. He knew already that he wasn't going to like what he heard. "Last month, there was a storm. They dropped a bag on the path up to the bluff and they didn't come back for it."

There was a thick silence. "Where's the bag, Isobel?"

She visibly swallowed. "I took it to Campbeltown and sold the contents to the pawnbroker. I know it was wrong. I know it. I really needed the money and I knew they weren't doing anything legal. But I still shouldn't have done it." Her eyes filled with tears. "I stole from them. You may as well know that about me too. As well as having unprotected sex with inappropriate men, I'm a thief."

She seemed to shrink, as though to protect herself from the condemnation she seemed sure was coming. She wouldn't get it from him. He was more interested in the fact that there was something in the bag Isobel could take to a pawnshop. Callum had imagined the boat sneaking in at night had been smuggling contraband—cheap alcohol and cigarettes from Europe was a common haul. Drugs were rarer, but much more dangerous. But neither haul was something she could have sold to a pawnbroker.

"What was in the bag?"

Her wide eyes blinked. Callum folded his arms and waited.

"Camera equipment, mainly," she said.

Callum felt the hairs on the back of his neck stand to attention. "Was there anything else in the bag?"

"Yes, but I only sold the things I recognised. The rest I gave to Jack to throw away. I asked him to take it over to the bin behind the shop, because I didn't want it anywhere near us." Her eyes flickered away from his. "You know, in case the men came looking for it, or the police found me with stolen goods. It didn't look like much anyway, just some parts from electronic equipment." She wet her dry lips. "Should I have kept them?"

Callum didn't bother pointing out that she shouldn't have touched the stuff in the first place. "What kind of camera equipment was in the bag?" Callum heard buzzing in his ears and knew it was his instinct screaming at him. Everything about this situation was wrong.

"They looked like the kind of cameras the paparazzi use. We googled some of the names, and it was high-end stuff. Very expensive new."

The wistful tone she used when mentioning its worth made Callum add the pawnbroker to his list of people to have a chat with. From the look on Isobel's face, she'd been ripped off when she'd sold the stuff. He stilled as the thought registered. What the hell? He was annoyed because the woman he'd had sex with didn't get a fair deal selling her stolen goods? He was losing his bloody mind. He told himself to keep out of her business, to let the issue of her needing money drop. It was a sensible plan. Unfortunately, it wasn't one his mouth agreed with.

"You stole to pay the loan shark, didn't you?"

She winced. "How do you know that?"

"You mentioned him when you were ranting about being a guest on Jerry Springer."

There was silence. Isobel looked everywhere except at him.

"Have you paid him in full now?" It was obvious that Isobel Sinclair was swimming in trouble and barely keeping afloat.

Her back went straight at the question. "That isn't any of your business. All I need from you is advice on what to do with the body." She sounded so prissy that it almost made him smile. Which shocked the life out of him, as it'd been months since he'd felt the urge. Knowing that the subject of her debt would only lead to an argument, Callum returned to the more pressing issue—the criminal in the freezer, and the contents of the bag she'd found.

"Was there anything in the bag that looked like a two-way radio?"

"Walkie-talkie?"

He gave her a terse nod.

"Yes, but there was only one of them, and we thought the pawnbroker wouldn't buy it if it wasn't part of a set. So we threw it out."

Callum pinched the bridge of his nose and closed his eyes. This kept getting worse. The equipment in the bag was most likely surveillance gear, and the radio was the owner's way of keeping in touch with his team. Callum wouldn't have been surprised if the stuff Isobel threw out turned out to be listening devices or equipment to infiltrate security feeds.

"This is much worse that I thought it was, isn't it, Callum?"

Callum stilled. He knew he should tell her that it was far worse than she imagined. He should scare her into calling the police. He should hand her over to the authorities and step back. But the sight of her sitting there, wide-eyed and desperate, made all of his protective instincts roar to life. He couldn't hand her over to someone else to protect. His eyes flicked to her stomach. Whether he liked it or not, for the time being, she was *his* to protect.

"Was there anything on the beach beside the body?" he asked, instead of answering her question.

She bit that bottom lip again, making him want to soothe her. He actually broke out in a sweat with the effort it took to stay in place.

"We didn't see anything," she said. "But we weren't looking. It was dark and we were too shocked and worried about the…" She gestured to the freezer.

"I need to look at the spot where you found the body, before the tide comes in and wipes the area clean."

Isobel stood, wrapping her cardigan tightly around her, in a gesture that suggested it was more for comfort than warmth. "There's a path at the back of the garden that leads down to the beach." She looked back at him as she headed out of the garage. "Nobody uses this beach. The public path is overgrown and in need of repair. I haven't seen anyone else in this cove since we moved into this house. Most folk in Arness hang out at the beach farther down the coast. It's easier to access and much prettier."

She wasn't telling him anything he didn't already know, but he let her chat as she led him to the end of the garden. She produced a key to remove the padlock from the gate. "I had to lock it to keep Sophie from escaping and falling off the cliff. She's just turned three and has a tendency to wander into trouble."

She seemed proud at that statement, so Callum didn't bother pointing out that Sophie's mother had exactly the same tendency.

They went through the gate and turned into the narrow path that ran along the top of the cliff until it met the public trail leading down to the cove below. The road lay beyond the path at the top of the bluff, with an overgrown parking bay nestled behind some fairly tall bushes. The whole area screamed abandonment. It was the perfect setup for anyone wanting to come in from the sea unseen. They could have a car waiting to pick them up and no one from town would be any the wiser. The only house near the path was Isobel's, and even she couldn't see the parking bay from any of her windows. Callum felt his jaw clench. What the hell was a woman with two young kids doing living somewhere so isolated? Scratch that. He already knew the answer. Isobel

Sinclair seemed to be lacking in the common sense department.

Callum turned and looked back at the house. The small two-storey cottage was one of the generic houses thrown up quickly in the fifties and sixties. With its grey stucco walls, small windows and, most likely, equally small rooms, the homes had been built with function rather than luxury in mind.

"You can see into the cove from that window, can't you?" He pointed to the one on the top left of the building.

"My bedroom," Isobel confirmed. "I can see the water, part of the path and a tiny bit of the beach."

"If you can't see all of the cove's beach, how did you know about the body?"

Isobel gave her answer to her feet. "I saw the boat come in, and saw them offload something into their dinghy. It was a clear night; plenty of moonlight. I was suspicious, so I crept out to the point where I could see the beach."

Callum knew what was coming. He was right. The woman was genetically deficient—her common sense gene was missing. "Which point would that be?" He kept his voice even, a sure sign for anyone who knew him, that there was a good chance he was going to blow.

Isobel pointed along the fence line of her garden. About halfway along there was a flat ridge outside the boundary of her property. The narrow ledge fell into a sharp drop at the cliff's edge—the crumbling sandstone cliff. For a second, Callum actually felt lightheaded at the thought of her being out there in the dark. She could have slipped and fallen to her death. The cliff could have given way beneath her. Hell, she could have accidentally stepped off into the darkness.

"Are you out of your mind?" he yelled, making her gaze jerk back up to his. "You could have died, woman. It's a miracle you're still alive. What kind of irresponsible mother sneaks around on a cliff edge in the middle of the bloody night? Do you have a death wish? Do you?"

She jerked her head back as though she'd been slapped, and for a second he thought she might burst into tears. She didn't. Instead, her shoulders went back, and her eyes blazed.

"Go to hell, Callum McKay. You have no idea what it takes to be a single parent. So don't go judging me. In fact, don't bother talking to me at all. Go on back to your hermit existence. I don't need you or your help. I'm sorry I told you about the body."

She spun on her heel and strode towards the gate. Callum took a step forward, his hand shooting out to curl around her arm.

"Well, you did tell me, and now we're both in this mess you call a life. You might not want my help, but you damn well need it. You don't have the sense God gave a fly. You're a walking disaster zone, woman."

"Stop calling me woman! I have a name. Isobel Sinclair. Use my name."

Callum stepped into her space, close enough that they were breathing the same air. Close enough to become enveloped in her subtle fragrance, and to feel the heat from her sensuous curves. Close enough to see the blazing defiance in her eyes and to feel that look heat his blood.

"You dragged me into this mess," he said. "Trust me when I say that I didn't want to get involved. I was happy living my life away from everyone else. I didn't come to you. You sought me out. You cannot even begin to conceive how much trouble you've stumbled into here. There's a member of the Russian mob in your freezer. Your prints are all over their surveillance equipment, equipment you sold to a local pawnshop, so it's easy to track. On top of that, you have a death wish that makes you skulk around the cliff edge in the dark. You don't just need my help, *woman*, you need a keeper. And after what happened between us this morning, that keeper is me. I don't care if you like that arrangement or not. All I care about is keeping you alive until we find out if you're carrying my child."

"I'm not pregnant!" Isobel shouted.

"Mum?"

Callum and Isobel spun towards the voice. There was a teenage boy standing on the other side of the gate, and he had Isobel's eyes.

Isobel made a strangled little mewl of pain, jerked her arm from Callum's hold and rushed towards her son. She held her hands out in front of her, as though it would calm the beast that was obviously rearing inside the boy.

"I can explain," she said.

The boy's eyes stayed firmly fixed on Callum. He didn't flinch, even though Callum had a few inches of height on him, and a whole lot more muscle. The teen was at that difficult stage where his body had grown, but hadn't yet bulked out to take on the form of a man.

"Seems to me you're not the one that needs to explain," the boy said evenly to his mother, gaining Callum's respect. He kept his eyes on Callum. "Who are you, and what are you doing with my mum?"

Callum didn't look away. He stared the boy down, giving him the respect of treating him like an adult. "That's between your mother and me."

The boy's jaw tightened and his fists clenched. He didn't like that answer at all. But he kept hold of his temper, and Callum's respect went up another notch. The boy had the potential to turn into a fine man.

Isobel was through the gate and was practically running to get to her son. "Come with me." She grabbed his arms and turned him towards the house. "I'll explain everything." She looked over her shoulder at Callum. "I'll see you down on the beach." She turned back, giving her full attention to her son.

But the boy wasn't done with Callum. His eyes held a message. He planned on talking to the man who was messing with his mother. Callum inclined his head in agreement. He'd be waiting for a visit.

Callum watched until the pair disappeared into the house before he turned back to the cliff path. It was steep and uneven, strewn with rocks and clumps of razor grass. It was exactly the kind of path he'd have run down years earlier, without giving it a second thought. Now he hesitated.

His new prosthetic legs were top-of-the-line, with articulated knee and ankle joints, and a computer that kept everything functioning properly. He could walk up and down steps, one leg in front of the other—an impossibility with most other prosthetics. He could stride over uneven surfaces and even swim wearing the damn things. For all intents and purposes, they were as close to having flesh-and-blood legs as he would ever get. But he still couldn't run down the path to the beach. He'd have to go down steadily, careful to place his feet in the right spots, otherwise he would have a repeat of his experience in Peru—where he'd lost a prosthetic when he'd slipped off a boulder and got his leg jammed in a crack.

Rage simmered, and he fought to contain it. There was no getting past the fact he wasn't the man he used to be. He couldn't do the things he used to do. And he needed to face that truth. He'd tried pretending that nothing had changed, that he was capable of everything he'd done when he still had his legs. All that had happened was he'd been proven wrong in a situation that could have resulted in everyone around him being killed.

He was glad Isobel wasn't with him as he started down the path. Glad she didn't see him work his way to the beach with the care an octogenarian would take. Part of him was shamed that he'd had sex with the woman and she didn't even know he was half a man. The rest of him was glad that his secret was safe. Right now, Isobel looked at him as though he was the man he used to be. She looked at him as though he was able to do everything she thought he could do. She didn't look at him like he was an invalid. There was no pity in her eyes. And Callum planned to do everything within his power to keep it that way.

CHAPTER 8

"You said you were done with men," Jack said as soon as Isobel had led him into their kitchen.

His fists were clenched at his sides and his brow was furrowed, making his peridot-coloured eyes seem even more luminous than usual. In that moment, he looked so like his father at the same age that it made Isobel's heart hurt. Darren had missed out on knowing his wonderful son. He'd missed out in a big way.

"I *am* through with men," Isobel said as calmly as she could, considering she was a basket case on the inside.

Jack smirked. "Right. That's why he's talking about you being pregnant."

"I am *not* pregnant." She mentally crossed her fingers and hoped. "And I really don't want to talk about my sex life with my son."

He turned green and held up a hand. "Never use that word."

"How do you think a woman gets pregnant?" Isobel suddenly felt faint. "Please tell me you know how babies are made?" It wasn't as though the conversation had ever come up, something Isobel had been incredibly grateful for, and she'd assumed Jack had found out at school. The same way she'd found out about the birds and the bees. There had been absolutely no chance her parents would have given her the information. Isobel's mother still insisted that she bought her four children at the local department store. Apparently Mairi had been on sale.

"I know what sex is." Jack looked disgusted. "I just don't want to think about you doing it."

"Good." Isobel sank into a kitchen chair. "Let's keep it that way."

"How am I supposed to do that when you've got the local nut job shouting about you having his kid? Don't you know about condoms?"

"Jack!" Isobel felt her cheeks burn and fought the urge to run. Jack would follow her anyway. There was no hiding from your kids when they wanted to know something. A fact she was reminded of every time she wanted to go to the toilet alone and her three-year-old followed her in.

"Who is this guy? What's his deal? Have you been seeing him? How long? And when? You're always here, or at the shop. When did you have time for a guy?"

Isobel could practically see his brain working. She tried to change the topic. "Why aren't you at school?"

"Half day. I told you this morning. Are you going to marry this guy? They talk about him at school. Laugh about him. Everybody knows he's brain-damaged from the war."

"He isn't brain-damaged!" Isobel was more outraged on Callum's behalf than she was about her son thinking she'd jump into another marriage. Hell, she was still suffering from the last one. "I think he has PTSD."

He frowned.

"Post-traumatic stress disorder. It's when you have mental health problems after you experience something awful, like war." In truth, she had no idea why Callum was living like a hermit in Nowhere, Scotland. All she knew for certain was that he'd been in the armed forces. And that he had muscles and he knew how to use them. Her cheeks heated again.

"Oh, sick, you're thinking about him!" Jack pulled open the food cupboard and came out with a family-sized bag of crisps.

Isobel made a mental note to get more snacks. She was always making mental notes to get more snacks. Jack ate enough for ten people, and she could barely keep up. Where he put it all, she didn't know. He'd stretched up the past year, towering over her now, but he was still pretty much skin and bone. Sometimes it stole her breath just thinking that she had a sixteen-year-old son.

"I don't want to talk about Callum." Isobel used her eldest-sister voice, which didn't seem to work as well on her son. "I'm an adult and have a right to a private life."

He snorted. "Yeah, right. Can we talk about the freezer in the garage instead? Why's it suddenly got a padlock on it?"

Isobel groaned and rubbed her temples. She needed aspirin. Lots and lots of it.

"Does it have anything to do with the guys who visit the beach at night?" Jack studied her and didn't miss her shock.

"What do you know about that?" She'd done her best to shelter him from the things she had to deal with—the boat people, the loan shark, the money problems. Her face hurt from faking a smile twenty-four hours a day.

"First, you asked me to get rid of a strange bag and not look in it. I looked. Of course I looked. Seriously, mum, did you really think I wouldn't?"

"Yes. I *really* thought my son would do what he was told!"

He gave her a pitying look as though she was sorely deluded. "Secondly, I'm a teenager. We don't sleep at night. I see you sneak out. I know you're watching the cove." He stilled. "Unless you're meeting the weirdo down there."

"What? No! I barely know Callum. I'm not sneaking out at night to meet him. And don't call him a weirdo."

"How come you're having his baby if you don't see the guy?"

"I am not pregnant!"

"I can hear you halfway down the street," Mairi said as she came into the kitchen carrying Sophie. There was chocolate all around the three-year-old's mouth.

"Where's m–" Jack started.

"Here." Mairi smacked a paper bag against his chest. "Bottomless pit. That's what you have instead of a stomach." She put Sophie down, and she ran straight at Isobel.

"I's had a choccy doughnut!" Her grin melted Isobel's heart as she wrapped her in a tight hug.

"So I see." She kissed her daughter's cheek. "Why don't you go watch Mickey Mouse in the other room? Jack can put the TV on for you." She grabbed a cloth and wiped her daughter's face.

Jack had already demolished his donut and, unlike his sister, there was no evidence around his mouth.

"Whatever." Jack held his hand out for his sister. "But I'm coming straight back. Come on, Soph."

Sophie took his hand and chattered all about her day as they headed into the living room.

"How can you be pregnant?" Mairi asked as soon as they were gone. "You don't have a life. You don't know any men. Unless…" She narrowed her eyes. "Did you sleep with the Arness Outlaw to get him to help us?"

"No!" Isobel was seriously beginning to think that everyone she knew had a very low opinion of her.

"Then why does the kid think you're pregnant?" Mairi filled the kettle and switched it on.

"Because," Jack said as he strode back into the room, looking far older than his sixteen years, "the local weirdo was shouting it from the cliffs, while he had his hands all over her."

"No way." Mairi's eyes were wide. "You did sleep with him for help."

"No!" This was getting totally out of Isobel's control.

"Did you or did you not have sex with Callum McKay?"

Isobel could feel her face heat. She looked pointedly at Jack, trying to tell her sister by telepathy that she was not going to answer questions about Callum in front of her son. She was fairly certain Mairi didn't get the message.

"Mum doesn't think you should talk about this in front of me," Jack told Mairi. His lips quirked as though he was fighting a smile. "She just asked me if I knew how babies were made."

Mairi burst out laughing, which made Jack grin and Isobel groan. With only nine years between the two of them, Mairi and Jack acted more like brother and sister than aunt and nephew.

"Go to your room," Isobel ordered, which made the two of them laugh harder.

"So what's in the freezer?" Jack asked Mairi, changing the topic away from Callum, but picking something else Isobel didn't want him to know about.

"Dead body." Mairi reached for the teapot as Isobel gasped. "We found him on the beach this morning and needed some advice on what to do with him. That's why she slept with the outlaw."

"Mairi! You can't tell him about the body. He's a kid."

The two of them shared a look again. One that clearly said Isobel was woefully out of touch.

"At his age, you were alone with a baby," Mairi said. "He's hardly a kid."

"That's why I want him to have a childhood and not worry about adult things." Isobel knew only too well what it felt like to be sixteen and woefully ill-equipped for adult life.

"You mean like the guy who comes around asking for money?" Jack pinned her down with a condemning stare.

"How do you know about that?" And yes, she sounded hysterical.

"Mum, you're rubbish at sneaking around. I saw you talking to him behind the shop a few weeks ago. Him and that pumped-up steroid freak he's got protecting him. What is he?"

"The steroid freak?" Mairi said. "No idea, but I'm leaning towards him being a genetic experiment between a hippo and a gorilla."

"Helpful," Jack said before looking back at Isobel, "but I mean the guy in charge. Who is he and what does he want with you?"

"He's a man that Robert owes some money to, that's all. H-he was j-just here asking where R-robert might be." Damn that stutter.

Jack shook his head at her, clearly disgusted. Isobel wasn't sure if it was with the situation or her lack of ability to lie. He turned to Mairi. "What's the real story?"

"Loan shark." Mairi was texting at the same time as following the conversation. "She's paying off Rob's debt."

"Do you even understand the concept of secrecy?" Isobel asked. Mairi shrugged it off.

"Why didn't you tell him to get lost? Or call the cops on him?" Jack was outraged again.

Isobel wasn't about to explain that Eddie Granger had threatened her family if she did just that. The loan shark had friends who were willing to hurt Isobel's sisters and kids if she didn't comply. And not for one second did Isobel doubt that he would carry out his threat.

"That's what we said." Mairi held out her phone, pouted and took a selfie. "Rajesh has upped his demand for selfies. I need more clothes. The guys don't like it when I post the same photo for each of them."

Jack frowned. "Let them whine. Bunch of losers have to pay for a pretend girlfriend, they have no right to complain."

"Thanks," Mairi said drolly. "That's helpful. I'll tell them that next time I email. I'm sure that will increase my income."

"Welcome." Jack nodded. "Now, you want to tell me why there's a dead body in the garage and why this Callum guy thinks you're up the duff?"

"No. I don't." Isobel stood. "Forget about the body. We're dealing with it. You just concentrate on school." She pointed at her sister. "You watch the kids. And by watch them, I mean make sure Jack stays in the house with you. I need to go down to the beach and show Callum where we found the body, and I can't deal with your version of the inquisition while I'm doing it."

"You can't ignore me," Jack said. "I have the right to know if I have another brother or sister coming."

Isobel groaned and strode past them.

"Why aren't you more freaked out about the body?" she heard Mairi say behind her.

"Grand Theft Auto," Jack said.

"Oh man, you better hope your mum doesn't find out you play that game," Mairi said.

And Isobel made a mental note to confiscate her son's Xbox.

CALLUM DIDN'T NEED Isobel to show him where she'd found the body—a trail of vomit led right to the spot. The tide had started to come in, and waves were lapping at the rocks and sand, which meant the spot where the body had lain had already been washed away. All Callum could make out were the footprints leading up to the water's edge.

Most were small and had obviously been made by the Sinclair sisters, but he could still make out at least one set of prints that came from larger boots. A few feet from the edge of the water, where the body would have lain, was another large indentation. Something had been placed on the ground. Which meant there had to have been at least two men on the beach the night before, and one of them had been carrying something other than the body. Something large and heavy.

It didn't make sense. Why dump a man out in the open like that? Especially one that had obviously been murdered. The killers couldn't have known who would find it, or what they would do when they did.

"Have you found anything?" Isobel asked as she came up beside him.

Callum had heard her coming down the path, long before he could see her. Silent she wasn't. He glanced at her flushed face, noting that her hair tie was long gone and her hair was flying about her face. It was long, past her shoulders, and tousled from the breeze. She looked as though she'd been thoroughly tumbled. Callum cleared his throat and wrestled his thoughts back under control. He pointed at the large oval indention in the sand. Something about the mark, with the boot prints beside it, was familiar to him.

"What is it?" Isobel said.

"Tell me what you see." His voice was still husky, carrying a sexual note that he couldn't hide.

She bit her bottom lip, and her lashes lowered. Beautiful. She was beautiful. And a complication he really didn't need.

"I see the spot where someone stood and put their bag down," she said.

Callum stilled as recognition became crystal clear. He was looking at the familiar soles of military-issue boots, and the mark left behind by a heavy duffel bag. A long, heavy bag. A body-shaped bag.

"Are you sure it was a body you saw them carry from the boat?"

She bit at her bottom lip as she thought about it. "No. I saw a long, body-like shape over someone's shoulder. And then I found a body. Two and two make four, right?"

"How many men got off the boat?"

"Two, if you don't count the body."

Callum followed the footsteps up to the path leading out of the cove. Most were obscured by the women's prints, but there was definitely only one set.

"I don't think you saw two men with a body," Callum said. "I think you saw two men with a duffel bag. I think there was an altercation on the beach. One killed the other and then took off with the bag. Did you see any blood when you were here?" There would have been a lot of blood, seeing as the man's throat had been slit.

"No, it was dark."

It was possible the blood had soaked into the sand under the body and Isobel had assumed it was water. There wouldn't have been any colour in the moonlight.

"When did you come into the cove? How long after you saw them get off the boat?"

"I waited at the top of the cliff until I heard the car roar away. The driver seemed to be in a hurry. Then I called my sisters."

Callum pinched the bridge of his nose. This was one helluva mess, and she'd landed smack dab in the middle of it.

"What's going on Callum?" Isobel said softly.

He let out a sigh. "I'm guessing here, but I think the guy with the bag had a delivery to make and he was on a tight schedule. I think he intended to come back and deal with the body."

She wrapped that ugly cardigan tighter around herself. "And while he was gone, we took it away."

"Aye. He knows the police didn't take it. If they had, the whole place would have been cordoned off and crawling with investigators for days on end. The fact it isn't, means someone else had to have taken the body. Someone who was watching them. He'll most likely try to figure out what the agenda of that person is."

"There was no agenda. All I wanted to do was make sure Jack didn't find the body, and the cops weren't called."

"Aye, but now this mob are aware that someone knows about them."

"Oh." Big eyes blinked up at him. "That isn't good."

"No. It isn't." He resisted the urge to shake her. "Now would be a good time to call in the police."

She shook her head. "I can't, I told you that. You need to believe me when I say I don't want the police involved. I can't risk that they'd arrest me and take me away from my kids. I sold stolen goods. I didn't report the sneaky boat activity. And now I have a body in my freezer. There is no way they won't arrest me."

She had a point. "I know a lawyer—"

"Callum, I can't afford a lawyer. I can barely afford to feed my kids. People like me, people with no resources, don't get away with breaking the law. They get sent to jail, and I can't let that happen. I need to find another way out of this mess. That's why I came to you. You have to help me. You will help me, won't you?"

"I'm trying to help you. This is bigger than I thought. We need help. You need to call the cops."

"I can't. Don't make me. I'm the only parent my kids have ever known. I can't let myself be taken away from them. They would feel as though I'd abandoned them too. And if they lock me up, I won't be able to pay off the loans. The moneylender said he'd hurt my family if I can't pay him back. I can't talk to the police unless I take my kids and sisters and we run first. Then, once we're safe and hidden, I could maybe make an anonymous phone call. What am I thinking?" She threw up her hands. "I don't have money to run away and start afresh. Maybe I could sell a kidney? Is that legal?" She was all too serious.

"No, it isn't legal," Callum said.

She nodded, appearing utterly crestfallen that she couldn't sell a body part. "Then I'm stuck here. With a body in the freezer and a moneylender threatening my family. I don't know what to do. That's why I came to you. I honestly don't know what to do, and you're the scariest person I could think of. The only person I could think of who might know what to do with a dead body. You *are* going to help me deal with the body, right?"

Callum stared at her before sighing. "Aye, I'm going to help you. But we can't deal with this alone. I'll need to call in help." Which meant contacting the team he'd run out on. He wanted to curse a blue streak at the thought. There was a good chance they wouldn't take his call. They say you shouldn't burn bridges for a reason, and he'd taken a nuclear bomb to his.

"Not police help, right?"

"Not right now."

"Not ever."

"I can't promise that. But I'll try to sort this for you without involving them."

"Because I can't get taken away." The look of absolute resolve on her face made Callum wonder what she would do if he called in the cops. "What do we do about the body?"

"Leave it where it is for now," he said. "At least until I do a bit of investigating and see how deep this hole is that you've stumbled into. You need to go stay with one of your sisters for a few days. Just in case these guys come back and decide to look for the person watching them."

"That isn't possible." She shook her head adamantly.

Callum was losing his patience. "Is there anything I suggest that you feel you can do? Because if you aren't going to take my advice, I don't see the point in me being here."

"Mairi and Agnes share a tiny one-bedroom flat over the town's garage, and Mairi is up all night working. Agnes has a college exam tomorrow that she can't fail. And Donna is live-in staff at the mansion house. She isn't allowed to have people stay over. That's why I can't go to them. Plus, I can't put them in any more danger than I already have. I'm not trying to be difficult. This is just the way things are."

She stood there looking at him with those oversized eyes that begged him to rescue her. Although he was fairly certain she wasn't even aware that's what she was doing. His eyes flicked to the spot on her belly where his baby could be growing, and he felt his own stomach clench. He deeply regretted opening the door to her that morning. Things had gone from bad to worse since he'd done it. And now, instead of her being someone else's problem, she was most definitely his.

"Woman, your life is a mess."

"I know," she wailed.

Callum expected tears, but she pulled herself together. She looked small, fragile and completely overwhelmed. And he couldn't stand it. With a sigh, Callum wrapped an arm around her and pulled her to him. He awkwardly patted her back and hoped she didn't start to cry. He'd rather crawl on his belly through a war zone than deal with a weeping woman. Especially one as soft as Isobel, who was fighting her tears and trying hard to be brave. She might not have any common sense, but she did have courage, he'd give her that.

"I'll spend the night at your place," he said with heavy reluctance.

There was a little hiccup. "On the couch."

That didn't even merit a reply. Of course he was sleeping on the couch. She had two kids in the house, and touching her had caused enough problems already. He grasped her shoulders and set her away from him. "I'm going back to my place to pack an overnight bag. I'll be back in an hour. Try not to get into any more trouble while I'm gone."

She lifted her chin. Her eyes were blazing at him through unshed tears. "I'll see what I can do."

With a snort, Callum turned his back on her and started the slow climb back up the cliff.

CHAPTER 9

Sophie had fallen asleep wearing her green dinosaur onesie, with a pink tutu on top. She had a shark motif swim cap tugged onto her head and ski gloves on her hands. Isobel grinned at her unconscious three-year-old. She was never quite sure what she would find when she went in to check at bedtime. As soon as the light was out, Sophie dressed in what *she* thought was appropriate for bed, and it was never what Isobel had put her to sleep in.

After softly closing the door on the bedroom she shared with her daughter, Isobel knocked on her son's door. There was a grunt, which Isobel took to mean "come in". Jack was sitting on his bed, his headphones around his neck and his tablet computer in his hands. He'd retreated to his room after dinner, once Isobel had explained that Callum would be spending the night. He hadn't said a word to her since.

"You still in a huff?" Isobel wished he would still let her kiss him goodnight and ruffle his hair the way he'd done when he was little.

"About your boyfriend moving in?" He gave an exaggerated shrug. "Why would I be upset about that?"

"It's not like that. He's only going to stay tonight to make sure we're safe."

"The same way he made sure you were safe when he jumped your bones?"

"Jack!" Isobel felt her cheeks heat.

"What? I'm not allowed to talk about how some random guy might be the father of my new little brother?"

"There's no baby. I told you that. I'm not going to explain what happened between Callum and me; that's between us."

"Sure. Will it still be between you two when he walks out on us, like everyone else does? Don't know if you noticed, Mum, but I live here too. I need to deal with the crap they leave behind when they run, just like you do."

He was breaking her heart. "I know you do. I'm really sorry that my bad judgement has hurt you. I never meant for that to happen. You know I love you, Jack, right? You're the best thing that ever happened to me, and I wouldn't change a second of my life if it meant you weren't in it."

His cheeks turned pink and he looked away, suddenly mesmerised by his computer screen. "If he hurts you, I'll make him suffer. I'm not a little kid anymore. He doesn't get to hurt you."

"I know." Isobel itched to touch him. "How about a hug?"

"No!" But he did give her a smile.

He put the headphones back in place and tuned her out, his eyes fixed on the screen in front of him.

Isobel closed the door silently and pressed her forehead against the shabby cream paint. She was screwing this parent thing up again. Who knew what sort of long-term emotional issues she was passing on to her son? And really, she couldn't blame him for anything he said. She was a disaster as a mother. Sure, she did her best, but it was never good enough. Even she could see that. They lived hand-to-mouth, relying on her sisters for extras, like tablet computers for school and second-hand games consoles, so that her teenage son would fit in with his friends.

She turned and sat on the top step, pulling her knees up to her chest and wrapping her arms around them. Of course Jack was upset about Callum. It was yet another man Isobel had dragged into their lives, even though she didn't want him in it any more than he wanted to be there. She'd screwed up. Again. And her kids would suffer because of it. Again.

"What are you doing sitting up there?" Aggie called softly. "Come down here, where we have cake."

Isobel tried to surreptitiously wipe away her tears as she painted on a fake smile. Aggie wasn't fooled; her eyes filled with sympathy as she walked up the stairs to meet Isobel halfway.

"Don't mind me, I'm having a pity party." Isobel forced another smile.

"It's going to be okay," Agnes said as she wrapped an arm around Isobel.

"Jack's angry with me."

"Jack is a teenager. He's angry with everybody." They headed down the rest of the stairs together.

"I've made a mess of his life. His dad didn't even want to meet him, and then I married Rob thinking he'd make a good father for Jack. How could I have been so dumb? Why am I such a terrible judge of character?"

Her other two sisters jumped up to hug her when she entered the kitchen. For a moment, the comfort of being in the middle of them all made her burden lighten. Without these three amazing women, she wouldn't have survived.

"We're all terrible judges of character." Donna stroked Isobel's hair. "It's the Sinclair curse. We're genetically incapable of telling a good man from a bad one."

"It's why the rest of us are single," Mairi agreed. "We

know if we pick someone, he'll likely be a dickhead. You were the only one brave enough to try."

"Dumb enough," Isobel corrected.

"We were all fooled by Robert." Agnes tugged Isobel out of the group hug and guided her into a chair. "We all thought he was a great guy. None of us saw the slightest indication that he was a gambler."

"He had a good job," Donna agreed as she placed a huge wedge of chocolate cake in front of Isobel. "He'd had it for years. We thought he was stable."

"Plus, let's be honest," Mairi said as she sat down beside Isobel. "He wasn't that good looking, and we all thought he'd be more dependable because of it."

The sisters stared at her in stunned silence.

"What?" Mairi said around a mouthful of cake.

"We didn't think that," Donna said. "Did we?" She looked at Agnes and Isobel, who shook their heads.

"No, we didn't," Agnes said. "Why would we think the fact he was skinny and had bad hair meant he was stable and honest?"

"Because he had to work harder to be popular. Because he should have been grateful he landed someone as gorgeous as Isobel and treated her fabulously because of it. Because he had no muscle mass and wasn't able to fight off anybody who came after him. You'd think the inability to defend himself would mean he wouldn't get into trouble in the first place." Mairi sat back with a triumphant smile, as though she made perfect sense.

"I worry about you," Agnes said. "You don't think like normal people."

"Like you would know what normal is," Mairi scoffed, before digging back into her cake.

"Robert wasn't bad looking and he wasn't skinny. He was lanky," Isobel felt the need to point out. "He was handsome in a kind of geeky way. The way that guy who owns Facebook is handsome."

"He is not handsome," Donna said.

"Yes, he is. He's handsome, but not hot or sexy. There's a difference, trust me. I know. Jack's father was hot. Robert was handsome in an understated way." And Callum was sexy as hell. But she kept that last part to herself.

"Have you had your eyes tested lately?" Mairi asked with such seriousness that the rest of them burst out laughing.

"Callum McKay is hot *and* sexy," Agnes said with a sneaky smile at Isobel. "Isn't he? How on earth are you going to keep your hands off him for a whole night?"

"Oh!" Mairi sat up straight. "I nearly forgot. Jack said Isobel already had sex with Callum."

"What?" Agnes said. "I was kidding about keeping your hands off him. Isobel?"

Isobel squirmed in her seat. "Jack didn't say that," she said as firmly as she could.

"That's right," Mairi said as her thumbs flew over her phone, "he said you could be pregnant. That Callum was shouting about you carrying his child." She shrugged. "I guess the sex part was implied."

Isobel glared at her youngest sister, but it was wasted on her.

"You slept with the outlaw?" Donna screeched. "When?"

"This morning," Mairi said. "To pay for his help."

"He wanted sex for his help?" It was Agnes's turn to screech.

"I did not sleep with him to pay for his help!" Isobel practically shouted.

"Then why did you sleep with him?" Donna demanded.

"Because he's hot!"

There was silence. Isobel realised what she'd said, and her face burned.

"You really did have sex with Callum?" Mairi said. "I thought Jack had misunderstood and I was winding you up."

Isobel groaned, put her elbows on the table and dropped her face into her hands. "Kill me now."

"Somebody should," Agnes snapped. "What were you thinking?"

"I wasn't thinking," Isobel snapped back. "That's the whole point. I wasn't thinking at all. It was a rerun of Jack's father. Only worse. Much worse. Callum kissed me, and I didn't have another thought until it was over." She threw up her hands. "But what difference does it make? I thought long and hard before I married and slept with Robert, and look how that turned out."

"You didn't think long and hard," Mairi said. "You married him three weeks after you met him, and he charmed himself into your pants a whole lot earlier than that."

"We're not talking about Robert," Agnes said. "We're talking about Callum McKay. A man you barely know, who you somehow still managed to have sex with."

"You only went over there to feel him out about helping us," Donna said incredulously.

"She felt him out, all right." Mairi grinned.

Isobel scowled at her. "Not helping."

"Please tell me you used protection," Agnes said.

There was silence. It was pointless lying. She'd stutter and they'd know the truth anyway.

"You didn't," Donna whispered. "Are you insane?"

"How could you?" Agnes demanded. "You of all people? The poster child for teenage pregnancy? Didn't you learn from that mistake?"

"Apparently not!" Isobel pushed back her chair and stomped to the sink. She needed a glass of water. No, she needed alcohol. But seeing as she didn't drink, she'd have to make do with water. She really needed to start drinking.

"Wait a minute," Donna said. "Callum could have thought about protection too. Didn't he say something? Suggest you use something?"

"We were too busy for the topic to come up." And didn't that make Isobel sound like the world's biggest tart?

"Are you pregnant?" Mairi asked.

"You can't tell in a matter of hours," Agnes said. "Don't you know anything?"

"I know enough to use a condom," Mairi said.

"Could you be pregnant?" Donna asked. "Is it possible?"

Isobel gripped the glass of water tight enough to make her knuckles turn white. "It's possible, but not probable. The timing is off."

"I can't believe you did this," Agnes said. "I really can't."

"You can't believe it?" Isobel felt her temper flare. "I was there and I can't believe it! I'm a cliché. An uneducated woman with no morals, who jumps into bed with any man who comes her way."

"You've slept with three men," Donna pointed out. "Including Callum. And the only reason you didn't finish school is because of Jack."

Isobel ignored her. "I'm one of those women on daytime TV. On those chat shows where they use polygraphs to find out if the boyfriend is sleeping with his best friend's wife. I'm one of those people. I mean it. What else would you call a person who has children to three different partners?"

"Unlucky in love?" Donna said.

"A slut?" Agnes said.

"Mr President," Mairi said.

There was a second of silence, before they all burst out laughing. Isobel sat back down at the table with her sisters and pulled the rest of the chocolate cake towards her.

"Guess I have no other choice but to wait and see if baby number three is on the way."

"To be fair," Donna said, "babies one and two are totally awesome."

"There is that," Isobel said. But she wasn't encouraged. She knew nothing about Callum McKay, other than what he ordered at the shop, and what the rumours said about him. She didn't know if he'd be another deadbeat dad who ran out on his kid the first chance he got. Did she even want him in her children's life? He was sexy, and terrifying, and dangerous, but was he honourable? Probably not. Otherwise, he wouldn't have jumped her in his hallway and he wouldn't be hiding in Arness.

"This is a mess," she said around a mouthful of cake.

"Aye, and it gets worse every day." Agnes reached for the pot of tea to top them all up.

"I don't like any of this," Donna said. "I think we should pool our money and move away. Start again, somewhere new, together."

"We don't have a lot," Mairi said, "but it would be enough to get us all settled. I've always fancied living in a city. You know, somewhere where there's work and I could get a job where I didn't talk rubbish to men online all day long."

"You love talking rubbish online," Agnes said. "We'd need to move somewhere cheap, though; a city would be expensive. I hear Wales is cheap. We could probably buy a whole town there for a couple of pounds."

"Oh, I hear Welsh guys are hot," Mairi said with a grin. "I can move to Wales."

"Mmm, probably best if we kept away from the hot men," Agnes said, her eyes sparkling with mischief. "Our eldest sister can't keep her pants on. We wouldn't want to exhaust her by providing too many options."

"Funny, oh so funny," Isobel said.

Isobel's three sisters reached over and covered her hands with theirs.

"Whatever happens," Donna said, "we're in this together. You won't be alone."

"I love you guys," Isobel said as she fought back tears.

"We know," Agnes said.

"Aye," Mairi said, "we love you too. Even though you're a loose woman. Maybe one of us should spend the night while Callum is here? Just to make sure you keep your underwear on. I vote for Agnes."

Agnes threw a tea cosy at her head.

There were four women waiting for Callum when he returned to Isobel's house. Four women, and one very angry teenage boy. Jack Sinclair stood at the bottom of the staircase, his hands in the pockets of his jeans, and his dark eyes filled with resentment. Callum didn't blame him one bit.

"Later," Callum said to the boy, who nodded tersely. They understood each other.

"Later what?" Isobel's worried gaze flicked between the two of them.

"Never mind that," the woman beside her said. "I'm Mairi. I'm the youngest sister. And we want to know if you plan on keeping your pants on overnight, or if someone has to stay here to chaperone?"

"Mairi!" Isobel spun on her sister.

"What?" Mairi said. "I'm just saying what everyone is thinking."

"Not me," the one beside her muttered. "I was thinking that he looks like he could kill a man with his bare hands." Her eyes shot to Callum's, and she blushed. "Which is good. You'll keep them safe. Right?"

"Donna," Isobel said.

For a second Callum thought it was a rhetorical question,

but Isobel's three sisters seemed to be waiting for an answer. "That's why I'm here."

"So you're not here to sleep with Isobel, then?" Mairi said. "Just to clarify."

A low growling noise came from Jack, and Isobel smacked her hand over her sister's mouth. "Ignore her. Her mouth works independently from her brain." Still holding her sister's mouth, Isobel gestured to the angry-looking blonde. "That's Agnes. The only sister I have who knows how to keep her mouth shut." She looked back at Mairi. "Stop licking my hand! Are you going to stop talking or do I have to tape your trap shut?"

Mairi nodded and Isobel removed her hand. Which didn't make any sense, because technically she'd agreed to both options. Callum decided that mental health issues ran in the family.

"How exactly do you plan on protecting my sister and her kids?" Agnes asked. "There are lots of rumours about you. We don't know what's true. Are you even able to protect them?"

"I take it back," Isobel said to the ceiling. "None of my sisters know when to shut up."

"I was an SAS soldier. I can handle myself in an altercation. Is that enough information for you?" He kept his eyes on Agnes, who wasn't the least bit intimidated by him. It wasn't a reaction he came across often, and he respected it.

"Are you involved in anything illegal?" Agnes said.

"Aggie," Isobel almost wailed.

"No," Callum told Agnes. "Unlike you four."

Agnes cocked her head in acknowledgment. "Do you have any criminal convictions? Are you on any watch lists? Were you kicked out of the armed forces?"

"No."

"Kill me now," Isobel said as she sat on the steps beside

her son. "You might as well. I'm going to die of humiliation anyway."

"Oh, get a grip," Mairi said, "she's only asking what we all want to know. Although there is one more question I think is important." She looked up at Callum. "Will you take responsibility for your kid, if Isobel is pregnant, or do you plan to run like every other rat bastard we know?"

"Out!" Isobel was on her feet and storming towards the door. She threw it open and waved her sisters towards it. "Out now. He answered your questions. You don't have to worry. Now leave."

When no one moved fast enough, Isobel came up behind them and started shoving her sisters towards the door. They complained and shouted more questions, but Isobel was ruthless. She slammed the door after them.

"No more chocolate cake for you!" someone shouted, but then Callum heard their footsteps echo down the path.

"Interesting family," Callum said when Isobel turned back to him.

"Don't start." She strode past him and into the living room, Callum and Jack following her. "This is the couch." She pointed at it, in case he was confused. "It isn't very big, but you'll have to make do. There are only two bedrooms in this house. I share one with Sophie, and Jack has the other."

"I don't share," Jack snapped.

That wasn't a surprise. "The couch is fine. I've slept on worse." Callum put his bag on it. He didn't plan to sleep anyway. He planned to stay up and keep watch. He glanced around the room—it was small, with only a couch, an armchair, a wooden coffee table and a chest of drawers with a TV on top of it. Heating was a cheap gas bottle heater, which couldn't do much to warm the place during a Scottish winter. On the walls were photos of Isobel with her kids and her sisters. They were in mismatched frames, but in each and every one, they looked happy.

"I'll get bedding." Isobel gave them a worried look. "Be nice to each other while I'm gone."

Jack and Callum stared at her until she left the room, muttering about men as she went. As soon as she was out of earshot, Callum turned to Jack.

"Let's hear it."

"You mess with my mother, I'll mess with you."

Callum was impressed. The boy stated his threat as though it were fact. There was no posturing. No emotional outrage. No inflection at all. Only confidence.

"How are you going to do that, exactly? I have a lot of years and a tonne of experience on you."

Jack's eyes narrowed. "I'll find a way."

Callum nodded. He had no doubt that the boy would do exactly what he said he would. "Fair enough. I don't intend to mess with your mum."

"Yeah, I've heard that before. This time I'm big enough to do something about it." Jack took a step closer to Callum. The boy was almost tall enough to look him in the eye, and he hadn't finished growing yet. There was evidence of muscle building, too. In a few years, Jack Sinclair would make a formidable foe. "Don't think you can use her for sex. She isn't some cheap night out."

Callum stilled. "Do people say that about her?" If they did, he was going to put a stop to it pretty damn fast.

Jack searched Callum's eyes, looking for something he obviously found, and his shoulders relaxed slightly. "She has two kids to two fathers. Both men ran out on her. People talk."

Callum's fists clenched. "They talk to you?" *About his mother?*

Jack shrugged, like it was nothing, but he couldn't quite

keep the emotion from his face. It wasn't nothing. It was a huge bloody deal. "I handle it. But people will talk if you're here. And don't think they won't know. Someone will notice. Rumours will spread. You need to be gone before that happens."

"I plan to be gone in the morning." Although, for some reason, the words seemed to stick in his throat as they came out.

Jack nodded and his eyes hardened, but not before Callum saw a flash of vulnerability that reminded him that Jack was still very much a boy. "And if there's a kid on the way?"

Callum opened his mouth to say that he'd never turned his back on a responsibility in his life. Then he remembered walking out on Benson Security and closed it again.

"That's what I thought," Jack sneered. "You're just like the rest."

There was nothing Callum could say to that. He couldn't make promises he wasn't sure he could keep. He couldn't tell the kid that he was a reliable bet when he knew he wasn't. He couldn't offer him anything at all.

"Let's see what the future brings first," Callum said, and heard exactly how pathetic he sounded.

"Sure." Jack turned away. "Whatever."

Callum felt the boy's obvious dismissal like a blow. He wasn't entirely sure why Jack's opinion of him mattered, when the opinions of most people didn't, but he had to bite his tongue to stop from making promises he couldn't keep. To stop from trying to convince the boy that he was a better man than he knew himself to be.

"Here you go." Isobel walked into the room, her arms full of folded bedding, and looked at them both. "What's going on?"

"Nothing," Jack said. "I'm going to bed."

He kissed his mother's cheek, which, from the look of shock on her face, wasn't something he did every night, and then sauntered from the room. Isobel placed the bedding on the couch, and her fingertips brushed the spot where Jack had kissed.

"You have a good boy," Callum said.

"I know," she whispered before clearing her throat. "I'll show you around."

"Good. I need to get a feel for the place. And I want to make sure the house is secured."

"I thought you might. Do you need to go upstairs? Sophie's asleep, but we could peek into the room if we're quiet."

"I want to check all the windows and doors." He'd already noticed that she had no alarm system and that she didn't even own a dog. The lane leading up to her house was only lit by one low-wattage orange lamp, and the path to her front door was flanked by overgrown bushes. It was a security nightmare.

"Callum." She hesitated in the doorway. "I know you didn't want any of this. But thank you. I mean it. Thank you for being here tonight."

She looked so earnest and vulnerable standing there with her hair wild about her face, and that oversized purple cardigan pulled tight about her. She looked like she was drowning in the thing. Or hiding in it. And Callum had never seen a sexier sight. Without thinking about it, he took a step towards her. Her eyes went dark and the tip of her tongue flicked out to moisten her lips.

Callum had never wanted to taste a woman more than he wanted Isobel right then. Her gaze flickered between his eyes and his lips, and he knew she was thinking the same thing. He knew she was feeling the same intense pull.

"Callum?" she whispered.

For one second, it felt like time had stilled and there was nothing else in the world except him and Isobel. He knew, without a doubt, that if he kissed her right then, she would return the fire he felt burning inside of him. He knew she wouldn't reject him, wouldn't turn away. He knew because he could see the same desperate need in her eyes as he felt growing inside of him.

But they couldn't.

He took a step back. There were tremors running throughout his body. The need to touch her, to take her, was so great that it almost brought him to his knees. But he couldn't lose his mind over her. Not again.

"Show me the house." His voice was husky and low, a declaration of what he desperately wanted, but a reminder of what he wouldn't allow.

She swallowed hard, her cheeks flushing a pretty pink. "Of course." Her dark eyes met his. "I… We… I mean…"

"No." Callum strode towards the doorway, making her follow him. "Show me the house. There is nothing else. There can't be."

For a second, he thought she might argue. Instead, she nodded and followed him into the kitchen. Callum felt strangely bereft. He knew there was no future for them. Their brief past had been a huge mistake. And yet…and yet her soft scent had him mesmerised, and the memory of her body pressed to his, had him in agony. He suspected that Isobel Sinclair had managed something that morning that no other person had ever managed with Callum. She'd managed to get inside of him. And he was very much afraid she could never be removed.

CHAPTER 10

Callum was gone by the time Isobel got up the following morning. The bedding sat on the couch where she'd put it, untouched. There was a tersely-written note on top of it.

Investigating.

It was followed by his cell number. He didn't say whether she could call him, he'd just given her the number. Isobel wasn't sure what to make of that, but she tucked the number into the front pocket of her jeans.

"He's done a runner already, then," Jack said as he came into the room.

The look of pure disgust on his face made Isobel ache for him. All of the male figures in his life so far had been unreliable. Of course he'd assume Callum was the same. And Isobel didn't know Callum well enough to reassure Jack that he was different.

"I told you he wasn't staying. He only spent the night because I was worried about sleeping with a body in the garage."

She shivered, then pushed the thought into the back of her mind, locking it behind the door labelled *denial* in big red letters. Her denial closet was beginning to bulge, and Isobel knew there was a limit to how much more of her life she could pretend didn't exist.

"We don't need him. If you're worried, you can rely on me. You should have told me. I would have watched over you and Soph last night."

Isobel looked at her son with a mixture of pride and sadness. "I know you would have. But you shouldn't have to. I don't want you to grow up too fast." Like she'd had to.

"Mum, I hate to break it to you, but I'm already there. In a few months I can leave school, get a job, drive, get married if I want to. You need to let me help. I can't stand around and do nothing. This is my family too. You. Sophie. You're it."

He was so earnest, so sure of his own abilities, and he wasn't even fully grown yet. Memories of caring for him as a baby, when she was the same age as he was now, came flooding back. She'd been so young. So desperate. So hopeful. She remembered the long hours trying to work part time and take care of him. She remembered her mum helping out as much as she could, behind her dad's back. It still smarted. Over sixteen years and her dad had yet to say one word to her. She'd shamed him coming home pregnant at fifteen and he'd never forgiven her.

"I'll make more effort to include you, okay?" It was the best she could do. "Now hurry up and get ready or you'll miss the school bus." And she didn't have the petrol money to get him into Campbeltown if he did.

"I'm ready." He picked up his bag. "Be careful with this Callum guy. We don't know him, Mum, and the rumours around school are heavy. I'm not sure he's someone you can trust."

"I know."

Although she wasn't sure there was anyone she could trust. She was just as leery as her son when it came to bringing a man into her life. It was best for all of them if she kept Callum at a distance.

With a wave, Jack headed for the door, stopping briefly to say goodbye to Sophie, who was watching the Wiggles in the living room and dancing along.

Isobel was washing up the breakfast dishes when Mairi let herself in the back door. As usual, she was texting.

"Hey you," Mairi said. "Did you manage to keep your knickers on last night?"

Isobel threw a wet cloth at Mairi and it smacked her on the forehead.

"That was uncalled for," Mairi said. She stopped looking at her phone long enough to notice Sophie wasn't in the room. "Where's the monster? I thought we'd hang out at my place while you're at work. Agnes has gone to Glasgow for her exam, which means Sophie and I can make a mess without disturbing grumpy bum. Plus, I get the heebie-jeebies thinking about the guy in the freezer so I don't want to spend the day here."

"She's watching TV." Isobel dried her hands. "I'm hoping Callum will have a plan for moving the body later today. I'd feel a whole lot better knowing it wasn't here."

She had visions of her sisters and her out in the dead of night, digging a hole for the guy.

"We need new shovels," Mairi said, proving yet again that the Sinclair women were on the same wavelength.

"I'll see if they have any at the shop." Isobel picked up her keys and phone from the table and popped them in her second-hand hobo bag.

There had been four messages from the loan shark waiting for her when she woke. She'd ignored them all, but she knew from experience that it was only a matter of time before he came around in person. And she was sick at the thought. There was no money for the next payment and no prospects of getting any. She couldn't even think about what he would want in exchange for letting the payment slip by.

"You okay?" Mairi's attention was away from her phone for once, but she was frowning at Isobel. "You're pressing your hand to your stomach. You aren't suffering from morning sickness already, are you? Is that even possible?"

Isobel hadn't been aware that she was holding her roiling stomach. She forced a smile. "I need to get you a book on pregnancy. You really don't have a clue."

"And I plan to keep it that way." Mairi strode off down the hall to get Sophie.

It took a few more minutes to pack all the toys Sophie wanted to take to Mairi's house, which meant they were running late by the time they left. As they turned into the road at the end of the lane, the women looked out over the water. The sky was a heavy grey that promised rain, and the wind had whipped up the waves. The smell of salt was thick in the air and the gulls circled overhead looking for food.

"Did they come back last night?" Mairi said.

Isobel's grip on Sophie's hand tightened at the thought of the boat visitors.

"I don't think so. I don't know. I was out cold for most of the night."

Mairi's eyebrows shot up. "With Mr Broodylicious on the sofa? I thought, at the very least, you'd be up all night fantasising about him."

"Actually, it was the opposite. I was asleep pretty much as soon as my head hit the pillow. Not even an X-rated dream."

"Well, that's disappointing. Guess he must be rubbish in bed if he's that easily dismissed." She gave Isobel a hopeful look and waited for details.

Isobel didn't give her any. The truth was that having Callum in the house made Isobel feel secure. She was used to being her small family's last line of defence. For years she'd slept with one ear open, listening for problems and ready to deal with them. With Callum in the house, Isobel's subconscious had decided he could take the watch for the night, and her exhausted body had slipped into a deep sleep. For one aching moment, when she awoke, she'd felt like she had a partner, and the weight of her family hadn't been pressing down on her. And then reality had slammed into her, along with the cold awareness that she was on her own.

Isobel parted company with Mairi and Sophie outside of the village's only shop. Sophie waved all the way across the road to the garage, where Agnes and Mairi shared the flat upstairs. The sight of her daughter's wide smile and unique dress sense made Isobel grin. Her daughter was wearing a cheap princess dress, fairy wings, gumboots and a woolly hat.

As soon as they were out of sight, Isobel entered the shop, the chirpy bell signalling her arrival. Her late arrival.

"Nice of you to bother turning up," Edna McPhee said, as though Isobel was hours late instead of fifteen minutes.

"Sorry." Isobel stashed her bag under the counter and pulled on the burgundy tabard that Edna insisted was the shop uniform. It didn't matter that Isobel was her only employee and that Edna herself refused to wear the hideous polyester thing.

"Do you have a reason for being late?" Edna sounded exactly like a teacher Isobel had when she was in high school. She hadn't liked that teacher any more than she liked Edna.

"Kid problems." It was the only excuse she was willing to give.

Edna's eyes became tiny dots under her heavily furrowed brow. "I knew I shouldn't have hired a single mother."

"Edna." Isobel tried hard not to let her irritation show. "I've worked here for almost three years, and in that time, I haven't missed a day. Not to mention, you can count the times I've been late on one hand."

Edna sniffed and patted her bleached blonde hair, which accentuated the lines on her face. "There are shelves that need cleaning." There would be no apology. There never was. No matter how many digs she made about Isobel's kids, or the men in her life running out on her.

Isobel did what she normally did. She gritted her teeth, swallowed her pride and worked like a dog for minimum wage, all the while reminding herself that she was lucky to have a job so close to home. Lucky that her sister worked from home and could look after Sophie. Lucky that she could walk to work when she couldn't afford to fill her car. Yeah, she was so freaking lucky.

"Did you hear about Janice and Clyde?" Edna pulled a bright pink lipstick from the drawer beside the cash register and touched up her already thickly made-up mouth.

"What about them?" Isobel gathered her cleaning supplies and started with the shelves nearest the counter—the ones stocked with chocolate and sweets. She knew from experience that Edna liked her to start her work where she could see her, so that she could give her advice on how to do it properly—while she flicked through magazines and fiddled with her hair. But, as owner of the place, Edna could, and did, do whatever the heck she pleased.

"They had someone sneaking around their property last night. Gave them the fright of their lives."

Isobel stilled, her dust rag suspended in front of the shelf. Clyde and Janice were the elderly couple who lived on the bluff, along from Isobel's house.

"Did they see who it was?" She tried hard not to let the fear she felt come through in her voice.

"No." Edna leaned forward, folding her arms on the counter and leaning her sagging bosom on it. Although

Isobel didn't know Edna's true age, she did know the woman was old enough to have the need of a decent bra. Unfortunately, this wasn't something Edna knew. As far as she was concerned, the only thing of importance in buying a bra was that it showed enough cleavage. If that cleavage was around her waist, that was neither here nor there. "Whoever it was ran off when Clyde let the dog out. He said he shouted after one of them, but the blighter just legged it out of there."

"That's terrible." Isobel made a big deal out of dusting every item she removed from the shelf. "Did they call the police?"

"No, they thought it was teenagers messing around. You know, like your boy Jack."

Isobel ignored the snide comment as she tried to control her breathing. It couldn't be a coincidence that her neighbours got a visit from someone right after she'd removed the body from the beach.

Edna had obviously lost patience while waiting for Isobel to react to her dig about Jack. "They should have called the police, because Marty Jackson told me that the Redfern family had someone try to break into their place last night too."

Isobel's hands began to shake and she had to cling to the shelf to stop them. Slowly, methodically, she moved the duster over the now-empty shelf. There were five families overlooking the cove. Clyde and Janice and the Redferns were two of them.

"Hugh Redfern called the police and they checked the property." Edna lowered her voice as though conspiring, instead of sharing local gossip. "There were tool marks around their front door lock and their garage had been broken into. But Hugh didn't notice anything missing, so he thought it might have been teenagers messing around as well. Although how he would know if anything was missing with the state of his garage, I wouldn't know. Linda Redfern keeps a filthy house. I don't know what that woman does all day long, but it isn't clean."

Isobel thought she might vomit. There was no mistaking the intent of the men lurking round her neighbours' properties. They had to have been looking for the body she'd removed. Or worse, looking for the person who'd been watching them.

Isobel got to her feet, on legs that were weak. "I need to make a call," she said. "I'll be back in a sec."

Edna jerked straight. "Where do you think you're going? You just got here. Don't think I'm paying for your time when you aren't working. I'm docking this from your wages."

Isobel wasn't interested. Her attention was on her phone. She pulled the piece of paper with Callum's number out of her pocket and started to dial as she left the shop. Her concentration on her phone, she walked around the corner to the little car park, hoping to find a private corner.

"Hello love," someone called, making her stop dead. "I was wondering when you were going to come out of the shop. Thought I'd have to send Raymond here in to get you. Ain't that right, Ray?"

Isobel felt the blood drain from her face as she backed away from the car that Eddie Granger was climbing out of. The loan shark was smiling at her with lots of teeth and cold, flat eyes. He wore a black suit and black shirt. The jacket gaped over his pot belly, and Isobel inanely wondered if it was even possible to button it shut.

"You didn't answer my messages, Isobel." Eddie swaggered over to her. "Ray here was worried. Ain't that right, Ray?"

"Aye." Ray looked like the type of man who'd rather hit someone than talk to them. He was a genetic mutant of a man. Short and stocky with far too many steroid induced muscles for his body shape. His eyes never stopped moving, assessing. He wore jeans and a Celtic football shirt. There were heavy rings on every finger, and Isobel didn't have to ask, to know that they would act as knuckle dusters when he punched. And she got the impression that Ray very much liked to punch.

"We need to have a word about what you owe me," Eddie said as he stepped close. Too close. Isobel had to suck in her stomach to stop any part of her body from touching his.

She tried to swallow, but her throat was dry. "I still have three days. You'll get your money." How, she didn't know. She mentally went through everything she owned, looking for something to sell, and came up empty. She had absolutely nothing of value.

"I know money is tight," Eddie said with saccharine sweetness. "I'm a thoughtful guy. I don't want to put you under any undue pressure to get the cash in time. I'm willing to negotiate." His eyes slid down her body, lingering over her breasts, and he licked his bottom lip. "I'm willing to let you work off the debt."

Isobel fought the urge to shudder. "That's kind of you, but I'll have the money."

Eddie grinned, showing stained and broken teeth. "You hear that, Ray? I'm kind."

Ray didn't answer; he was too busy looking around. Whether he was keeping an eye out for a threat to his boss, or looking for something to hit, Isobel couldn't even begin to guess.

Her attention was dragged back to Eddie, when he ran a fingertip down her cheek. Bile rose in her throat, burning and making her want to gag.

"See, here's the thing—as I said, money is tight all round right now." He gave her that fake sympathetic smile. "I can't let you just pay the interest anymore. I'm going to need the whole amount on Saturday."

Isobel gasped. "I can't. I don't have that kind of money." She didn't have *any* money.

"I understand; I do. Times are tough. I've tried to help you out by letting you pay what you could, but I can't do that no more. I need the rest this weekend."

Isobel's mind raced. What he was asking was impossible, and he knew it. He was enjoying this; she could see it in his eyes.

"Thirty-four thousand by Saturday." He looked at her and his eyes hardened. "Best get one of your sisters to look after the kids, because when I come back here, I'll be collecting, one way or another. And it will take a *lot* of paying off to square with me."

His fingertips trailed down her throat, over her collarbone and across the swell of her breast.

"I'm gonna enjoy collecting from you, Isobel Sinclair." He turned towards his car then looked back at her. "Saturday." He nodded at Ray. "Drive the message home. But restrain yourself. I have plans for her."

"No," Isobel said as she tried to press herself into the wall and disappear entirely.

Ray took a step towards her. His smile was serpentine.

CHAPTER 11

Campbeltown only had one pawnshop, but it was doing a thriving business, which said a lot about the state of the economy in the area. Although anybody could have guessed that people were struggling, by the amount of empty shops on the high street. As far as Callum could see, the only businesses doing a decent trade were the second-hand shops, the pubs and the pawnbroker.

The shop was crowded with goods people had either sold, or had pawned and then were unable to buy back. Callum took his time perusing the stock, paying particular attention to the camera equipment. He didn't see anything particularly high-end, which made him think that the things Isobel had brought in had already been sold. As he pretended to shop, Callum kept a close eye on the guy working the counter.

He was in his fifties, and what muscle he may have had, had turned to fat. His grey hair was sparse, but he'd grown parts of it out to form a comb-over. He also had the same ingratiating smile that lying politicians wore. Callum didn't need to listen to him fleece his customers to know he was a conman—it was written all over his arrogant face. He was exactly the kind of man that Callum detested: the kind who thought it was okay to take advantage of the poor and desperate.

When a young woman, carrying a baby and selling her old laptop, was given the absolute minimum, Callum decided he'd had enough. As he passed the woman on his way to the desk, he put a hand on her shoulder.

"Wait outside," he said. "He owes you some money. I'll make sure you get it."

She looked startled for a moment, before her eyes welled up and she nodded. Callum watched her scurry from the shop. Her clothes were hanging on her frame, but the baby looked fat and healthy. It didn't take a genius to figure out that the woman was sacrificing for the child. Which made what the pawnbroker had just done even more repugnant.

"What can I do for you?" the man behind the counter said as he assessed Callum. His eyes lit up when he came to the conclusion that a man looking like Callum wasn't there to sell anything, which meant he must be there to buy. Callum could almost see the man salivate, and would bet he'd just added twenty percent to everything in the store.

"A woman came in a few weeks ago selling camera equipment," Callum said. "I need to know what she sold to you and if there is anything left."

The smile appeared again, but the eyes were calculating. "Are you with the police?"

"No." Callum smiled back and watched the man pale. There was nothing ingratiating or friendly about Callum's smile. It was all about the promise of pain. "I'm with a security organisation. Tell me about the equipment."

"I'm not sure what you're talking about," the man said. "I get a lot of items through my business. How am I expected to remember everything?"

"I suppose some financial encouragement would prompt your memory?"

The man inclined his head and looked pleased that Callum understood.

Callum understood, all right. "I have other ways that will prompt it." He reached to the small of his back and pulled out the gun he'd tucked there. He placed it on the counter in front of him.

The owner took a step back, his tongue flicking out in a nervous gesture. "I don't know what you think you're doing, but I have cameras in here."

Callum reached into the pocket of his leather jacket and produced what looked like a small TV remote. "I jammed the feed." He put the jammer on the counter beside the gun.

The owner's eyes jumped to his. Now he looked nervous instead of smug. It was a huge improvement. "Who are you?"

"I'm the man asking the questions. Camera equipment, brought in by a woman called Isobel Sinclair." Callum saw recognition flicker in the man's eyes. "Do you have anything left?"

The owner's attention kept straying to the gun. "You won't shoot me. This is all a bluff."

Callum pulled a silencer out of his other pocket, picked up the gun and slowly twisted it on. "I have absolutely no problem with taking out your kneecap. To start."

The owner shuffled back again—from the green sheen of his face, he understood that Callum was perfectly serious. In fact, Callum was hoping the guy would prove difficult, as he'd enjoy putting a bullet in him.

"There's no need for threats. I know who you're talking about now. Everybody knows the Sinclair girls."

"Go on," Callum ordered.

The owner licked his lips. "She brought in a bag of stuff. Camera bodies, lenses, extra memory, that sort of thing."

"What kind of lenses?" Callum said.

"BLAH mil."

Long distance. "Did you look at the camera memory? Was there anything on it?"

"Nothing." The man shook his head. "It was blank. Like it was brand new."

"Do you have anything left?"

"No. It sold fast." He couldn't quite keep the smug look off his face, and Callum would bet he'd made a good profit from Isobel's haul.

"Who bought it?"

"I don't know, and they paid cash."

From the way he said it, Callum assumed that he'd asked for cash so that there was no record of the transaction and he wouldn't have to pay tax on it. This guy was scamming everyone.

"And there's nothing left from the bag Isobel brought in? Nothing?" Callum saw a flicker of guilt in the man's eyes and didn't give him a chance to lie. "Get it for me. Now," he barked.

The owner reached under the counter, pulled open a drawer and rummaged around a little. He came up with a little black box that fit in the palm of his hand. There were wires protruding, and a serial number and make on the back. But Callum recognised it instantly. Everything within him stilled.

"Do you know what that is?" he asked the guy, keeping his voice even.

The owner wet his lips again, a habit Callum was beginning to hate. "It's military, I know that. The company here"—he pointed at the label—"they supply military technology. I haven't figured out what it is exactly yet."

Callum knew. "Put it beside the jammer."

His tone brooked no argument, and the man hurried to

do as he was told. Callum looked up at him once he'd placed the device on the counter. "How much did you give Isobel?" The man paled even further and started to bluster. Callum pulled out his phone. "I can call her and ask, but I'd rather you told me."

The owner looked at the phone, then at Callum. "Four hundred pounds."

Callum cocked an eyebrow. "I will be checking this with Isobel."

The man's cheeks flushed. "Okay, two hundred. But it was obviously stolen. She had no idea what it was or what it was worth. She couldn't even tell me where it came from. And everyone knows the Sinclair sisters can't afford equipment like that. It was obvious that her delinquent son had stolen it and his mother was hawking the goods." He looked disgusted by that. Callum wasn't buying it. The guy had bought what he knew were stolen goods. Not exactly the moral high ground.

"How much did you sell the stuff for?"

"I don't have to tell you that!" His face was a deep red now.

Callum lifted the gun and pointed it at the man's knee, keeping the barrel steady. "No. You don't."

"Put the gun down," the man screeched. "I sold it for three thousand."

Callum had to fight the urge to pull the trigger. He placed the gun on the counter, but kept his hand on it. "You owe Isobel two thousand eight hundred. I'll take that now."

"I don't have that kind of cash around here." The owner threw his hands up. "And what about my cut? I found the buyer. I was the one who sold it. It's not my fault the stupid bitch didn't know its worth."

"Make that the full three thousand," Callum said evenly. "Cash."

"You're being ridiculous," the owner shouted.

Callum picked up the gun again. "I'll take whatever you have on the premises right now and I'll come back for the rest. And you can add three hundred to the total to make up for the money you just conned that young mother out of."

"You can't do this!" The guy made no move to get the cash.

Callum shifted the gun slightly to the left and pulled the trigger. The bullet made more noise hitting the cupboard than it had coming out of the gun. The pawnbroker clutched his chest and looked like he might be having a heart attack. Callum didn't give a crap.

"I'm going to count to three, and then the next bullet goes in you. And I will still want every penny I've asked for."

It took the man exactly two minutes to empty his till and remember that he had a small safe in the back. Callum got every penny he asked for. After warning him to keep his mouth shut, Callum walked out into the afternoon sun to find the woman waiting like he'd asked her to.

"Here." He handed her the extra three hundred pounds she should have been given on top of the hundred she'd received.

"Thanks, mister." She pocketed the money.

Callum nodded and headed back to his car.

CHAPTER 12

Isobel leaned over the tiny basin in the staff toilet of the store and looked at the reflection above it. Her eyes were red and swollen, but at least she'd managed to stop the tears. Her throat was still raw from emptying her stomach into the toilet, and she was shivering. Slowly, gently, she lifted the hem of her shirt to see the damage.

She gasped at the sight of the darkening bruise developing low on her ribs. Blinking back yet more tears, Isobel gently prodded the red area and winced. It was too sensitive to tell if Ray had cracked any ribs. The only way to know for sure was to get an x-ray, and there was no way she was going anywhere near a hospital. The doctors would take one look at the fist mark, complete with ring imprints, on her side and call the police. What she needed to do was get home and put some ice on it. But that wasn't going to be possible until she finished her shift.

With a wince, Isobel lowered the shirt and leaned forward to press her forehead against the mirror. She should have been thinking about her ribs, or about the body in her freezer, or about the slight possibility she could be carrying

Callum's child. Instead, all she could think about were ways she could possibly get the money for Eddie. Her sisters weren't much better off than she was; none of them had the money to give her to pay off the loan shark. But somehow, someway, she had to find the cash. She swallowed a sob that threatened.

After Ray had hit her and her knees had given way, he'd held her up and whispered to her, "When Eddie's done with you, you're mine." And then he'd sauntered back to the car while she leaned against the wall.

The whole thing had taken seconds. No one had witnessed the assault. No one had run to help. She was on her own, as she usually was.

"Are you going to stay in there all day?" Edna shouted as she thumped on the door. "I'm not paying you for this. You haven't done any work today."

Isobel blinked away her tears, splashed water on her face and opened the door. Edna had her arms folded under her bosom and was tapping the toe of her gold sequined heels.

"I'm s-sick." Isobel couldn't look Edna in the eye. "I'll be out soon."

"I heard you vomit," Edna said. "Don't tell me you're pregnant again. Who does it belong to this time?"

"I ate something that disagreed with me." Isobel wished Edna would go away. "I'll be fine in a minute."

"Uh huh." Edna's voice held a smirk, making it clear she didn't believe a word Isobel told her.

No doubt, everyone who came through the shop would hear about how Isobel Sinclair had managed to get herself knocked up again. Isobel was past caring. On her list of worries, Edna ranked pretty low.

"I'm not paying you for the time you waste," Edna called. "I'm keeping a record."

Isobel sat on the toilet lid and pulled out her phone. With

shaky fingers, she tapped Callum's number. It rang twice before he answered.

"McKay," he barked, and the antisocial tone was a strange comfort to Isobel.

"Callum, it's me, Isobel." She worked hard to keep her voice from giving away that she was hurt and upset. As tempting as it was to throw herself on Callum's strength and beg him to fix everything, Isobel was beyond the age of believing in white knights.

"What's wrong?" He sounded alert, and she could hear traffic in the background, which meant he was driving somewhere. She had a sudden moment of panic that he might be driving to get away from her and her problems. She swallowed it down.

"Edna told me that two houses on the bluff had people sneaking around them last night. One was broken into."

"Cops called?"

"Yeah, but nothing was taken and no one was arrested. The police think it was kids messing around." She took a deep, shaky breath and wiped away the tear that was rolling down her cheek. "They're looking for the body, or the people who took it, aren't they?"

"Aye."

"Callum, is it possible we're wrong and the guys assumed the body had been taken out to sea?"

"Your sisters' and your footprints are all over the area. It's clear from looking at them that you were carrying something heavy back up the bluff."

"This is bad, isn't it?"

"Aye." A pause. "But I have a plan."

Isobel swallowed hard at the utter confidence in his voice. What would it feel like to have such confidence? To not feel as though life buffeted you continuously? To feel in control of the things that were happening instead of being forced to react all the time? She couldn't even imagine a life like that.

"I'm sorry I was forced to pull you into this," she said. "But I'm really glad you're here."

There was silence for a moment.

"I'll be at your place this evening," Callum said.

"I'll make dinner," Isobel said, but he was already gone.

There was a loud smack at the door. "Are you coming out of there? Or are you talking to the father of your new bairn?"

"There's no baby!" Isobel put her phone away and splashed water on her face. When she threw open the bathroom door, Edna was smirking at her.

"Whatever you say," she said.

Isobel pushed past her and got back to work.

As soon as Callum ended the call with Isobel, he knew what he had to do. He was just putting it off until he had the words he needed to do it. They were in over their heads. Whatever Isobel had stumbled into was much bigger and much more dangerous than he'd first thought.

He rubbed his thigh and wheeled his chair into the kitchen, where he'd left his phone. Once back from Campbeltown, knowing he'd be at Isobel's house for another night, he'd taken the opportunity to give his legs a rest from his prosthetics. He also needed to charge the things, something he hadn't quite gotten used to. But the processor that powered the legs and made them function almost exactly like real legs needed to be charged. He thought of Isobel and what her reaction might be if he told her he needed to take his legs off and recharge them. Not that she would ever find out about his missing limbs. But he thought her reaction might be humorous. He could see her getting a kick out of saying, *Callum's charging his legs.*

He looked at the clock, knowing he was running out of time. It was now or never. It was time for him to swallow his pride and ask for help from the people he'd turned his back on months earlier. Callum swivelled his chair towards the bedroom, to pick up his legs, and hesitated.

Since walking out of Benson Security four months earlier, Callum had only seen and spoken to his partner Lake Benson. He'd avoided everyone else. He'd ignored calls, deleted emails and refused to open his door when they called. Part of him wanted to continue to keep them at a distance, to write an email asking for help, or leave a message. But they deserved more than that. They deserved to see him in the raw, without pretending to be something he wasn't. They deserved to see him face reality. And that reality was that he was half a man, in need of help.

With determination, or bloody-mindedness, Callum rolled to the corner of the kitchen and stared up at the camera, the one he'd been too damn busy to remove.

"Elle? You there? I need you to listen to me. I figure, knowing you, that you'll have some software running to alert you if I suddenly start ranting about killing myself. So I'm going to sit here and say every word I think might trigger your program, until you text me and let me know you're listening. And, for the record, Betty, I know you're watching too, and I don't want you to call. This is between me and the London team."

There was silence. Callum kept his eyes on the camera and started a list of words that would freak Elle out. "Death, suicide, gun, bullet to the brain…"

He didn't get very far before the phone in his pocket vibrated. Callum dug it out and found he was holding his breath as he read the message:

We're here.

Good. That was good. Okay. He could do this. He'd done

worse. He could do this. He broke out in a sweat and had to fight the urge to rub his palms on his jeans.

"Thanks," he said to the camera. "So here's the thing. I have a bit of a situation and I…I need help." He folded his hands tightly against his chest, aware that if they were loose in his lap, Elle might see the tremble.

He'd rather crawl through a war zone, with enemy fire aimed at his head, than lay himself bare before anyone. But he owed them this. He owed them honesty. He owed them part of himself—even if it meant he had to tear off a bloody piece and hand it over.

"One of the local women, Isobel Sinclair, has stumbled into something dangerous. It looks like there are smugglers using the local cove for access to the road system. Yesterday these unknown men left a dead body on the beach. And Isobel, in her infinite wisdom, thought the best thing to do with it was put it in her freezer and call me instead of the cops."

He looked around for a second, searching for the right words. None came to him. All he could do was stumble on. Were they laughing at him? Were they scoffing about his sudden need for help when he'd been so quick to kick them out of his life months earlier? He swallowed hard. Damn, he wished he could look them in the eye and see how they were taking this. He'd never humbled himself before anyone in his life, and here he was doing it to a camera instead of a person. Anxiety made him want to rage, to tell them he'd changed his mind and storm away to be alone. But he'd spent too much time by himself already. Now he needed help. He needed his team.

He looked back at the camera. "I know I was a bastard when I left. I haven't changed. Don't think that. I didn't ask to be involved in Isobel's problems and I wish I wasn't. I'd walk away if I could."

He wet his suddenly dry lips. "I think Isobel might be pregnant. With my child. Until I know for sure, one way or the other, she's my responsibility and this mess is my mess. Which means I'm asking one of you to step into my personal situation—and you know how I feel about running personal missions for the team." Memories of whining about helping Dimitri find his sister and Julia get her grandmother out of jail flooded his mind. "Like I said, I'm an arsehole."

It was humiliating coming face to face with the reality of just how much of a dick he'd been.

"I don't know what I'm dealing with here, but my instincts are going crazy. I know you're overloaded with work." More so since he'd walked out. "Any help you can spare would be good. I'll pay the going rate."

There was nothing else to say. Either they forgave him, or they didn't. It was out of his hands now. "Let me know what you think. I'll be at Isobel's and I'll have my phone."

He turned away from the camera and rolled down the hall to the bedroom, feeling painfully raw and vulnerable. He tried to tell himself that he didn't care whether or not they wanted to help him. If push came to shove, he could phone Lake and organise for him to send a man from the Invertary office. Or he could go it alone. Which was what he'd wanted when he kicked everyone he knew out of his life. But the truth was that he didn't want some random guy he didn't know from Lake's team. He wanted his team at his back.

His hand was on his bedroom doorknob when his phone buzzed. With trepidation, Callum checked the message.

On our way.
Boss.
And Callum smiled.

CHAPTER 13

Isobel was putting dinner on the table when Callum arrived. He had a sports bag over his shoulder and a grim look on his face.

"We're having spaghetti bolognaise." Isobel threw the door wide for him to come in. "There's plenty. Come eat."

"You don't need to feed me." He followed her into the house.

"Have you had dinner?"

He paused as he put his bag on the sofa, where the bedding from the night before was still neatly folded. "No."

"Then don't be an idiot and come eat."

Callum grunted something that Isobel wasn't interested in and followed her down the narrow hall. As they entered the kitchen, Jack looked up and frowned at Callum.

"Behave," Isobel told him.

She grabbed an extra place setting before taking her seat at the table. She handed the plate and cutlery to Jack to put in the spot for Callum. He looked like he was handling a nest of wasps.

There was a large pan of food in the middle of the table,

and Isobel reached for the spoon to dish it up. Callum was still standing in the doorway, watching them all as though they were a science experiment he had to monitor. Isobel glanced at Sophie and saw she was looking at Callum in exactly the same way.

"This is Callum," Isobel told her daughter. "He's a friend of mine and he's going to eat with us, if he ever sits down."

"Clalumm," Sophie said, her eyes still on him.

"Callum," Isobel corrected.

"Claaaauuuum," Sophie said.

"Whatever," Isobel said as she reached for her daughter's plate.

With the same sort of caution a bomb disposal expert would employ, Callum pulled out the last chair at the table and sat down. Sophie continued to stare at him, and Callum did his best to avoid her eyes. Isobel dished out food for everyone, making sure the boys got plenty, before she sat back in her chair. It'd been a long time since they'd had a man at the dinner table. It felt strange, and the tense atmosphere wasn't helping to make it better.

They ate in silence as Sophie stared at Callum, Jack glared at him and Callum ignored them both and looked around the room. Isobel let her gaze scan the room and tried to imagine what Callum saw. The kitchen cupboards had been installed sometime in the eighties and were dated and worn. Their burnt-umber colouring was the fashion of the time, but now it just looked dirty. Since her landlord wouldn't let her paint them, she'd concentrated on trying to brighten up the rest of the room.

She'd painted the walls a pale blue, bought cheap white curtains with blue daisies on them for the windows and found some blue pottery at the second-hand shop in Campbeltown, which she displayed on the counter. There were chips in the pottery, but Isobel didn't think anyone would notice. The floor was clean, but the linoleum was curling up in places—another thing her landlord wouldn't fix. The table and the chairs they sat in were another thrift store find. None of the set matched, but Isobel had painted it all white to make it look like it belonged together. Overall, Isobel thought she'd done an amazing job with very little. She was proud of what she'd achieved. She'd made a home for her family. It might not be the richest, or the most sophisticated, but it was cute and welcoming, and that was all that mattered.

"You're making my mum self-conscious," Jack said.

Isobel stopped eating. "No, he isn't."

"He's looking at the place as though it's a dump," Jack said.

Isobel looked at Callum, who had yet to touch his food. She cocked her head and considered him. "I don't think so. I think he's probably stayed in places that were a whole lot worse than this. I'd say he's either thinking about how fast he can run from the table or about how secure the house is."

Callum's eyes bored into hers. "You should have replaced that window. Glass is more secure than wood. Glass makes a noise when someone breaks it."

"Security, then," Isobel said. She looked over at the narrow, boarded-up window beside the back door. "I asked the landlord to replace it. He never got around to it, so I painted it white and hoped for the best. I don't think it looks so bad."

He scowled. "It isn't about looks. It's about safety. A two-year-old could get into this house."

"I'm three," Sophie told Callum proudly.

Callum considered her for a long moment, as she waited for his response. "Well done?" he said at last.

Jack shook his head.

"Eat your food," Isobel told Callum. "We don't waste food around here."

Callum obediently picked up his fork and started to eat.

"What's you got on your face?" Sophie leaned towards him as though she might grab the stubble covering his chin.

He backed up. "Hair."

Sophie frowned at him. "It's in the wrong place."

Isobel smiled at her daughter. "Men can grow hair on their faces, baby."

"Why?" her three-year-old demanded of Callum.

For a second, his badass outer shell slipped and he looked genuinely flummoxed. "I don't know."

"Huh." Sophie wasn't impressed.

There was a heavy silence as Callum, Jack and Isobel finished their food and Sophie painted her face with hers.

"I went to the pawnbroker in Campbeltown today," Callum said.

Isobel stilled, unsure where he was going with this. "Oh?"

"I managed to piece together a little more information on the visitors to the cove. I didn't like any of it, so I called in some help. I've got a member from my old security team coming in tomorrow."

"Security team?" Jack said, and Isobel appreciated that he was talking. She was too busy worrying about dragging yet more people into her mess.

"I worked for a private security firm in London before I came here." Callum's face gave nothing away about how he felt about his job.

"You were a security guard?" Jack said mockingly.

"No. I was a security specialist. My area of expertise is hostage extraction and personal protection in hostile environments."

"You were a bodyguard?" Now Jack sounded more impressed than mocking.

"When I had to be. Mainly I supervised a team, worked on the logistics of operations and made sure my people got out in one piece when we went into situations that were dangerous."

Jack looked eager for a second, before he remembered he was a cool sixteen-year-old. "So you know hand-to-hand combat and stuff?"

"I have military training and a black belt in Krav Maga."

Jack's eyes went wide. "I have a brown belt in kung fu, but I've always thought Krav Maga was better. Is it?"

Callum looked like he was seriously considering his answer. "Krav Maga incorporates some kung fu moves. You'd do well in a fight with either. But if you still wanted to move over into Krav Maga, your experience would make a good foundation."

"Krav Maga is mean. If I knew that, I'd be deadly," Jack said wistfully. "It'd be seriously cool to be deadly."

"There's nothing cool about being deadly." Isobel glared at her son. "We're pacifists. I think. Unless we're attacked. Then we aren't. Just you concentrate on schoolwork and forget about being deadly. Now clear the table while I get Sophie ready for bed."

Jack rolled his eyes but did as he was told. Isobel scooped Sophie up and carried her from the room. As she passed through the door, she thought she heard Callum say, "It *is* seriously cool to be deadly."

By the time Isobel had put Sophie into bed, Callum had secured the house for the night. She'd spotted him going from room to room, checking windows, with Jack trailing behind him. It was obvious that Jack was interested in everything Callum was doing. It was also obvious that he was trying hard to hide his interest.

"Homework time," Isobel said as she walked into the living room, where Callum was raking through his bag. "Don't spend the time chatting online with your friends."

"As if." Jack made a detour to the kitchen to stock up on snacks before heading upstairs.

Isobel knew he wouldn't hang out online. They had the cheapest internet connection they could find and had to be very careful about how much data they used. Basically, their connection was enough to allow him to do his schoolwork and not much more. She turned back to Callum.

"You got everything you need?"

"Aye." He ran his fingers through his hair. "I didn't want to say in front of the kid, wasn't sure how much he knew, but I spoke to the pawnbroker about the amount of money he gave you for the camera equipment."

Isobel felt her stomach plummet. "Did he tell the police I sold him stolen goods?"

Callum gave her a look that said he was questioning her IQ. "He bought those stolen goods, remember?"

"Oh, right." Now *she* felt like her IQ needed questioning.

"Anyway, the guy fleeced you, but he was happy to rectify his mistake."

He reached into his pocket, pulled out a huge wad of cash and tossed it to her. Isobel caught it reflexively. It was heavy and didn't quite feel real. She stared at the bundle. She'd never seen so much money in her life.

"How much is here?" Her voice was a silly croak.

"Three thousand pounds."

Isobel actually felt faint. Three thousand. It was nowhere near enough to pay off the loan shark. But it was more than enough for them to get from Arness and start somewhere else. She was looking at petrol money, the deposit on another rented house and food money for a couple of weeks until she found another job. He'd just handed her the chance to start again. And he'd done it as though it was nothing.

"I don't know what to say." She stumbled over the words as she tucked the money into the front pocket of her jeans and made a mental note to find somewhere more secure to stash it.

"Don't say anything."

"Okay."

But seeing as she still wanted to say thank you, she did it the way she'd been wanting to do all through dinner—with a kiss.

With no warning, she launched herself at Callum, and he caught her easily, his strong arms tightening around her as she assaulted him with her mouth. There was no hesitation on his part. As soon as their lips met, it was electric. Never in her life had she felt the way she did when she was touching Callum. Everything else fled her mind. Nothing else mattered other than touching this man.

They kissed with a desperation that bordered on pain. Tongues, lips, teeth. Isobel couldn't get enough. He was her addiction. She felt herself falling forward, and it barely registered that Callum had sat back on the sofa, with her straddling his lap. His mouth never left hers as his hands slid under her T-shirt and his palms covered her breasts. She moaned into his mouth, circling her hips and grinding herself against his hard length. More. She needed more.

As if reading her mind, Callum tugged the neck of her shirt down over her breasts and bent his head to suckle her nipple through her bra. She hated that bra. It needed to go. Now.

"Mum."

The small voice vaguely registered for Isobel—she was still deep in a fog of need—but Callum stopped instantly.

With his hands firmly on her hips, he lifted her off him and put her on her feet. Isobel was shaking like a junkie needing her fix.

"Mum." Sophie's voice penetrated Isobel's daze, and she realised her daughter was calling for her.

"I'm coming," Isobel shouted. She cleared her throat and looked down at Callum.

His hair was tousled, his eyes were dark and his lips were swollen. She saw the same desperate need in his eyes as she felt burning inside her.

"Woman," he said in that husky voice of his, "you don't have any sense."

Isobel couldn't agree more. When it came to Callum, all sense and logic flew out the window. Without another word, she tugged her shirt back into place and, even though every cell of her body wanted to be back on the couch with Callum, made herself walk out of the room and upstairs to her daughter.

CALLUM STAYED SEATED on Isobel's deeply uncomfortable sofa and wondered, yet again, what had just happened. There was no middle ground with her. Either they were keeping their distance from each other or they were all over each other like a poison ivy rash. She was the itch he continually wanted to scratch, and he was going insane with it.

But he wasn't there to get physical with Isobel Sinclair. He was there to protect her. It worried him that there had been people snooping around the other houses on the bluff. It was too much of a coincidence to dismiss. Which meant there were people out looking for the body. It wouldn't take a genius to figure out that the houses overlooking the cove were the most likely place to find it. And even if the body didn't turn up in one of them, Arness was tiny, and they were bound to find it if they kept on looking.

Callum picked up the remote and flicked through channels on Isobel's tiny TV. It looked to be about a million years old and only had the free-to-air programmes. Which meant there was nothing on that he wanted to see. If he'd been back at his house, he could have watched a football game while he waited the night out. But no, he'd been leery about letting them invade his space, worried Isobel might take it the wrong way and think he was looking for a relationship. Now he wished he'd stopped being a coward and taken them home. At least there he could protect them properly, and he had the sports channels.

"I'm going to bed," Isobel said from the doorway.

He almost laughed at the sight of her nervously keeping her distance. He could have told her it didn't matter. He'd spent months getting hot just from the glimpses he'd seen of her through his kitchen window.

She seemed to be waiting for a response, so he said, "Okay."

"There are snacks and coffee in the kitchen. Help yourself." She shuffled from foot to foot. "If you're cold, you can put on the fire." She pointed to the ancient gas heater with the bottle poking out the back. "Or I can get you an extra blanket if you'd like."

"I'm fine." He wasn't about to tell her that since losing his legs, he never felt cold. It had something to do with heat trying to disperse over less surface area. All he knew was that he didn't need any sweaters.

"I don't know why I keep jumping you," she blurted, and then flushed a deep shade of red.

"Because I'm irresistible?" He arched his eyebrows and wondered what else there was to say.

Her smile was wide, and her shoulders relaxed. "It must be that. But"—she pulled her bottom lip in between her teeth—"I don't want a relationship, Callum."

For some reason, that statement irritated him. Even though he'd just been thinking the same thing. "We're on the same page. No relationships."

Her whole body relaxed at his agreement, which was kind of insulting.

"Good, that's good. I've got enough to deal with, and I'm obviously rubbish at relationships. I've decided being alone forever is the way to go. It fits me."

Her words could have come straight out of his own mouth. Hearing them come back at him made them seem ludicrous. "I never asked for a relationship." Now he sounded irritated with her, when really it was irritation with himself.

"I know." She held up her hands. "I'm glad we're on the same page. I'll try to control myself around you. I promise."

Now that really annoyed him. When he scowled at her instead of answering, Isobel let out a little sigh.

"Okay then." She backed up into the hall. "Guess I'll see you in the morning."

Callum grunted and she disappeared. He reached for the TV remote again, before remembering there was nothing to watch. All he could do was clean his gun and hope he got a chance to use it. The short conversation with Isobel had really gotten under his skin. Logic told him that they understood each other, that neither of them wanted the baggage of another person in their lives. But logic didn't explain the need riding him, a need that only Isobel could satisfy. It also didn't explain why his first reaction at hearing her say she didn't want him, was intense disappointment.

With a growl of frustration, he started dismantling his gun.

CHAPTER 14

Isobel woke to a hand covering her mouth and tried to scream.

"Stop. There are people in the house. I need you to listen."

Callum. It took a second for his words to register.

People in the house.

She was instantly awake, her eyes latching on to his. She felt panic rise and knew she had to stop it. She had to be calm for her kids. She stared into his calm eyes and worked at breathing evenly. He was her lifeline.

"I'm going to remove my hand. It's okay. You're going to be fine."

She nodded to let him know she understood. His hand disappeared. Isobel fought the disorientation she felt. It had taken hours to get past feeling sexually frustrated and fall asleep. She glanced at the clock beside her bed—four a.m.

Callum loomed over her. "Get your daughter. Keep her quiet. I'll be back in a second. I'm going to get Jack."

He turned away, and Isobel had to fight the urge to reach out and grab his arm to keep him with her. He disappeared through the door, moving as silently as a stalking cat. Isobel pulled jeans and a sweatshirt over the underwear and T-shirt she slept in, slipped her feet into the sneakers beside her bed and leaned over her daughter.

"Sophie baby," she whispered, "you need to wake up."

All her daughter did was turn away and burrow herself deeper under her bedding.

"Sophie." Isobel tugged at the blankets until she'd unearthed most of the child. Sophie was cuddling her favourite soft toy, a giraffe, and was wearing the matching onesie. "Sophie. Get up now. Come on. This is important."

"Don' wanna," the little devil muttered, refusing to open her eyes.

Isobel didn't know what to do. She couldn't make any noise, and she was worried if she pushed Sophie much more, she'd wake up screaming her protest. She felt a whisper of air behind her and turned to find Callum and Jack. When had Jack become so silent and deadly looking? It felt as if the whole world was upside down.

"Get her up," Callum ordered.

What did he think she was doing? "I'm trying. I don't want her to start crying."

"Move." He stepped into her space, reached into the bed and lifted Sophie out of it.

For a second, the three-year-old looked sleepy and disorientated, and then she realised there was a strange man holding her. A flash of panic rushed across her face. She took a deep breath and opened her mouth.

"Don't. It's me, Callum."

Her eyes went wide but she didn't scream. She froze, staring at Callum, no doubt thinking he was a monster. Isobel put her hands on her child, cooing gently at her, letting her know that her mother was there. Sophie's eyes never left Callum's. It was as though she was mesmerised.

"Clam?" she whispered.

Callum nodded. "That's right. Your mum needs help. You can't make a sound or the bad people will find us. You need to be very quiet. Can you do that?"

Her eyes flew to Isobel, who forced a smile and nodded her agreement. Sophie looked back at Callum.

"Are you a bad man?" she whispered.

Isobel's eyes shot to his.

"No." Callum was intensely serious. "But I'm not a good man either. I can, however, get you and your mum out of here safely. Do you understand me?"

She nodded, and Isobel felt like she could breathe again.

"Jack too," Sophie whispered.

"Jack too," Callum said solemnly.

That seemed to be enough to reassure Sophie, who, still clutching her giraffe, turned and launched herself into Isobel's arms.

"Be very quiet, baby." Isobel kissed her head, and Sophie curled into her, resting her head on her mum's shoulder. Isobel held her tight and looked up at Callum. "What now?"

"I go hunting," he said.

She felt a shiver at the deadly intent in his face.

"What do you want me to do?" Jack said.

Callum turned to her son, who was almost as tall as him, and handed him a weapon Isobel didn't recognise. "Take this. It works two ways. Either press it to your opponent and fire or aim and pull the trigger. It will work in close quarters. Fifteen feet at most."

Jack looked down at the weapon and nodded. "Combination stun gun and Taser. Nice."

Isobel wanted to ask how he knew what it was, but kept her mouth shut. Now wasn't the time for questions.

"You know how to get out using the bathroom window?" Callum said.

Jack nodded, but Isobel was confused. "The bathroom is upstairs. You can't get out that way."

"I'll show you, Mum," Jack said before turning back to Callum. "I'll get them out. I've done this loads of times. I can carry Sophie, and Mum's fitter than she looks."

Isobel opened and closed her mouth a few times as she tried to decide what she should say.

"Good," Callum said. "Run to my house. The alarm is on." He rattled off a complicated code. "Can you remember that?"

"Say it again," Jack said, sounding strangely like Callum. Callum did, and Jack nodded. "Got it."

"Go down to the basement. As soon as you're in there, lock the door. You'll be secure. If I don't turn up within an hour, call the emergency number and tell them where you are. Okay?"

Jack nodded grimly, but Isobel was not okay.

"Why are you telling my sixteen-year-old what to do instead of me?" Isobel didn't even like the thought of Jack being in danger, let alone handing him a weapon and giving him responsibility for his sister.

"Because," Callum whispered, "Jack is bigger than you, he sneaks out of the house all the time, he has a brown belt in kung fu and he knows how to throw a punch." He cocked an eyebrow at her. "You aren't the only one who hears gossip."

"How?" The man never left the damn house. How did he hear gossip? And why was Jack sneaking out? And who was he punching?

"Go," Callum said to Jack, who nodded.

Callum turned towards the door, reaching for the gun Isobel noticed was tucked into the back of his jeans.

"No." Isobel grabbed his arm. "You come too. We can't leave you. You need to come with us."

For a second, his eyes softened and Isobel thought he was on the verge of smiling. "Don't worry about me. I know what

I'm doing. You concentrate on getting your family to safety. I'll see you there soon." He looked at Jack, and something passed between them in that look. Obviously at some point, without her noticing, Jack had learned to speak in silent men talk.

Without another word, Callum was gone.

CALLUM HATED everything about Isobel's house. He hated that there was only one set of stairs to the first floor and no other emergency exit. Which meant Isobel and the kids had to climb out the bathroom window, onto the tiny roof of the portico and then lower themselves to the ground. He hated that the garage door didn't shut properly, so it had been all too easy for the intruders to get inside and find the body. A cheap padlock on the freezer wouldn't stop them for long. And he hated that the locks on the house were worse than useless. But most of all, he hated that her good-for-nothing landlord hadn't bothered to replace the broken glass in the window beside her kitchen door. Because that meant all the intruders had to do was pop out the wood covering the empty window frame, reach in and open the door. Breaking into Isobel's house was child's play. Sophie could have done it.

If Callum hadn't been lying on the living room sofa, no one in the family would have known someone was in the house until it was too late. But Callum had been wide awake when the asshole broke in. He'd snuck up on the man in the kitchen and knocked him out, before sliding him into the large pantry. A few seconds later, he had the guy's hands and feet cable tied and his mouth gagged. Callum had shut the door and slid a chair up under the handle to keep the man there. When this mess was finished, Callum had a few questions for him.

Locking up one of the men wasn't perfect—he was still able to make noise when he woke up—but it had bought Callum enough time to see that the guy had come with four friends, all of whom were in the garage. After that, Callum had run upstairs to get everyone out.

Now it was time to hunt.

It was time to find out exactly who these men were and what they wanted.

The house was eerily silent as he made his way back down to the kitchen. He kept an ear out for Isobel and her kids, prepared to run to help if they needed him. It didn't sit well with him that he'd entrusted a sixteen-year-old kid with their safety. With no backup team and no other option, he had to rely on the boy. But Callum had a sneaking suspicion that Jack was no ordinary kid. When he'd crept into Jack's room to wake him, he'd found the kid fully dressed and in a position to defend himself. He'd taken one look at Callum's face and said, "How many are there?"

Callum didn't know what Isobel had done to raise the kids, but whatever it was, it was damn good. Jack was a son anyone would be proud to have.

At the bottom of the stairs, Callum stilled and listened. There was noise coming from the backyard. Slowly, silently, he made his way through to the kitchen. Isobel wasn't one of those women who put lace curtains up in every room. Her kitchen window only had a faded roller blind, and it hadn't been pulled closed. Even though the light was off, Callum was aware that movement would be spotted through the window, so he kept to the side as he edged closer.

The men had found the body, which was no surprise. Two of them were hauling it down the lane towards the road, where they must have parked their vehicles. The other two were headed straight for the house. All of the men were nondescript in appearance, their features generic. They could have been born anywhere. The only other thing they had in common was that they moved with confidence. Not training, exactly, but the confidence that came with experience. These men had been in situations like this before.

One of the men signalled to his partner to go around to the front of the house while he took the back. Callum couldn't allow that. The front of the house had the portico over the door that Isobel and the kids were using to escape. He turned and made his way through the house, to head the guy off before he stumbled on Isobel.

Callum opened the front door as quietly as he could and slipped out into the crisp night air. Jack spun on him immediately, his hand coming up, weapon aimed at Callum. There was just enough hesitation for Callum to signal to him to be quiet. Jack nodded and turned his attention back to the roof above the front door, motioning for his mother to hand Sophie down to him.

With a glance up to Sophie and Isobel, Callum left Jack to get the job done, and silently moved to the corner of the house, ready to intercept the enemy when he appeared.

Terror was riding Isobel. The night was black. There were no lights on in her house, and the light from the lane barely cut through the darkness. Jack had lowered himself off the portico roof and was waiting for her to hand Sophie down. Suddenly, he signalled for her to get down. She did so immediately, flattening herself and Sophie to the narrow roof as Jack slipped into the shadows at the side of the doorway.

Isobel turned her head and watched as two men appeared from the back of her house, carrying the dead body. They moved quickly past the front of the house and down the lane to the road. As soon as they were out of sight, she heard Jack whisper for her. He motioned for Sophie, and just as Isobel was about to lower her daughter, Jack's hand came up and he pointed the stun gun at someone coming out of the house.

For the longest second of her life, Isobel waited, unbreathing, as her son faced down the enemy. And then his arm lowered and Callum appeared. He glanced up at them and nodded before making his way to the corner of the house. Isobel's heart was beating so loudly that she actually panicked that someone might hear. Sophie tensed in her arms, as though she was going to call out to Callum, and Isobel gently covered her mouth.

"Shh, baby," Isobel whispered against her ear. "I'm going to hand you down to Jack. Don't make any noise. This is just like when we play hide and seek. Only we don't want the bad men to find us. Nod if you understand." Her dark curls bobbed. "Good girl. Now hold my hands and I'm going to lower you to Jack. When I let go, he'll catch you. Okay?" The trust in the answering nod almost made Isobel weep.

Without hesitation, Isobel lowered Sophie to Jack's waiting arms, sending up a prayer of thanks that her three-year-old took after her and was slight enough not to pull Isobel over the edge with her. Jack was tall and his hands were around Sophie's waist before Isobel had to lower her too far. He held his sister to him and signalled for Isobel to come down next.

Isobel had turned, ready to lie on her belly and lower herself, when there was a sharp whistle. She looked over her shoulder at Jack, who signalled for her to lie flat. He stepped into the shadow, holding Sophie to him. There was another low whistle and she peeked over the edge in time to see Callum signalling for Jack to run with Sophie. Isobel's breath caught, but she completely agreed—the kids had to get to safety. They couldn't, *shouldn't* wait for her. Jack pointed to Isobel, clearly meaning that he didn't want to leave her. Isobel let out a hiss to attract his attention and waved him off. From the way Callum was pointing his gun at the corner of the house, someone was coming, and Isobel wanted her kids gone before they arrived.

Jack shook his head stubbornly, but before she could shoo him off again, Callum made a growling sound and pointed at himself, then her hiding spot, making it clear to Jack that he'd look after his mother. Jack nodded reluctantly, gave one last look to Isobel and then turned and ran with Sophie. The whole thing took only a matter of seconds, and Isobel kept her eyes on her kids until they disappeared into the night. Heart racing, she looked to Callum for reassurance, but his focus was on whoever was coming their way.

Isobel wasn't stupid. Whoever was coming was dangerous. Otherwise Callum would have allowed her to get off the roof. She placed her forehead on the cool concrete beneath her and prayed her kids would be safe. Her kids *had* to be okay. *Please keep them safe...please keep them safe...please...*

She heard gravel underfoot and peeked over the edge. A man strode around the corner of the building—straight into Callum. They clashed with a ferocity that forced the air out of her lungs. She'd never seen anything like it. Never. It was the raw power of tempestuous waves striking at immovable rock. And yet it was also like a brutal choreographed dance.

There was no sound except the odd grunt. Neither man used a gun, although both were clearly armed. Instead, there was the sound of flesh smacking flesh. Bone striking bone. They circled each other, striking fast and hard. Callum dodged a punch to his jaw and caught the man in the stomach. The man stepped back, spun and came out with a knife. Callum growled, low, mean, feral. If he'd been dangerous before, then this was something else. This was the nuclear option. His demeanour changed somehow, and his movements became tighter, more efficient. He dodged the knife, stepped back, spun and kicked the man's wrist. The knife went flying.

There was a yelp, like a dog in pain. The man grasped his wrist, which was hanging at a strange angle. Callum had destroyed it with one kick. He didn't relent. His next kick took out the man's knee. He crumpled, howling now. For a second, it seemed as though Callum was going to walk away. He lifted his eyes to hers. Those dark, deadly eyes. But a flicker of movement brought his attention back to the man on the ground.

He had a gun in his good hand, and it was pointed at Callum.

"No!" Isobel was up, ready to jump off the roof and save him. Somehow.

Callum kicked out. The hand with the gun crumpled with another agonised howl. Callum knelt beside the man, said something Isobel couldn't hear and reached for his head. When Callum stood, the man was dead.

When he turned to Isobel, it was as if she was seeing him in slow motion. There was blood on his jaw. Blood on his knuckles. Sweat glistening on his brow. His muscles were tense and ready. His eyes were hard. This wasn't a man who whispered soft words. This was a Viking. A warrior. A hero.

He strode towards her, covering the distance in silence. "Down," he said, and held up his arms for her.

Isobel snapped out of her daze and realised she was still lying flat on the tiny roof. Her whole body shook. Her brain couldn't process the violence she'd just witnessed.

"Isobel," he growled, a command she didn't dare defy.

She turned and lowered her legs over the side until she felt the edge of the roof bite into her stomach. It pressed against the bruise left by Ray's fist, and for a second the world turned white. She broke out in a sweat with the pain, but fought through it, praying that the ribs weren't cracked and that she wasn't making the damage worse. Grasping the edge and flexing her meagre biceps, she lowered herself further. Before she could extend her arms and hang from her fingertips before dropping to the ground, Callum was there, his strong hands at her waist. He took her weight and lowered her to safety. As his hands pressed against her ribs, Isobel winced and stifled a moan.

He stilled, before turning her in his arms. Slowly, he lifted the edge of her shirt. His eyes went hard when he saw the bruise.

"We'll talk about this later."

Isobel's mouth was dry. Her body was shaking. She curled her fingers into Callum's T-shirt and held on tight. His hands ran up and down her arms, warming her, comforting her, but there was no softening in his eyes. Her attention strayed to the body. "You killed him, didn't you?"

"I didn't have a choice." Fingers on her jaw gently turned her head. "Look at me. Not at him."

Isobel swallowed and nodded. She knew he hadn't had a choice. She knew it. She'd watched the whole thing. And still, her eyes were drawn back to the body.

"No." He turned her head again.

"I've never seen someone die before." She hoped he realised her words were a confession, not a condemnation. She knew he'd had to do it. The man was going to kill him.

"I need you to run to my house," Callum said.

Her hands tightened in his shirt. "You're coming too."

"I need to deal with the men who're still here. I have questions."

"No. You need to come with me."

"Think, Isobel," he snapped. "The kids need you. I can take care of myself. Go. I'll be there soon." He pried her fingers from his shirt and pushed her in the direction of the path through the trees—the one her kids had taken, the one that didn't go near the road, where the other men might be waiting.

"Go." With one last order, he turned and strode towards the house.

Isobel scurried into the cover of the trees and felt torn. What kind of person would she be if she left him there to face this alone? He was outnumbered. What if he got injured? What if he needed her help getting back to his house?

She pulled out her phone from the back pocket of her jeans and texted Jack. *Are you okay?*

The answer was immediate: *In Callum's house. Heading for the basement. We're safe. You?*

On my way. Waiting for Callum.

There was a pause and then, *Don't do anything stupid.*

Isobel chewed at her lip. There was absolutely no guarantee she could give. *You're sure you're safe?*

Absolutely.

I'll be there soon.

She stopped texting Jack and dialled the emergency number. Her thumb sat over the call button as she waited for Callum. She could give him ten minutes. Ten minutes to see if he needed her to call in the cops. Even though she didn't want them there, she would bring them in—for Callum. All she had to do was make it through the next ten minutes.

CHAPTER 15

The bastards had filled the house with gas. The smell hit Callum full force as soon as he was through the front door. His eyes stung and he had to fight the urge to cough as he made his way along the hall to the kitchen. He wanted to get his prisoner out of there before the place blew. It was a courtesy these guys hadn't afforded Isobel and her kids. It was obvious they'd intended to get rid of them from the moment they'd set foot on her property.

As he passed, Callum scanned the living room, gun in hand. There was no sign of life, and the gas bottle from the heater was sitting with its valve wide open. Holding his breath, he barely made it to the kitchen. The house was filling up fast. As soon as he opened the kitchen door, he knew trying to get his prisoner out wasn't going to be possible. Time had run out. Gas from the oven had filled the room, and a small incendiary device sat in the middle of the kitchen table. There was a crude timer attached to the device.

With ten seconds on the clock.

Callum turned and ran for the front door. He propelled

himself through the house and hit the night air just as the device went off. Gas ignited. A blast ripped through the building. It hit Callum square in the back, lifted him from his feet and propelled him across the yard. He landed hard beside Isobel's overgrown bushes.

For a second, Callum lay there, gasping for air. He felt like his whole body had taken a beating, but at least his legs were still in place and seemed to function. With effort, he rolled over to lie on his back. A minute. That was all he needed. A minute to catch his breath, and then he would check on Isobel and the kids. At least they were safe in his house and not in the inferno before him. There was nothing to save from Isobel's home. The whole structure had been blown to bits, and what little was left was now ablaze.

"Callum!"

His name came at him as though he was hearing it under water. He turned his head to see Isobel fall to her knees beside him. Callum groaned. So much for her being safe in his house. The woman really needed to be vaccinated against stupidity.

"Are you okay?" Her hands roamed his chest, presumably looking for injuries. "Of course you aren't okay. You just got blown up!" Her voice went up an octave at the end, taking it into the realm only dogs could hear.

"I'm fine." It came out as a croak, which irritated his throat and set off a hacking cough. The gas had done a number on him.

"You're not fine." She lifted her phone. "I'm calling an ambulance. And the police. I should have called them in months ago. I'm an idiot. I'm going to get everyone killed, including the only man who's ever fought for me."

"No." Callum took the phone from her hands. "No cops. We need to regroup. We need to know where we stand. I have someone coming to help. We'll wait until we know more before involving the cops."

Isobel placed a palm on each of his cheeks and leaned down until her face was above his. "Callum, there's no keeping this from the police. The whole of Arness will have heard that explosion. The cops will come anyway. We should get in there first. I'll tell them the dead guy was self-defence. Better yet, let's not mention him at all. Maybe they'll think the intruders killed each other."

Callum felt strength return to his remaining limbs. "There are no intruders. They're gone. Just like we need to be." He fought to sit up, scanning the area around the house. No sign of a body, just as he'd expected. "They took the guy I killed with them."

"Why would they do that?"

"The same reason they took the other guy. They don't want anyone to know they were here."

She scowled at him. "Well, they shouldn't have left him on the beach in the first place. That's just bloody irresponsible. You can't wander around leaving dead bodies where you please. And if they wanted to be covert, blowing up a building isn't the way to do it. Even I know that!" She was shaking, her pupils dilated and her skin pale. She was struggling with shock.

He had to get her somewhere warm and safe. He had to get her to his house. "We need to get out of here." Callum climbed to his feet, somewhat ungracefully, with Isobel hovering over him.

"You're bleeding!" She lunged for him, pulling his shirt up to get at the wound.

A strange tenderness unfurled inside Callum. He covered her hands with his. "It's nothing. We'll deal with it at the house." She searched his eyes, desperate for reassurance. For once, Callum didn't hesitate in giving it. "It's nothing. It's going to be okay. I promise."

Callum couldn't resist pulling her into his arms. He held her tightly, aware of how right she felt against him. She buried her face in his chest and wrapped her arms around him. They clung to each other, and Callum wasn't sure who was giving comfort to whom.

"It's okay," he said as he stroked her back. "It's the adrenalin making you shiver. It'll pass."

He wanted to stand there forever, revelling in the comfort of her soft body, reassuring himself that she was still alive. Still with him. But he couldn't. Already he could hear sirens and voices in the distance. He kissed her hair. "We have to go, sweetheart."

She nodded, and he felt her take a deep breath, pulling herself together. Callum wondered how many times over the years she'd had to do exactly that. How many blows could one woman take before she stopped bouncing back? He really didn't want to know. The thought of Isobel losing her courage, and drive, was too much to contemplate.

"I'm ready." She stepped away from him, leaving him cold without her.

Callum took her hand. He told himself she needed the connection, but deep down, he knew he needed it almost as much she did. They headed for the path into the trees between Isobel's property and his.

"I can't believe what I saw," Isobel said as they ran.

"There was a lot of gas in the house," Callum said.

"Not the house. The way you took that guy apart. I've never seen anything like it. All that power and precision. It was amazing." The last word came out on a sigh that made Callum stumble.

"Your body is amazing," she continued. "The way your muscles move when you fight. All that strength." Her teeth pressed into her bottom lip, and Callum stifled a groan. "I haven't even seen you without a shirt yet."

That was it. He'd had enough. "Stop talking and run."

"You practice that martial arts stuff, don't you? Do you do it shirtless? Can I watch?"

He did groan this time. "You're having a reaction to the adrenalin. You needed it to help save your life. Now it's looking for an outlet. Ignore it. It will pass."

"Maybe it would pass faster if we both got naked and spent five minutes working it off? We can spare five minutes, right? I mean, the kids are safe. Right?"

"Woman, I'm beginning to think your default setting is recklessly horny."

"It's my curse," Isobel agreed. "But it seems to be worse when I'm around you."

"Stop." Callum's jeans were getting tight and it was becoming hard to run. "Don't say another word."

He glared at her to get the message home, and she smiled sweetly. At least she stopped talking.

Callum led her through his house to a door at the back of the kitchen that she'd assumed led to a pantry. It didn't. It hid a set of stairs that led under the house.

"Oh, is this your granddad's famous bunker?" There weren't many houses in the area that had basements, and the McKay one was particularly well known, because old man McKay had spent years fighting with the council over it. He'd needed planning permission to turn it into a bomb shelter, or something like that. The place had become an urban myth around Arness, with everyone wondering what exactly lay under the old man's house.

Isobel felt jittery. She was aware that she was fidgeting a lot, but she couldn't seem to stop. Every inch of her skin felt hypersensitive. Her blood seemed to fizzle in her veins. There was too much energy in her body. She felt as if she'd explode if she didn't get rid of it. And the only way she wanted to do that was with the man at her side. He was driving her crazy. The scent of him, so masculine and musky. The way his body moved. The ripple of his muscles. She wanted to feel the rough rasp of his stubble against her skin. She wanted to bite into those strong muscles. She wanted to feel him moving inside her until she couldn't think from needing him.

"Will you stop it?" he growled as he stalked down the stairs in front of her. He hadn't even looked around. He couldn't possibly know what she was thinking. And she didn't care if he did anyway. Her mind was on other things. Mainly the way his butter-soft jeans cupped his firm backside. Damn it, her mouth was actually watering.

Callum spun to face her, and Isobel walked right into him. Because she was on the step above him, she could almost look him straight in the eyes. She licked her lips. If she didn't taste him soon, she was going to go insane.

"Woman. Your kids are through the door at the bottom of the stairs. They need comfort. Even I can figure that out. You need to focus and stop thinking about sex."

Oh my goodness, that rumbling voice set off mini-orgasms. She closed her eyes and moaned.

"Hell," Callum muttered. "You're killing me."

She couldn't think. Her brain was hazy. She rocked towards him, breathing him deep. Callum clenched his jaw and let out a stream of curses.

"Just one little taste," Isobel whispered.

She saw the hesitation and then the angry resolve. "One of us has to be sensible. I can't believe it's me."

He spun on his heels and strode down the rest of the steps, leaving Isobel feeling somewhat desperate. She blinked several times and tried to clear her mind. He was right. She needed to focus. She could do this. She could.

Callum pressed a code into the keypad on a box beside the door. There was a click, and he tugged the door open. The very thick, reinforced door. Once through the doorway, Isobel was confronted with a long and narrow living area, with four doors equally spaced on the left-hand side of the room and another door on the far wall. The walls were painted white and the floors were wood. The lighting was soft and almost made her forget that she was in a basement.

They were standing in a compact kitchen, which flowed into a dining area. There was a seating area at the far end of the room, complete with large leather sofa and a massive TV. Jack had been sitting watching TV, and must have jumped up when the door opened. While Callum started rummaging through the kitchen cupboards, Isobel rushed to her son and wrapped him in a tight hug, whether he liked it or not.

"Are you okay? Where's Sophie?" She ran her hands over his shoulders and arms, searching for injuries.

"I'm good. Sophie's in bed." He cocked his head towards one of the doors on the left-hand wall.

When Isobel opened it, she found a small bedroom. It had a freestanding closet, a dresser, a chair and a set of bunk beds. Sophie was out cold on the top bunk. Isobel stroked her daughter's hair before closing the door quietly behind her. She turned to find Callum going through the largest medical kit she'd ever seen.

"Why do you need all that gear?" she said. "Is it in case you get stuck in here during a nuclear winter?"

Callum looked at her like she was nuts, before turning to Jack. "I need you to call your aunts. Tell them you're all fine and that you're here. But ask them not to rush over. I want them to spread the word that your mum took you two away for a few days and you weren't in the house when it blew."

"The house blew up?" Jack's jaw fell.

"You didn't hear it?" Callum said, attention still on the medical kit.

"I was down here, in the bunker, putting Sophie to bed."

"It isn't a bunker. It's a…granny flat." He seemed pleased at that description.

Jack shared a smile with his mum. It was definitely a bunker.

"Did Sophie go to sleep okay?" Callum pulled out some sterile wipes, tugged up his shirt and started dabbing at the wound on his side.

Isobel rushed over and took it out of his hand. "I'll do it." There was a deep gash along the line of his bottom rib. It was still bleeding a little, and there was dirt embedded in it. "You need a shower. This needs to be washed out properly."

"There are clean cloths under the sink," Callum said. "See if you can get the dirt out here."

Isobel wasn't happy with that plan, but she went searching for a cloth, listening to Callum and Jack as she ran it under the tap.

"Sophie," Callum said. "She okay?"

"I told her Mum was with you." Jack smirked. "She seemed to think that made Mum safe, so she went to sleep. What happened at the house? What do you mean it blew up?"

"The intruders filled the house with gas. There isn't anything left of it." Callum paused, as though unsure of how to say anything else. "I'm sorry," he said at last.

"Yeah, me too." Jack looked a little lost. "I'll go upstairs and call the three witches."

"You can do it from here." Callum nodded to the old-style phone on the wall. "Use the landline. I need to go up and get a change of clothes and deal with this wound."

Jack nodded and headed for the phone. He stopped when

he saw it. "Dial? It has a dial? When were you born? The Stone Age?"

Callum grunted and gathered up his medical supplies.

"I'll come with you," Isobel said. "Help clean you up."

"What?" Jack dropped the phone receiver, and it dangled by its spiral cord.

Isobel felt her cheeks burn. "I don't mean shower with him. I mean bandage his wound."

Jack frowned and looked like he didn't quite believe her. Whatever. She grabbed the rest of the medical kit and looked at Callum. "You coming?"

With a shake of his head, he followed her. They went straight to the master bedroom, with its en suite. Isobel put the kit on the dresser before walking over to Callum. Wet cloth in hand, she tugged up his shirt.

Callum's hand covered hers, and she stilled.

"I don't need help," he said. "It's stopped bleeding."

"Let me take care of it." *Let me take care of you.*

She hated to see him injured. She hated even more that she was the cause of it. If she hadn't dragged him into her mess, he would have been safe at home instead of dealing with the intruders at her place. The thought of the intruders reminded Isobel of watching Callum fight, and her mind turned to darker, sultrier places.

Slowly, Callum released her hand. She reminded herself that she wasn't there to gawk at his perfect abs, she was there to clean out his wound, but as soon as she saw the tattoo around his belly button, that thought flew out the window. Suddenly, the gash on his side wasn't the most interesting part of him.

"You have a tattoo?"

"Several," Callum said.

"Oh." She was distracted, her attention firmly on the tribal design that curved over his stomach and framed his belly button. She traced it with her fingertips and watched his muscles ripple under her touch. "Does it mean something?"

He cleared his throat. "Not that one."

Isobel tore her eyes away from the black ink. "Where are the other ones?"

He stared at her, and she felt herself falling into the depths of his eyes. Slowly, his eyes not leaving hers, Callum continued to lift his shirt. There was a Celtic knot emblazoned on his pec, done in the same black ink as the tattoo on his stomach.

"Take off your shirt, Callum." Isobel was the one giving orders for a change.

"This isn't a good idea," Callum said, but he sounded needy, uncertain.

"What isn't?" She dropped the wet cloth and leaned in to swirl her tongue around the curves of the Celtic knot.

He cursed and ripped off the shirt. Isobel's hands were on him before the shirt hit the floor. All that hot, smooth skin covering firm muscle—he was a work of art. She traced the ridges and valleys of his stomach.

"I want to memorise this with my tongue," she said.

Callum groaned as his fingers worked into her hair and tightened. "I need to tell you something."

"Tell me later." She twirled her tongue around a hard nipple and then bit down hard.

"It's important."

"Later." Nothing was more important than tasting this gorgeous man.

He cursed, and the grip in her hair tightened, pulling her away from his chest and angling her face up to his. His lips met hers with a furious clash. All of his strength, all his ability was poured into the kiss. She felt him reach behind her and heard the click of the lock. After that, all that registered was Callum. His tongue plundered her mouth, spearing in and out, making her thighs press together. She pressed her fingernails into his shoulders, hard enough to leave marks. She needed him. She ached for him. She wanted to taste him, inhale him into her soul. She wanted to feel his weight over her and feel his hard length inside her. She wanted all of it.

His stubble rasped at her chin as he deepened the kiss. He was feeding on her, their gasps and moans melding into a symphony of unadulterated desire. She pressed her palm flat in the middle of his chest, feeling the soft hairs against her smooth skin. She wanted to feel them rub against her breasts. She wanted to feel his skin against every inch of her skin.

Desperate, she pressed her hand down his body and over the bulge in the front of his jeans. She moaned into his mouth as the heel of her hand rubbed at him, feeling the firmness press back. She'd imagined going slower this time. Learning his body. Luxuriating in all that muscle and hot, hot skin. But that would have to wait. She needed him now. Desperately needed him.

Frantically, she popped the button of his jeans and unzipped him. She tugged at the waistband of his underpants, freeing the smooth crown of his cock. Callum ripped his lips from hers and let out a stream of curses.

"Slow down," he ordered as he tightened his grip in her hair.

That wasn't going to happen. Isobel wrapped her hand around his length and stroked, luxuriating in the size of him. She wanted to touch him like this for hours. She wanted to wrap her lips around him and suck and lick until he begged for mercy. But most of all, she wanted him inside her. She was empty, desperately empty, and only Callum could fill her.

Her hand still holding him, she licked and kissed and bit at his chest, tasting the salt and musk of him on her tongue.

She walked forward, making him back up towards the bed. She needed him now. She was past waiting. The need that had been building since she'd kissed him in her living room hours earlier had reached explosive proportions, and there was only one thing that could give her relief.

The back of Callum's knees hit the bed and his balance teetered. Isobel gave him a hard shove and watched him fly back onto the bed. He was perfection. Broad shoulders, tattoos, washboard abs and a smattering of hair. And underneath it all, poking out of his jeans, was her prize.

Isobel didn't wait a second. She ripped off her jeans and underwear and climbed on top of him. Her mouth slammed onto his as she felt the head of his cock slide through the swollen and wet lips of her sex. She clenched and groaned at the stark empty feeling inside her. She couldn't wait a second more. Wrapping her fist around him, she positioned him where she needed him to be and sank onto him.

Callum ripped his mouth from hers. "Condom."

"In a second." He felt too good. Too, too good.

She felt Callum root around in his pocket.

"Up," he ordered as he brought the square packet to his teeth and ripped.

"Just a little longer." She ground down on him.

He wrapped his hand in her hair and tugged her down to look in his eyes. The look on his face was a mixture of amusement, need and something else. Something soft. Something she was scared to name.

"Woman, focus. You don't want to get pregnant."

For a second, she was lost in his eyes, the feel of him inside her overwhelming. In that moment, nothing else mattered other than being with Callum. Than feeling Callum. Than knowing him.

"Crazy woman," he muttered, then tugged her face down

and slammed his mouth on hers. One taste. One touch. She was lost. She melted into him, boneless and at his mercy.

"No sense," he mumbled against her lips, and then she felt his fingers grasp her hips and he lifted her off him and onto the bed beside him.

"No." Isobel climbed right back on top of him. This time, he was sheathed. It felt different, less intimate, but definitely safer.

Isobel whined her complaint, aware deep inside of her that she was acting insane.

"Move, darlin', move." Callum's dark order brought her right back into the moment.

This was what she needed. Perfection. Nothing felt like Callum. Nothing. Her hips moved as she ground herself down on him, keeping up a relentless pace. He clenched her hips, but didn't try to take over. Isobel sat back, her fingers raking over his abs.

Luscious green eyes stared up at her, and she found she couldn't look away. He was perfection. Brutal strength and raw masculinity. Her body was on fire. Sparks of electricity ran across her skin, from her fingers to her toes. She moved faster, circling her hips every time she pressed down on him.

"Yes, yes, yes." Her head fell back and the chants became more desperate. She felt as though she was floating away, leaving her body and everything else behind. Wave after wave of sensation rippled through her. She felt him thicken inside her. His panting grew more desperate. She felt his muscles tense beneath her as she roared towards the precipice.

"Callum," she wailed as she flew over the edge.

She collapsed on top of him as he arched up to meet her. His hips moved, once, twice, before he grunted his own release. Shocks rippled through Isobel as she floated back down to earth. She was limp. Sated. Replete.

Callum's arms wrapped around her as she lay on top of him. Her face pressed into the curve of his neck. "If we ever manage to do this with foreplay, I'm going to die," he said.

Isobel started to laugh, and felt his chest move under hers. He kissed her head.

"You need to move. I have to deal with this condom."

Isobel moaned, pressing her forehead into him. "I can't believe I forgot again."

She struggled to sit up and climbed off him. She was still wearing her sweatshirt and bra, and Callum still had his jeans on. But at least he'd managed to remember to protect them. It was almost as though she *wanted* to get pregnant. She looked at Callum to find him watching her.

"I lose my mind around you," she confessed.

He stroked his hand over her hair. "It isn't only you. I haven't forgotten to glove up since I was a teenager. I blame you. You need to stop jumping me. I can't think straight."

"Me?" She climbed off the bed. "This insanity is all your fault. Stop…" She waved a hand at him to signify everything that was Callum. "Stop being you!"

For a second he looked stunned, and then he burst out laughing. Isobel was so shocked by the sound that she almost forgot she was mad at herself. And then something else occurred to her.

"Are you clean?" she asked as her stomach lurched.

Callum grinned at her. Why he suddenly thought this was funny, she had no idea. Because it wasn't funny. Not at all.

"Sexually. Are you clean?" She pointed at him. "Do you have any sexually transmitted diseases?"

"Woman, these are the things you ask *before* you jump a man."

Isobel lifted her jeans and underwear and glared at him. "I'm being serious. Are you clean?"

"Aye. Are you?" He cocked an eyebrow at her.

"Of course I am! I don't have sex. Ever. The last man I slept with was my ex-husband. Before that, it was Jack's father." She waved her jeans at him. "I am the most responsible person I know. I don't take chances. I can't afford risk. I'm a mother. And then you come along! And every sensible thought in my head disappears. Seriously! Why is that? It's like I want to sabotage my life. Well, what's left of my life." She pointed at him. "You mess with my mind. You…you…seducer of common sense, you!" She stomped towards the bathroom, slamming the door behind her on Callum's laughter.

"Don't think I've forgotten about that bruise on your side," Callum called after her.

"Idiot," Isobel muttered as she ran the shower. And she wasn't talking about Callum. Teenagers had more sense than she did. She'd almost had unprotected sex. Again. She shook her head in disgust and squealed when the door opened behind her.

"Do you mind? I'm trying to shower here." She wasn't. She was standing in the middle of his bathroom, castigating herself while wearing a sweatshirt and nothing on the bottom.

"Let me see." Before she could stop him, he reached out and tugged up her sweatshirt, exposing the bruise.

Isobel didn't look at it. She was of the firm belief that if you couldn't see something, it didn't hurt. Instead, she stared at Callum's illegally hot bare chest and tried to come up with a way to immunise herself against the sight. She shivered when he gently traced the mark Ray had left.

"Punch to the ribs. Looks like the guy wore rings." Callum looked up at her. "You need an x-ray."

"It's fine. Just bruised." She hoped.

"Who did it?" His voice was soft, but Isobel wasn't fooled.

"That's got nothing to do with you. I only asked you to

help with the body. Now that the body is gone, you don't need to be involved at all. You can call your team and tell them we don't need the help anymore." It made her sick to give him the out, but it was the decent thing to do. She hadn't invited him in to fix her life. She was pretty sure that wasn't even possible anyway.

"This isn't over. The body might be gone, but you're on the radar of some seriously bad people. People who tried to kill you tonight," he said evenly.

"And they probably think they succeeded, which means we're safe."

"As soon as you surface again, they'll know they didn't get you, and that safety will come crashing down."

"You don't need to worry about that. I only asked for help with the body. The rest has nothing to do with you."

"I'm in this until it's finished. You need my protection even more than you did when you asked for my help."

"Fine, do what you like." She threw up her hands and took a step back. "Now get out. I want to shower."

"Not until you've told me who hurt you."

"It's not your problem."

"I'm making it my problem."

"What are you going to do? Pull my fingernails until I give up the information? Go away and let me shower in peace."

Callum's eyes narrowed. "I think I'll just call your sisters and ask them who hit you."

"They don't know."

"I bet they could make an accurate guess."

"Why do you insist in knowing this? Are you so dead set on making all of my problems your problems? Haven't I complicated your life enough? You don't need to know who did this. I'm handling it."

His palm slid over her hip and down to rest over her lower abdomen. "This makes your problems my problems."

"You don't even know if there is a baby. Why are you even waiting around to find out? Why aren't you running as fast as you can?" She held her arms wide. "I mean, look at me. I'm in my thirties with a teenager and a toddler. I have a crappy job that I probably lost today because I couldn't keep my problems out of my workplace. I don't have a house. Or belongings. I don't even have a change of clothes. And on top of all that, I don't have the sense to have protected sex."

"You aren't the only one that made that mistake. I didn't protect you."

His willingness to taking responsibility for his part in their mess melted her frustration, but she had to make him see reality. "Callum, think about this logically. What will you do if there is a baby?"

"I'll take responsibility for it."

"And what does that mean exactly?"

His eyes shifted, looking around the room. When he looked back at her, there was only resolve in his face. "I'll look after you and our child."

Her heart actually melted, and part of her soul jumped towards him, desperate to have him look after her. Desperate for a partner to help raise her family. Desperate for a role model for her son. But she'd done this before. She'd married Rob thinking he'd be a nice, stable influence on Jack, thinking he'd never leave her and that she'd live a content, perhaps a little boring, life with the man. She wasn't making that mistake again.

"You're obviously a good guy, Callum. And I appreciate that your honour won't let you walk away. But it wouldn't just be me and the baby. It's Sophie and Jack too. It's my three sisters and my crappy life. You don't want that." She snorted. "Heck, there are days when even I don't want it. Don't worry, I'm sure there isn't a baby. But if there is, and you want to be a part of things, I'll let you contribute and I'll make sure it spends time with you too. Now, I really need to get cleaned up."

"We'll talk about the baby later. Right now, I need you to tell me who hit you."

"You aren't going to let this go, are you?"

He just stared at her.

"Fine." She was worn out by everything, including Callum. "The loan shark paid me a visit today. He wants the balance of what's owed to him by the weekend. Or…" Her eyes went wide. There were things Callum really didn't need to know, and tiredness was making her talk without thinking. She hurried on, hoping he didn't notice the slip. "One of his guys, Ray, reinforced the message with his fist. So there you have it. Can I shower now?"

"Or what? You started to say something and stopped. Tell me the rest. Now."

Isobel almost went breathless at the sight of him. This was the Callum who'd fought circles around the guy outside her house. This Callum was brutal, deadly and unstoppable. And although she knew he'd never hurt her—not physically, anyway—she also knew he would never stop until he got what he wanted.

"If I don't have the money, I get to repay the loan on my back." There. She'd said it. She'd even said it as evenly as possible, in the hope she wouldn't betray just how horrifying that thought was.

Callum stilled and his fingers tightened at her nape. "Name. I need his name."

"Eddie Granger."

"Home base?"

"He works out of Glasgow."

Callum nodded. Curtly. As though making a decision. "He won't be a problem for you again. Him or this Ray guy."

He dropped his hand and turned to leave. Isobel reached out for him, grasping his bicep. When he looked back, she could see the barely-contained rage burning deep inside of him.

"You can't kill him. They'll put you in jail." She was terrified that was exactly what he had planned. "I don't want you getting into trouble because of me."

His face softened slightly. "I know other ways to deal with this. Trust me." He glanced at her belly. "It's the least I can do. Now get showered and catch some sleep. Use one of the bedrooms in the basement. They're more secure. I've taken the middle one, but the other two are there for you and the kids. I'll talk to you later."

Isobel wanted to ask him what he planned to do, but he was already gone, leaving her shivering at the loss of his heat.

CHAPTER 16

For some reason, Rachel had arranged a flight to Scotland for the middle of the night. Elle thought it was because she was just as eager to get there and get Callum back to the office as the rest of them. They arrived at Campbeltown airport as the sun came up, stopped briefly at a little café so Ryan wouldn't turn feral and eat the rest of the team, and then drove straight to Arness. Since there was no sign of Callum, Elle bypassed his alarm and they made themselves at home in his house. The general consensus was that if he called for their help, he'd expect them to move in with him anyway.

Yeah, Elle was pretty sure that was going to go down well with Callum when he returned.

"This place might as well be a cell in a monastery," Megan said as she dumped her holdall on Callum's kitchen table. "There's no evidence that anybody lives here."

"I don't think they call the rooms in a monastery cells." Elle swept Megan's bag onto the floor and set up her laptop in its place. Elle didn't care how Callum lived. All she cared about was that he was still alive. For a while there, she wasn't sure that would be the case.

"They do. I saw it on TV. They call them cells because living in them is a prison sentence," Megan said as she started opening and shutting Callum's kitchen cupboards.

"I can't stay here," Rachel announced as she strode into the room. Her Gucci bag was slung over her arm and her feet were shod in her usual red-soled pumps. With her sleek auburn hair, Chanel suit and Rolex watch, she looked so completely out of place that it wasn't hard to agree with her.

"There's a tent in the garage." Megan gave her an evil smile. "You could always pitch it in the backyard."

"I don't mean in this house, although that too. I mean Arness. It has all of five houses and one shop. We might as well be in stranded in Greenland."

"Greenland?" Elle said.

"There's nothing there either," Rachel said. "I mean, have you ever met anyone from Greenland? Ever? No. That's because there's nothing there. Nothing."

"Feel free to leave, then," Megan said. "We'll manage fine without your brand of encouragement."

Rachel pointed a talon at Megan. "Remind me why I haven't fired you? Again?"

"Please." Megan rolled her eyes. "You were fired along with me. If you didn't have the money, and the balls, to buy into the company, you wouldn't be here either. Plus"—Megan flicked her long blonde hair over her shoulder—"I like to think of myself as the positive force that balances your influence on the planet. The angel to your devil. The yin to your yang. The antimatter to your matter. The world needs both of us. If we separate, bad things will happen. Mark my words."

"Oh, for the love of Prada," Rachel muttered. "I don't have

time for this. We actually have real, paying clients that need our attention. Callum asked for one person and some of Elle's time. Why are we all here?"

Elle let out a sigh. Rachel knew damn well why they were there. She'd even insisted on coming and leaving Joe and Julia in charge of the London office. Rachel had said that she was the only person able to deal with Callum's temper, and they needed her to get the job done quickly. She'd even gone so far as to hire a private plane to get them to Campbeltown airport in record time. Although Elle was certain if Rachel was quizzed about her generosity, she'd have some other horrible reason why she had to do it. The woman was an alligator—she did everything she could to protect her soft underbelly, even if that meant snapping at everyone around her.

"Why are we here? *Because*," Megan enunciated her words, "we care about Callum and want him to come back to London."

Rachel shook her head as though mystified, before sitting beside Elle. She crossed her long legs and drummed her red nails on the table. "Where is he, anyway?"

"I don't know. He disabled the cameras after he spoke to me." Elle's fingers flew over her keyboard, but she paused to look out the window. There was still smoke drifting in the distance. "Anybody else notice the burned-out house on the way here? That didn't have anything to do with Callum, did it?"

"Nope, that was a gas accident," Megan said. "I made Dimitri stop the car and ask the cops. Faulty gas bottle. Thankfully, the family were away at the time."

"Is this the wall where Callum had sex?" Ryan called from the hall. "I think we should put up a plaque or something to commemorate it for him."

"Will that boy ever grow up?" Rachel sneered.

"That *boy* is the same age as you," Elle said.

"Yes, but I'm decades older when it comes to maturity," Rachel said.

Elle couldn't argue with that. "I have more information on Isobel."

"Let's hear it." Dimitri followed Ryan into the room. "Make coffee while you're over there, will you, babe?" Dimitri said to Megan.

"Do I look like your servant?" Megan's eyebrows shot up. "I'm your wife, not your slave. Make your own damn coffee."

"Baby," Dimitri crooned. "You make better coffee. And if you do it for me, I'll do that other thing for you later."

Megan clapped her hands and beamed at him. "Really?"

"Promise." Dimitri pressed a hand over his heart solemnly.

"Then you get coffee." She blew him a kiss before she reached for the coffee pot.

"Before anyone makes the mistake of asking what they're talking about," Rachel said, "know that I forbid it."

"We don't need to ask." Ryan's eyes were on Elle's laptop. "It's sex. They're all about the sex. They don't think about anything else."

"Hey," Megan said. "We're newlyweds. It's our right."

"Yeah, but does it have to happen right under our noses?" Ryan grumbled.

"You're just jealous," Megan said.

"As much fun as is it to listen to you bicker like children," Elle said, "I have news on Isobel. As far as I can tell, she's clean. No run-ins with the police, no parking tickets, nothing. She does, however, have sucky taste in men. She left school at fifteen because she got pregnant and the boyfriend did a runner on her. She hasn't heard of him since, which isn't surprising, since he OD'd in Edinburgh six years ago—heroin. Her second attempt at happy-ever-after ended miserably too, but this time she made it to the altar before she got pregnant. Unfortunately, this guy was worse than the last. He ran out on her as soon as the baby was born."

"What a dick," Ryan muttered.

There was general agreement before Elle brought up the rest of the report. "The husband filed for divorce from Glasgow and hasn't been back to Arness since. But, and this is where it gets really nasty, he didn't tell the rest of the world that he wasn't married to Isobel anymore. So when he borrowed money from his friendly neighbourhood loan shark, he made certain the guy knew Isobel was good for repayments. And then, guess what? He suddenly and mysteriously disappeared."

"Leaving Isobel with the debt," Megan said in disgust.

"How much are we talking?" Dimitri asked.

"Thirty-four thousand pounds, give or take a few hundred," Elle said.

"That's a lot of money for a woman like Isobel," Rachel said.

"That's a lot of money for everyone *except* you, Rachel," Ryan said.

Rachel's eyes narrowed and she opened her mouth, no doubt to spew acid all over Ryan, but Elle got in first.

"The point is," she said, "the ex, Robert Argyle—not his real name, by the way—has disappeared and the loan shark is making regular visits to Isobel to extract payment."

"We need to find this arsehole and make him repay his own debt," Ryan said.

"Yeah," Elle said to Ryan, "but as much as I'd like to make Isobel's ex pay his own debt, we can't. I managed to track him down. He's currently serving fifteen years at Her Majesty's pleasure. Armed robbery. I thought I had bad taste in men, but Isobel takes first prize. She's attracted to serious losers."

"And Callum," Megan said. "He isn't a loser, he's just…"

"Lost?" Elle said.

"Suicidal?" Dimitri said.

"Seriously bad-tempered?" Ryan said.

"A coward who ran away from his responsibilities?" Rachel said.

"Standing right here," Callum said.

All heads snapped to the doorway where Callum was standing, his arms crossed over his usual Henley, and his face in his usual scowl. Elle had never seen a better sight.

"Hi, boss." Elle grinned.

"Nice place," Megan said chirpily. "Minimalistic. But nice."

Callum frowned at them. "Don't you know how to knock?"

"We did. You didn't answer," Megan said. "Where were you, anyway? We've been right through the house."

"Basement. And keep the noise down. Isobel and the kids are still asleep down there."

The team shared a look.

"Uh, Callum, why do you have them in the basement when the bedrooms are up here?" Megan said, and then looked horrified. "Serial killers use basements. Please tell me that isn't your killing ground? You haven't been torturing kids down there, have you?"

"Babe," Dimitri said with a shake of his head. "Ignore her," he said to Callum. "Too much TV."

"There are bedrooms down there?" Elle said. "I wondered what was behind the security access. I thought weapons. Just sayin', if I'd had more time, I would have totally cracked that lock."

"Good to know." Callum leaned a shoulder against the doorjamb.

"It also explains why we don't have any footage of you sleeping," Elle said. "I was worried about that at first, then I thought you were camping outside."

Callum just stared at her.

"PTSD." Elle shrugged. The explanation made perfect sense to her. She'd even read up on the condition. If Callum had been sleeping outside, it wouldn't have surprised her. She'd always thought he was untamed and belonged with the animals. "I thought maybe being inside made it hard to sleep."

"Betty said someone told her I sleep in the nude," Callum said.

Megan put up a hand. "That would have been me. I just wanted to shut her up."

"Yeah, but it kind of backfired," Ryan said. "She wanted to make more money, and thought watching you in the buff was a way to do it. She was mad when she couldn't get it on camera."

Callum zeroed in on Ryan and the room temperature dropped a few degrees. Elle shivered and was glad she wasn't on the receiving end of that look. Ryan didn't seem fazed. Either that or he was too focused on the doughnuts he'd picked up in Campbeltown to care.

"Explain," Callum barked.

"She had someone hook up the live feed to her house and she's been charging the old folk to watch," Ryan said. "Lake only found out about it yesterday after a rumour went around town that Betty was showing live porn in exchange for pie and cake." He pointed a doughnut at Callum. "She told Lake *she* wants to be thrown up against a wall."

Callum didn't move an inch, apart from the tiny muscle in the corner of his jaw that throbbed.

"Somebody *should* lob her at a wall. I hope you shut that crap down." Callum's voice was low and even, a sure sign he was about to blow.

For once, Ryan seemed to notice something other than food. "You did when you ripped out the cameras."

There was silence. Callum stared at Ryan with a look that said he had better do something fast.

Ryan got the message. He stood, fishing his phone from his pocket. "I'll get Lake onto it now. Make sure Betty didn't save any footage or anything."

The twitch in Callum's jaw became more pronounced as Ryan left the room. He turned to Rachel. "Why are you all here? I only asked for one backup person. That's what I'm paying for."

"You aren't paying for anything. Suggesting it is, frankly, insulting." Rachel got to her feet. "You asked for help and you're going to get it. Joe and Julia would have been here too, but we needed someone to look after the office."

"I voted for Rachel," Megan said, "but she overruled me. Something about wanting to keep an eye on the plane she was paying for. Honestly, you blow up one itsy-bitsy plane and you never hear the end of it."

Rachel carried on talking as though Megan was invisible. "Once we're finished here, we plan to drag your miserable, self-pitying behind back to London so you can fix the mess you left in your wake, when you ran away like a hysterical pre-schooler."

"Subtle," Megan coughed into her hand before attempting to look innocent.

For a second, Elle could have sworn she saw the walls undulate with the tension in the room. She waited for Callum to start shouting about how he didn't need their help and how they should get lost. She could almost hear him saying, *"Never darken my doorstep again."* But instead of shouting, there was silence. Heavy, uncomfortable silence.

And then a tiny voice piped up. "Clam?"

Every set of eyes in the room focused on the little girl who'd appeared at Callum's feet. She wore a giraffe onesie and had a matching stuffed toy clutched to her chest. With the other hand, she rubbed at an eye. She was the most adorable thing Elle had ever seen and made her want to rush back to London and return with her own giraffe onesie so they would match.

"What?" Callum said gruffly. "Why aren't you asleep?"

The girl shrugged and then held her arms up to Callum, obviously expecting him to lift her. The shock in the room was clear. Everyone waiting to see what he would do. For a second Callum looked completely bewildered, before his face turned carefully blank. He made no move for the child. And she was having none of it.

"Clam, up," she demanded.

With an irritated growl, Callum bent and scooped the girl up. She burrowed against his chest and watched them all with big eyes. Callum was tense, his movements stiff. It was clear he wasn't quite sure how to hold her. Eventually, he gave her back an awkward pat.

"I'm taking Sophie back to her mum. We'll talk later. You can use any of the rooms up here." Callum turned towards the door, but Sophie sat back and pointed at the table.

"Doughnuts!"

With a growl, Callum made a detour to the table. He lowered the child so she could grab a doughnut and then he strode for the door. Sophie grinned at them as she bit into the powdery treat.

"Did that just happen?" Megan stared after them.

"Wow," Elle said.

"I think our boy is ready to come back," Dimitri said. "I'm so proud. I almost have a tear in my eye."

"Oh for the love of Prada," Rachel said. "He picked up a child, he didn't cure cancer."

"Hey," Ryan said as he came back into the room. "Who ate my doughnuts?"

CHAPTER 17

Isobel was fixing breakfast in Callum's bunker kitchen when he came striding in with Sophie in his arms. She was halfway through a giant doughnut.

"Doughnuts for breakfast? Really?"

"This isn't breakfast. This is a pre-breakfast snack. Right?" Callum looked down at Sophie, who nodded.

Jack was sitting on the sofa in the living area, texting furiously. He didn't look up from his phone. "I want a pre-breakfast snack. Or breakfast. Any food would be good."

"You know how to use the kitchen," Isobel told him. "If you're in such a hurry, you can make your own food."

"You don't say that to Soph. That's favouritism, that is," Jack said.

Isobel ignored him and reached for her daughter.

She shook her head as she gnawed at the donut. "Stay, Clam."

"That's brilliant." Jack snorted a laugh. "Hard shell. Brainless. Looks like snot. It's the perfect name for him."

"Jack!" Isobel glared at her son.

Callum cocked an eyebrow in Jack's direction before

placing Sophie on a kitchen chair. "You need to stay here. I have work to do."

"Wanna go with Clam," Sophie said.

"Callum," Callum corrected. "And you can't. You need to have breakfast."

She opened her mouth to protest, but shut it when Callum shook his head.

"I wish she'd do that for me," Isobel said.

Callum straightened and turned his attention on her, suddenly making her feel naked. Not a good feeling while she was in a room with her two children. His eyes darkened as though he could read her mind. "You sleep okay?"

Isobel nodded. It had only been a couple of hours, but it'd been sound. "What's with this basement, anyway? Was your granddad one of those doomsday people? Have you taken over where he left off? Are you sitting around down here waiting for the world to end? Is this what you've been doing all these months? You've been in here burrowing like a mole and preparing for Armageddon?"

"No." His lips twitched as though he might risk a smile, but it passed, making Isobel crave hearing his deep, rich laughter again. "My grandfather was the mole. This is his panic room. He wanted one after I was captured in Iraq. He thought there should be a safe place for me if I ever needed one."

She jerked back. "You were captured?"

"I was only held for a few days before my team got me out."

Suddenly, the fact that the underground mini-apartment seemed more lived in than the house upstairs made a lot more sense. "This is where you live, isn't it? You don't sleep in the bed upstairs. That's why it was so neat." He'd been hiding. From life and from himself.

Callum cleared his throat. "My team, I mean, the security team I used to work with are here." His voice was husky.

Isobel flushed and felt herself leaning towards him. Just hearing that tone made her skin ache to be touched. Which she shouldn't allow. She stepped away from him.

"A whole team? I thought maybe one person." She couldn't risk any more people. She couldn't. "I thought it was just one person coming to do you a favour."

Callum dragged a hand through his hair, which made his T-shirt tighten over those impossibly buff shoulders of his. Why did he have to be so damn hot? It wasn't fair. Where she had stretch marks on her stomach, he had washboard abs. Where she had cellulite on her thighs, she was sure he had only toned muscle. She was at least ten pounds overweight and had given up on ever losing it, whereas he looked like there wasn't an ounce of fat anywhere on him. It wasn't fair. Why did she have to crave the touch of a man who made David Beckham look ordinary?

"I don't understand why they're all here." Callum's tone was even, which made her pay closer attention. She got the feeling that whatever he was about to tell her was far more important than he was letting on. "I was partner in an international security firm. I managed the London office, and the people upstairs are the team I was in charge of. They've come here to help us get to the bottom of your situation. They want me to come back." He sounded bewildered.

"The whole team are here? All of them?" Isobel was horrified. "They're here like this is a proper job? I can't afford to hire a security team. You have to send them away."

"Mum," Jack said.

"No, Jack, you know I'm right. I can't owe anyone else. I can't." She looked at Callum. "Send them away."

"No. We need them, and you don't have to pay anything."

She balked. "You're paying?" She shook her head. "I can't

allow that. Things are complicated enough between us without involving money."

"Nobody's paying, you damn stubborn woman. They're doing it…out of the kindness of their hearts. I think. It doesn't matter. They don't want money. And they're the best in the business. Trust me. We need them, and they will find out what's going on here." He took a step towards Isobel, and she felt the room shrink until it was filled with only him. "These people will watch our backs. You and your kids are still in danger. To send them away would be gross stupidity."

"You think I'm stupid?" Seriously? He was insulting her? Now? When she was barely holding it together?

"I didn't say that." The vein in his temple began to throb. "But you don't have the common sense God gave a goldfish."

Isobel put her hands on her hips and glared at him. "Take that back. That's just rude."

Jack cleared his throat. "You two want to remember there are kids in the room?"

Isobel groaned. "We're having an adult discussion here, Jack."

"You might be. He's trying to get back into your pants."

"Jack!" Isobel put her face in her hands.

"Don't talk to your mother like that," Callum said. "If you have a problem with me, be a man and talk to me about it. I'm more than happy to clear things up for you."

"Callum!" Isobel glared back at him, but he was engaged in a stare-off with her son. "That's it." Isobel shoved Callum towards the stairs out of the basement. "Go talk to your friends. I'll be up once Sophie's fed." Callum walked away reluctantly. Isobel didn't care. She stalked over to Jack and took his phone. "You go too. Eat upstairs. I've had enough of both of you. Sophie and I need some testosterone-free time."

"Mum," Jack whined.

She pointed at the stairs. "Now!"

With a sigh that was Oscar-worthy, Jack followed Callum.

"You better have food up there," he said to Callum's back.

"No guarantee," Callum said. "Ryan's here. He could have eaten everything by now."

Jack muttered something, but Isobel was past caring about them. She waited until the door slammed shut behind the pair before she turned to Sophie, who grinned widely.

"I like Clam," she said.

Isobel groaned. She pulled yesterday's sweatshirt on over the T-shirt she'd borrowed from Callum and hung like a dress on her. Until her sisters brought replacements, she was stuck wearing jeans with grass stains on the knees. She closed her eyes briefly and fought to block out the worries that were pressing in on her. Everything she owned was gone. Everything she'd worked so hard for, the home she'd tried to build for her kids, all of it was gone.

She wanted to crumple in a heap and sob until she faded away. She wanted to throw up her hands and scream that she was giving up. She was tired of struggling to get back up every time she was knocked down. She was tired of all of it. Of owing money she hadn't borrowed. Of trying to keep enough food in her house. Of making repairs to a house she didn't even own, and coaxing another mile out of a car that was on the verge of suicide because it couldn't take anymore either.

And now, here she was, living in the bunker basement of the town's most notorious resident. Relying on a man she barely knew, while she waited to find out if her latest sexual indiscretion would follow her through life. She placed a hand low on her belly. She couldn't even think about that now. There were dangerous men after her, a loan shark who wanted her to pay off the debt on her back, and she was so damn tired of dealing with everything by herself.

"I want milk," Sophie announced.

Isobel looked at her innocent, smiling daughter, who was treating this whole thing like a big adventure. "I'll get you some milk, baby." She crossed the room to the fridge.

And then she'd make breakfast. And then she'd call her sisters and get supplies. And then she'd see what she could salvage from her house. And then…

…she'd keep going.

Because that was what she did.

"If you have issues with this situation between me and your mother, you take them up with me," Callum said as soon as the basement door had closed behind Jack.

"I already told you my issues. You said you weren't going to string her along, but I see how you look at her. You need to back off."

It was on the tip of his tongue to reassure the boy that he had no intention of going anywhere near his mother. Instead, he said, "This is between me and your mother. I have no intention of treating her with anything other than respect. Which is what you need to do too. Which means watching what you say to her. She's an adult. She deserves a personal life."

"And I suppose you think that personal life means you." Jack puffed out his chest. "She's had enough of men who use her and walk out. I'm not going to let that happen again."

"You have no idea what I intend to do, boy."

"You telling me that you're planning a happy-ever-after with her?" Jack barked a mirthless laugh. "Yeah, right."

"I don't know what I'm planning, and neither do you, so back off."

"Like you're the type of guy who'd take on a woman with two kids. A woman with no house, no money, no prospects.

What does she have to offer you except sex? Huh? Guess that's enough to keep your interest."

Before Callum could think about it, his fist curled into Jack's shirt and he had him pressed up against the wall. "Don't make me take you outside and teach you a lesson. You will talk about your mother with respect and you will stay out of her personal life. Got it?"

"No." The boy was brave and stupid. "Until you prove you aren't going to use her and run, you can teach me as many lessons as you like, but I won't butt out. I'll be watching every single thing you do. And when you hurt her, when you abandon her, I'm going to teach you a lesson. Or, more likely, die trying."

Damn if Callum didn't like this kid. "That's between you and me. But you keep your comments to yourself around your mother. That's non-negotiable. She's dealing with enough."

Jack searched Callum's eyes for a long moment before nodding. "You can tell your bodyguards to back off. I'll keep this between us, and you can bet I'm watching every move you make around her. I know where you sleep. If I can't get at you when you're awake, I'll get you then."

Callum released Jack and stepped back, only to find Dimitri, Ryan and Megan forming a line behind him.

"Having problems, boss?" Ryan asked.

"I'm not your boss," Callum snapped. "And this is between me and the boy."

"Stop calling me boy," Jack told him as he pushed past the group and headed for the kitchen. "Or I'm going to start calling you old man."

The team watched him go.

"I like him," Megan said. "Reminds me of someone else I know." She tapped her chin. "Mmm, who could it be?"

"Get in the kitchen. We have a job to discuss." Callum strode past her.

"I think the boss is a bit grumpy," Dimitri whispered as they followed.

"Guess he isn't getting any," Ryan whispered back.

"If I have my way," Jack said, "he won't get any until he can prove he'll do good by my mum."

"I'm Megan," Megan said. "I spent years making sure my big brother Don-Don didn't get any. Stick with me, kid, and I'll teach you everything I know."

Callum swallowed a groan and headed for the coffee. Once he had a mug, he leaned against the counter and considered his team. No, not *his* team. The Benson Security team. The longer he was around them, the harder it was to remember that he had walked away.

"Right," he said. "Let's get this briefing started."

The rest of the team pulled out chairs at his dining table, where Rachel and Elle were already seated.

"Is this something we should talk about in front of the child?" Rachel pointed a talon at Jack.

The kid instantly pushed his shoulders back, ready to face off with Rachel. *Ah, the recklessness of youth.* "Don't even think about taking Rachel on. You're just a tasty snack for her. You can stay. But everything said in this room stays here. No texting your friends or posting information on Facebook."

"Instagram." Jack relaxed again. "Only old people use Facebook."

Callum shook his head and sipped his coffee.

"I'll ask again," Rachel said. "Are you sure he should be here?"

No, Callum wasn't sure. But he was certain that if they kept Jack out of the loop, he'd go off and protect his family any way he saw fit, which would be dangerous for all of them.

"The boy has a family to protect. He needs to be here."

Rachel still wasn't convinced.

"I'm vouching for him," Callum said before she could object again. "He's my responsibility." He looked at Jack to see how he took that news. Jack was staring at him with a strange look in his eyes, as though he was trying to figure out what Callum's angle was. Good luck to him. Callum didn't even know the answer to that.

"How much do you know?" Callum asked the team.

Rachel leaned back in her seat and studied him. Callum kept his face expressionless and waited. Rachel wouldn't poke her nose into his business. Mainly because she didn't care.

"We know that Isobel has terrible taste in men," Rachel said.

"No kidding," Jack said.

Callum pointed at him. "You talk, you leave. Your choice."

He made a zipping gesture over his mouth before jumping up to sit on the counter.

Callum looked back at Rachel. "Carry on."

"We know she has a body in her freezer, one we're really hoping she didn't kill."

Callum was aware of Jack bristling, desperate to defend his mother, but he didn't say a word. "No, she found him on the beach and hauled him up to her house with the help of her sisters. He's one of a crew of men who've been sneaking into the cove for months. And before you ask, I don't know for sure what they're up to. Isobel has been watching them."

"Do they know she's been watching them?" Ryan asked.

"They didn't until she took the body," Callum said. "Then they went looking for it. They found it last night."

Isobel appeared in the doorway as Callum explained, and her cheeks flushed at the sight of the filled room. Sophie trailed beside her, her giraffe under her arm and paper and pens in her other hand. She walked straight over to Callum, plopped down at his feet and started to draw.

"Everybody"—Callum signalled to Isobel to come join the discussion—"this is Isobel Sinclair. Isobel, everybody. They can tell you their names later. Come on in. We're going over the situation."

She walked over to stand beside Jack, giving wary smiles to the team as she did so. "Jack, why don't you take your sister back downstairs?"

"I think he needs to be here for this," Callum said calmly.

"No, he really doesn't," Isobel said. "I'm his mother and I want to keep this side of life away from him for as long as possible."

"You can't." Jack sounded far older than his years. "I'm in it up to my neck. It's my mum who's selling stuff she found on the beach to pay off a guy who's threatening her. And my house that's been blown up. I'm in this, Mum. There's no sheltering me."

Isobel looked like his words were a blow, and it took physical effort on Callum's part not to reach out and pull her to his side. He reminded himself that Isobel didn't belong to him, and he was more than happy with that, and then he sipped at his coffee. The taste was suddenly bitter and the drink too cold.

Elle's head snapped up. "Your house blew up? That was your house? The police said it was a gas fault, that the family were away."

Isobel looked to Callum instead of answering, clearly unsure as to what to tell the team.

"That's what we want them to think," Callum said. "They rigged the gas to blow. Isobel and the kids got out before that happened. I had a guy bagged and tagged in the kitchen and planned to go back and ask him some questions. I don't know if he got out, but if he did, he knows Isobel had help. Professional help."

"He saw your face," Dimitri said.

It wasn't a question, so Callum didn't answer. "I managed to take one of them out before the place blew, but when I checked, he was gone too." He looked at Dimitri and Ryan, knowing they would understand why that worried him. "They took him with them."

"What the hell have you got yourself into?" Dimitri said.

"I don't know." Callum dug out his phone and tossed it on the table in front of Elle. "There are photos on there. The body. The beach where he was dumped. See what you can get from it. I also took his fingerprints and a hair sample. It's downstairs. Do we know someone who can run those for us fast? I want to see if we can get a hit from the prints or his DNA."

"I know a guy." Elle reached for the phone. "I've been using him to run the DNA on that David guy we met in Peru. Still don't have a hit on it, though. What I really need is a photo. I could run his photo through image-recognition software and find him that way. It might take years, but I'd get there."

"Focus," Callum snapped. "We're talking about the dead body, not your weird obsession."

Elle beamed at him. "I've missed you. Give me the samples and I'll get them to my guy."

"Clam!" Sophie shouted at him, reminding Callum that she was still drawing on the floor at his feet.

When he looked down, she stuck her arm in the air and thrust a scribbled drawing at him. A little bewildered, he took it from her. It was a green mess. He looked at Isobel, who smiled.

"It's for you," she said.

"Thanks?" Callum looked down at Sophie, but she was

busy working on her next masterpiece, so he put the paper on the counter beside him.

"What else can you tell us about the attack on the house?" Dimitri said, thankfully bringing Callum back into his comfort zone.

"Not a whole lot." Callum ran a hand over his face. "There was nothing about these guys that made them stand out. No unique facial features. No visible tattoos. Nothing. The two guys I got the best look at had olive skin tones, like they'd come from a Mediterranean country instead of further north. They definitely didn't have that blue sheen Scottish folk get because the sun is a stranger up here."

Jack laughed, and then pointed at his closed mouth when Callum glared at him.

"I don't think they were ex-military," Callum continued, "but I only went hand to hand with one of them. They were experienced though. They were fast, efficient and they didn't communicate with anything but hand signals."

"Middle Eastern, maybe?" Megan said.

Callum shook his head. "I don't think so. My first thought was Italian, which doesn't make any sense."

"Maybe mob?" Megan said.

"No. There were tats on the dead guy. Standard English prison and Russian mob."

A ripple of confused looks went through the room.

"Weapons?" Ryan asked.

"Knives, handguns. Nothing unusual. Nothing hard to get hold of."

There was silence. Callum looked at Isobel and wondered if she was even aware she'd placed herself firmly between him and her son. He wondered whether it was so that she could defend either of them, if needed, or so that they could protect her? Without really planning to, he inched closer to her, just in case she needed him.

"There's more," Callum said. "During one of their nighttime visits to the cove, the guys from the boat lost a bag on their way up the bluff." He felt Isobel stiffen, but carried on as though he hadn't noticed. "Isobel found it the following day and sold the contents to a pawnbroker in Campbeltown. It had been full of camera equipment. High-end stuff. Isobel said it looked like the type of gear the paparazzi would use."

"Surveillance," Ryan said.

"That's what I thought too," Callum said.

"I don't know what you mean," Isobel said.

Callum felt his face soften as he looked down at her. "They were watching someone, or something, at a distance, to gather information."

"Oh." Isobel clasped her hands in front of her.

"Clam!" Sophie shouted, and handed him another drawing. He took it and put it on the counter beside him without looking at it this time. Sophie didn't seem to need his input on her work.

Callum looked back at the team. "I had a word with the pawnbroker. There wasn't any camera equipment left, but he had this." He reached into his pocket and tossed the small black box onto the dining table.

"Is that what I think it is?" Ryan looked at Callum.

"Aye," Callum said.

"What?" Megan said. "What am I missing?"

Dimitri pointed at the box. "That's part of a SAM guidance system."

"Stop speaking army, speak civilian," Rachel snapped. "What do you mean exactly?"

"He means," Callum said, "in non-military speak, that you're looking at the remote-control mechanism for a handheld surface-to-air missile."

"Are you sure?" Elle said.

Dimitri caught Callum's eyes and nodded. "We're sure."

"That isn't good," Elle said. "Right?"

"No," Callum said. "It isn't good."

Isobel made a little whining sound and wrapped her arms around herself. Jack sat up straight, ready to protect his mother. From what, Callum didn't know. He did know that he couldn't stand watching her shoulders hunch, as though she was trying to curl in on herself.

"Come here," he muttered, and wrapped an arm around her shoulders.

He was surprised when she didn't put up any resistance, and even more surprised when Jack didn't object. Instead, the boy studied Callum and his mum for a minute before turning his attention back to the group.

When Callum looked at his team, they were uniformly trying not to smile. Well, apart from Rachel. Rachel was studying her manicure and looking thoroughly bored.

"Clam!" Another piece of paper was thrust up at him, and he added it to his growing pile of scribble art.

"So," Megan said, "we've got an unknown dead guy, who's obviously a criminal, but we don't know what kind. We also don't know where he's from or who he was working with. We have a whole bunch of surveillance equipment that was smuggled into the country a month ago. And we have part of a missile guidance system." She looked at each of them. "You all thinking terrorist? Because I'm totally thinking terrorist."

"Me too!" Jack grinned.

"Totally terrorist," Elle said.

"Definitely," Ryan added.

Callum held up the hand that wasn't around Isobel's shoulders. "No jumping to conclusions. We follow the evidence and see where it leads."

"Now I'm thinking *CSI*," Megan said with a grin.

"Ryan, see if you can get anything from that SAM tech," Callum ordered.

"Yes, boss." Ryan saluted.

Callum ran a hand over his face. "Rachel, set up a timeline."

That made her sit up straight. "Why me? Why can't one of the minions do it?"

"Because Julia isn't here and you're the only other one with project management experience," Callum said. If he'd still been a partner at Benson Security, he would have told her to suck it up, rather than explaining himself.

"Okay," she said begrudgingly, "but only this once, and I'm not doing it until I've arranged some decent accommodation. There are no hotels in town. Actually, there's no *town* in this town. It's only a few houses, a garage and a shop. How do people live like this?"

"Yeah," Ryan said. "How *do* people live without their servants running around after them? What do they eat when there's no caviar? Oh, the agony of the underclass…"

"Clam!" Sophie thrust another piece of art at him. Callum took it without even registering; his focus was on Ryan and Rachel and their new weird dynamic.

"Why don't you do what you do best and go eat something?" Rachel said. "Maybe you could hang out at McDonald's for the rest of the day and let the adults get on with things here. I can even give you some pocket money to spend while you're there."

Ryan glared at her, and the two of them seemed locked in some sort of stare-down.

"Should we do something," Jack whispered to Callum, "or are we waiting for their laser vision to kick in and for them to melt each other's heads?"

To his surprise, Callum had to fight a smile. "Cut it out, you two."

Ryan gave Rachel one last glare before turning to Callum.

"I'm glad you're back. I seriously can't take any more of Cruella."

"I'm not back." Sure, he needed their help on this one thing, but that didn't change anything else. "I sold my share of the business."

"No, you didn't." Rachel flicked some imaginary lint from her black suit pants. "Your partners decided your decision wasn't made when you were in your right mind, so we didn't buy you out."

Callum wasn't sure he'd heard right. "You did what?"

"Okay, that's my cue to leave." Ryan scooped the small black box from the table and fled the room.

"Take me with you," Megan called after him.

Callum ignored them both. "Explain," he demanded of Rachel.

"There's nothing to explain. You're still a partner." Rachel lifted her mug of coffee and toasted. "We saved you from yourself. You're welcome."

Callum felt his left eye begin to twitch, a reaction he'd developed the day he'd met Rachel. A soft hand curved around his forearm, and he looked down to find Isobel smiling at him.

"They were just doing what they thought was in your best interests," she said softly.

He wasn't so sure about that.

"Of course we were." Rachel had the hearing of a hawk when she felt like it. "We need you back at the office. The children"—she waved a hand at the rest of the team—"are driving me insane."

"We love you too, Rach," Megan said. "Although, to be fair, Callum, things have degenerated since you left. There's no one to monitor the bickering, and now we're getting on each other's nerves and everybody's being really bitchy." She wagged her finger at Rachel and Callum. "That's what happens when the parent leaves the kids alone without proper supervision."

Jack barked out a laugh and shrugged when Callum glared at him. For one heady second, Callum wondered if this was what it felt like to be the parent of a teen. The feeling passed just as fast as it had hit him, and Callum moved quickly along.

"I've missed this," Elle said. "I'm really glad you're back."

"We'll see about that," Callum muttered.

"Clam!" Sophie shouted, and held up more art.

CHAPTER 18

"Are you sure you know what you're doing?" Agnes said as she reached for the chocolate chip cookies in the middle of the small dining table.

Isobel burst out laughing. It became a little hysterical. Of course she didn't know what she was doing. Her whole life was one huge, out-of-control mess.

"I'll take that as a no," Agnes said before biting into her cookie.

They were sitting in the small apartment in Callum's basement because the house above them had been turned into "operation command". All day long, people had been rushing about, whispering into phones, tapping at keyboards, plotting world domination. Who knew what they were doing? All Isobel knew for sure was that she'd been the catalyst for all this drama, and now she was only in the way. Taking her kids, she'd retreated downstairs, and had been grateful when her sisters arrived.

They'd turned up armed with clothes for all of them and an activity set for Sophie. Sophie wasn't interested in the set, even though it was packed with her beloved stickers. She was currently raiding all of the cupboards in the house to find treasure. Ten minutes earlier, she'd appeared in the basement wearing a motorcycle helmet and carrying a large sieve. She was in her happy zone.

Jack, meanwhile, had hit it off with Ryan. Even though there was at least twelve years between the two of them, they'd bonded over their bottomless stomachs and a love of video games. They were sitting on the couch in the living room area playing Mortal Kombat on the PlayStation under Callum's TV. Everyone else was upstairs.

"So this is the famous bunker." Donna was wide-eyed as she looked around the basement flat.

"He doesn't like calling it a bunker." Isobel shook her head at how ludicrous her life had become that those words should come out of her mouth. "He lives between here and the house upstairs."

"I thought old man McKay never got around to finishing this place," Donna said.

"Callum finished it. I think it was a sentimental thing because his granddad started it."

Agnes stopped eating. "He finished off the bunker for sentimental reasons? Do you even realise how weird that is?"

Yep, she did. Isobel was also aware that, seeing as her house blew up, the only roof she had over her head at the moment was the floor of the house above her.

"What happens if the bad guys come back and blow up this house?" Mairi asked as she texted one of her online boyfriends. "Do you guys just get buried alive down here?"

Oh my goodness...

The thought was enough to make Isobel nauseated. She turned to the sofa. "Ryan? Is there another way out of this bunker?"

"Granny flat," Ryan said, his eyes still glued to the screen and his thumbs hammering at his controller. "Callum doesn't like it being called a bunker. He thinks it makes him seem like a weirdo hermit. Whereas a granny flat that is hidden under the house and has a steel-reinforced door makes perfect sense to him."

Mairi grunted, still texting. "Maybe you'll get a straight answer if you throw him a cookie."

Yep, they all had Ryan's number, and they'd only known him a few hours.

"Cookie?" Ryan's attention was pulled from the game.

"Is there another way out of here?" Isobel picked up a cookie and waved it as she spoke.

He cocked a thumb at the back wall. "That door opens up into a tunnel that leads out to the road. Now gimme the cookie."

"Yes!" Jack shouted as Isobel threw the cookie at Ryan. "You are dead, dude. Should have kept your mind on the game. Hey, where'd you get the cookie?" He turned to Isobel. "Do I get a cookie?"

With a shake of her head, she tossed one to her son as well, before turning back to her sisters. "We don't need to worry," she said, sounding slightly hysterical. "There's a tunnel."

"I thought the tunnel was a myth," Agnes said. "Old man McKay never got council permission to dig one."

"Obviously he decided to dig it without the permission," Isobel said. "I wonder how he did it. Do you think he had like a digger or a burrowing machine or something? Or maybe he scooped it out by hand, like he was tunnelling out of jail?"

"Burrowing machine?" Donna said as all three sisters gaped at Isobel.

"What? I'm sure it's a thing." Isobel reached for another cookie. "Didn't they use one to make the Channel Tunnel?"

"I hope the McKay tunnel is structurally sound," Donna said. "I wouldn't want you to get trapped in it."

"Don't worry. I'm sure Callum thought to check it out and reinforce it if need be."

"Honey, listen to yourself." Agnes leaned over the table and covered Isobel's hands with hers. "I hate to break it to you, but your white knight is a fruit loop."

"You mean her baby's father," Mairi said helpfully.

"Baby?" Ryan said. He'd snuck up on them and picked up the plate of cookies. He stood behind the women, shoulder to shoulder with Jack, working his way through the biscuits. "What baby?"

"Callum knocked up Mum," Jack said.

"Jack!" Isobel's cheeks began to heat again. "Go play your video game. Take Ryan with you. There's no baby. And this is none of your business, either of you."

Ryan shook his head and looked at Jack, who was the same height as him. "Dude, if you were ten years older, the things I could tell you about Callum."

"I'm mature for my age," Jack said. "Feel free to spill. But first we need more cookies and milk."

Ryan agreed, and they went off to get some.

"Mature my hairy backside," Mairi muttered. "Damn, I accidentally sent *hairy backside* to Karl. Must not talk and text…must not talk and text…"

"If she doesn't talk while she's texting," Agnes said, "she'll never speak." She thought about it for a second. "I totally agree, Mairi, you must never talk and text."

"Will you lot stick to the topic for a minute?" Isobel said. "We were talking about leaving. Are you packed?"

"I've packed up all my gear," Agnes said. "I still need to send an email to the university to let them know that I'm moving, and I'll send my contact details when I know them. Mairi, have you given the rental agency notice yet?"

"Not yet," Mairi said. "I've been busy. I will, though."

"Mairi, we need to get out of here before Saturday," Isobel said.

"I know," Mairi said. "I've got a lot on right now. I think someone has hacked my boyfriends' accounts. I'm getting weird emails, and I'm worried it'll affect my job."

"We've got three days to get out of here before that loan shark comes looking for thirty-four thousand pounds that none of us have," Isobel said. "You need to pack and sort out your flat. Worry about your online boyfriends later."

"Um." Donna squirmed. "I might have a teeny-tiny problem."

"What?" Isobel wanted to groan. Just once, she would like something to go smoothly.

"I need to give my boss two weeks' notice. He won't accept anything less and says I won't get a reference if I walk out before then." Donna's wide eyes begged them to understand.

They didn't. Donna wasn't known as the family doormat for nothing.

"He can't do that," Agnes said. "It wasn't in your employment contract. I know. I read it. Unlike you."

"I need that reference, and the lord of the manor won't give me one if I don't stay two weeks."

"Does he know you call him that?" Mairi said.

"Are you insane?" Donna said. "He doesn't know half of what we call him behind his back."

"Can we focus?" Isobel said, sounding strangely like Callum. "You can't give two weeks' notice because we need to leave in a couple of days."

"I'll follow you," Donna said. "You get settled and I'll be there two weeks later. It isn't that long."

Isobel shook her head. "I can't leave you behind. Everyone knows us here, and Eddie would use you to get to me. He'll hurt you, Donna. I can't let him hurt you. Either we all go together or we stay together."

"If you stay, he'll hurt *you*." Donna shuddered. "I can hide at the manor house. He won't be able to get to me."

"Yes, he will." Isobel knew exactly what Eddie Granger was capable of doing. "We need to get out now. Together. We need to start somewhere where no one knows us and no one can find us."

"Did you plan to tell me that you're running away?"

The voice startled everyone, and all eyes turned to the staircase leading to the house above.

Callum stood in the entrance, his feet apart, his arms folded and his jaw set. He was not pleased.

Isobel swallowed hard. "Yes. I planned to tell you."

"When?" The temperature in the room dropped, and Isobel shivered.

"I don't know. Soon." She squirmed.

"Before or after you disappeared?" His voice was deadly calm, and Isobel noticed that the room was suddenly very silent.

"Callum, we can talk about this later. We don't have any definite plans right now."

"Sounds definite to me. Donna is giving notice and Mairi is informing their landlord." His eyes were like lasers burning into her. "You didn't mention a deadline for the money when you told me about the loan shark hitting you."

"He hit you?" Jack was off the sofa and charging towards her, as though he could save her from something that had already happened.

"I'm okay," Isobel said. "It's nothing."

"It isn't nothing." Callum stood beside Jack. "She could have cracked ribs."

"Let me see," Jack demanded. He took a step towards Isobel, and Callum put a hand on his shoulder to stop him.

"Isobel!" Donna said. "You didn't tell us that."

"I was handling it," Isobel said. "I'm sure my ribs are fine."

"The same way you're sure you aren't pregnant?" Callum said. "You can't will things to happen just because you want them to be that way."

"I am not pregnant. I don't have broken ribs and I am dealing with everything." Her voice turned into a hysterical screech. People needed to back off and give her some space. She was coping with things as best she could. She would be doing a whole lot better if the problems stopped coming at her so damn fast.

There was a thud, and then the door to the bedroom Callum used crashed open. A second later, a wheelchair appeared with a stuffed giraffe sitting in the middle of it. Sophie's hands could be seen wrapped around the handles, but apart from that, the only other thing anyone could see was the top of her motorcycle helmet.

Callum went very still, and Isobel knew he was mad that someone had been in his bedroom.

"Sophie," Isobel said, "I told you not to go into Callum's room. Put that chair back at once." She looked back at Callum. "I'm sorry. I should have been watching her better."

"Jaffie likes the pram," Sophie shouted, muffled through the helmet.

"It isn't a pram, it's a wheelchair." Isobel rushed over to her daughter.

"Peese?" Sophie said.

Isobel hesitated. What harm would there be in letting her play with the wheelchair? Callum had obviously been injured at some point and had needed it, but he didn't need it now. She looked down at her daughter's large, pleading eyes, the only part that could be seen thought the helmet, and bit at her bottom lip. Her kids had nothing left—surely Callum would understand if she wanted to play with the chair?

Isobel turned and gave him the same pleading look as her daughter. "I'm sorry she went into your room, but can she play with the chair? I promise to make sure she doesn't damage it. It's clear you don't need it—would it really matter if she used it as a pram for a while?"

A strange look passed between Callum and Ryan.

"I promise not to let her cover it with stickers," Isobel said.

Ryan stared at Callum, clearly trying to communicate something that was lost on Isobel.

Callum took a deep breath. "There's something I need to tell you…"

"Callum," Elle shouted down the stairs. "I need you right now. You need to see this."

Ryan shook his head, as though telling Callum not to do something.

"I'll be right up," Callum shouted. "We'll talk later," he said to Isobel, before heading up the stairs.

"Can she use the chair?" Isobel called after him.

"Aye," he said, but he didn't sound pleased about it.

"Need cookie," Sophie shouted as she aimed the chair towards the table.

Isobel looked at Ryan. "Maybe she shouldn't play with it. Does it have sentimental value for Callum?"

"Something like that," Ryan said, then followed his boss up the stairs.

CHAPTER 19

"You should have told her," Ryan said as he stopped beside Callum. "It's going to be worse when she finds out."

Callum didn't say anything, because what could he say? Ryan was right.

They went through the door at the top of the stairs, and Ryan put a hand on Callum's arm to stop him.

"You need to tell her before she finds out some other way," Ryan said. "It's my experience that when you're missing a body part, or two, women like to know that kind of thing."

"Do you think I don't know that?" Callum felt the rage that was always present surge forward, trying to break free.

Ryan was unperturbed. "Look, I know you don't like to talk about personal stuff, or emotion, or, well, anything, but this is serious. You can't wait until you're getting into bed with her again and go, 'By the way my legs are metal.'" He froze. "Oh, dude, tell me you weren't just planning to drop your jeans and shout 'surprise'?"

Callum clenched his fists and fought the urge to lash out. Ryan took a step back. "You want to hit me now, I can see that, but it doesn't change the fact that you need to come clean with your woman."

"She isn't my woman," Callum said through his teeth.

"She's carrying your baby, dude. That's about as attached as you can get."

"Stop calling me dude. What are you, twelve?"

"I don't think he's even that mature," Rachel said as she came up beside them.

Ryan's easy-going attitude morphed into something far darker, and he scowled at Rachel. "We're talking about emotion, Rach. We don't need you for that. You need to be capable of experiencing some to have an opinion."

Rachel's eyes narrowed, and Callum held up his hands to stop them. "What is wrong with the two of you?"

"So many things," Elle called from behind them. "Now get in here. I have stuff to tell all of you."

"I'm coming too." Jack came up from the basement. "You can't make me stay down there. They're talking about PMS. I don't think it's good for my development to listen to that."

"Women." Ryan fist-bumped Jack.

"You can stay," Callum told Jack. "But the same rules apply. No talking. No telling."

"Basically, keep your mouth shut," Jack said. "Yeah, I heard you. Do you have any snacks up here?" He made a beeline for the pantry, Ryan in tow.

Wondering yet again how he'd managed to get from the professionalism of the SAS to this motley crew, Callum headed into the kitchen. The dining table had been claimed by Elle and was covered in computer equipment. Megan sat on the kitchen counter sipping from a mug of coffee. Dimitri stood beside her, leaning against the counter, but ensuring most of his body touched his wife's. For some reason, seeing them so cosy irritated Callum more than it usually did. And this time it wasn't purely because their behaviour wasn't professional. It took a few seconds for him to realise what he was feeling—it was envy. Ashamed and angry with himself, he turned to Elle. "What you got?" he barked.

Elle didn't seem bothered by his attitude. "I sent photos of the dead guy through to our contact in the government who has access to the face-recognition database that uses Harry's software." Harry was the fourth, and now silent, partner in Benson Security. He'd made a fortune developing security software for the government, then married his childhood sweetheart and was now setting up literacy centres in Africa. "It came up blank."

"Okay," Callum said. It was to be expected; the database wasn't exactly extensive. "Is that it?"

She gave him a look of utter disappointment and tapped away at her keyboard then turned the screen towards him. "The search on his fingerprints came up blank too."

Callum felt a tingle creep up his spine. The atmosphere in the room changed as each of them realised what Elle was saying.

"Did you try the Irish and European databases too?" Ryan said around a mouthful of peanuts.

Jack nodded. "We're a hub. Easy access to the Atlantic, Ireland and Europe. I don't know why we don't have more people here. Apart from the smugglers. Smugglers like to come here."

Callum shot him a look. "What'd I tell you?"

Jack slapped a hand over his mouth and gave Callum a thumbs-up with the other hand. Ryan handed him the peanuts. "Keep your mouth full. It helps."

Barely containing a groan, Callum turned back to Elle. "Did you try the other databases?"

"Do I look like an amateur?" Elle said. "Of course I did. He doesn't exist anywhere."

"That doesn't make sense," Ryan said. "He had prison and gang tats. If he has a record, his fingerprints are on file."

"Exactly, yet there's no mention of him anywhere," Elle said.

"What about DNA?" Rachel helped herself to some coffee. "I shouldn't be drinking this. It will keep me up all night."

"Cruella, you're a creature of the night. You don't need sleep," Ryan said.

Jack stifled a laugh that turned into a coughing fit when he almost choked on a peanut.

"Cut it out," Callum snapped at Rachel and Ryan. "Your bickering is getting on my nerves. Whatever is going on with you two, sort it out like adults and keep it out of the business."

Rachel and Ryan shared a look before both nodded. An uneasy truce. It was a better result than Callum had expected.

"DNA is going to take a couple of weeks. This isn't *CSI*," Elle said. "We can't get the results by the end of the show. But, to be honest, I don't think we'll get a hit there, either. I think someone has hacked the system and erased this guy."

"Who could do that?" Rachel asked.

"Governments do it," Elle said. "I think they did it to that guy David I've been trying to track down since we met him in Peru. But, to be honest, a very skilled and connected hacker could do it. Someone like Harry would have access to most databases, and the knowledge to hack into the ones he didn't."

"We need to eliminate the government possibility," Callum said. "I'll call Lake. See if I can get him to tap into the same network that produced David for us. Maybe someone there will have information on this guy."

"And if he is a government agent?" Megan said.

"Then we're in deeper than I thought. You can all kiss

goodbye to your freedom for the foreseeable future, because if he is government, there will be people locking us up until they get all the answers they need." Callum reached for his phone.

"If we're going to lose our freedom," Ryan said, "I need a last meal. There must be someone in Campbeltown who delivers out here. Anyone want pizza?"

The rest of the team shook their heads, but Jack held up his hand.

"If it isn't the government," Elle said, "it could be a thing this group is doing to stay off the radar. If I had prints from someone else on the team, I could see if their records have been erased too."

"Unfortunately, we don't have that. The house blew up taking any prints they might have left behind, with it," Callum said.

"What about the black box Callum got from the pawnbroker?" Dimitri said. "Couldn't you lift some prints from that?"

Elle shook her head. "It's been handled by too many people. There's no way to get decent prints off it now."

"It's a pity Isobel threw away the rest of the stuff in that bag," Callum said. "We might have lifted a print from something in there."

Jack cleared his throat and held up his hand. "Permission to speak," he said with sarcasm.

Callum ignored the tone and pointed at him. "See that? I like that. You should all do it before you open your mouth. What is it, Jack?"

"Mum didn't throw away the bag. She gave it to me to throw away." He hesitated and shuffled his feet. "I didn't exactly do what she asked me to do."

Callum stilled. "Spit it out."

"I traded the stuff for a video game I wanted." The words

came out in a rush, and his cheeks flushed a little when he realised he now had the undivided attention of everyone in the room.

"Traded it with whom?" Callum said.

Jack looked around before fixing his eyes on Callum. "Friend of mine. She's making a robot, and I thought she could recycle some of the gear. Use it for parts or something."

"Does this friend of yours still have the stuff?" Elle asked, practically bouncing with excitement.

"I think so."

"Where is she?" Callum said. "She local?"

"She's in Campbeltown," Jack said. "We go to school together."

Callum looked at Ryan. "Guess you're going to Campbeltown. Take Jack and get that stuff back. Pay for it if you have to."

"It's late," Jack said. "By the time we get there, we'll be waking her family up. Her dad will be mad. Can it wait until the morning?"

"No." Callum stared at Jack until he looked away.

"I'll tell Mum where I'm going." He dragged his feet out of the room.

"I'll come with you." Rachel picked up her black leather bag. "I managed to find a room in a hotel in Campbeltown that isn't too awful. You can drive me instead of me having to call for a cab."

"Thanks," Ryan muttered.

"If you don't need me," Rachel said to Callum, "I'll head back to London tomorrow. Something has come up that needs my attention."

"We'll be fine without you," Callum said.

"More than fine," Ryan muttered.

"I'll wait in the car," Rachel told Ryan. "Don't take too long." She strode from the room, expecting Ryan to follow.

He did so reluctantly, giving Callum a dirty look as he passed. "This is punishment for giving you great relationship advice, isn't it?"

"This is work," Callum said. "Nothing more. Suck it up and act professionally for once."

Ryan let out a sigh. "And even though you say stuff like that, I still prefer working with you to working with Cruella."

The door slammed behind Ryan and Jack as they went out to meet with Rachel.

"There are two bedrooms up here," Callum said to the three team members left. "Sort yourselves out in them. I'm sleeping downstairs after I call Lake, and the Sinclair sisters leave."

"Bagsy the one with the bathroom," Megan shouted.

Dimitri grinned at her. "Guess we're in the master bedroom."

"I don't care where I sleep," Elle said. "I have searches running, so I'll probably camp in here with my baby." She stroked her laptop lovingly.

"I wonder about you," Megan said.

"I wonder about all of you," Callum muttered, and headed off to find somewhere quiet to talk to Lake.

CHAPTER 20

Isobel couldn't sleep. Sophie didn't have the same problem. They were sharing a room with bunk beds, and she was out cold on the top bunk, snoring adorably. Isobel couldn't remember the last time she'd spent a night where she didn't listen to Sophie. As soon as she'd been born, Rob had run off and Isobel hadn't been able to afford the mortgage on the house they'd bought together. She'd sold the place for just enough to cover its cost, and moved into the only rental available in Arness—the two-bedroom house that had burned to the ground. She remembered well the nights lying in bed listening to her baby daughter breathe, wondering how she was going to make it through the next week—heck, the next ten minutes. But she'd done it. She'd built a life for her kids and had been fine. Until Rob's past was thrust upon her.

She tossed back the blankets and snuck out of bed. Jack was staying in Campbeltown overnight because his friend was away visiting family and wouldn't be back until the following afternoon. Ryan and Jack wanted to be there as soon as she arrived, to get the things Jack should have thrown out—things Jack had swapped for something he'd wanted, because Isobel couldn't afford even a second-hand game for her son. She felt her chest clench at the thought, and knew there would be no sleep that night. Her memories were just too close. She pulled on the woollen socks Agnes had given her and let herself out of her room, wearing only her underwear and an old grey T-shirt she'd borrowed from Callum.

The strange basement apartment was silent as Isobel made her way into the kitchen area. She glanced at Callum's room and saw that the door was still closed. She didn't know if he was in there. He'd been upstairs, plotting, when she'd gone to bed. Trying to be as quiet as possible, she took some milk from the fridge, poured a glass and popped it in the microwave, hoping a warm drink would help her sleep—or at least relax.

"Can't sleep either?" The rumbling voice wasn't a surprise. Part of Isobel had hoped Callum would be there.

He was standing in the doorway to his room, no shirt, but his jeans and shoes still on.

"You want some warm milk?"

He shook his head. "Wouldn't mind a whisky, but I don't keep that in the house."

"I remember." The microwave pinged, and she reached for her drink. It seemed like an eternity ago that she'd been sitting in his kitchen, having a mini-breakdown and begging him to help her.

"Did your team get any further in finding out who the dead man is…was?"

"No." He stalked towards her like a lazy cat. "The more we dig, the more anomalies we find. I don't like any of it."

Isobel felt a wave of guilt sweep through her and looked away from his too-perceptive gaze. "When we leave, will you let this drop?" There was no need for him to continue searching when the body was gone and she wasn't around to be at risk.

"No. There's something here that needs uncovering." There was steely resolve in his voice, and Isobel knew that Callum wasn't the type of man to walk away from danger.

"I'm sorry I brought this to your door." She raised her eyes to his and was once again astonished at how intense they were. He wasn't an easy man, and he didn't even try to hide that. She could imagine that he terrified most people, yet, for some reason, his dark intensity only drew her to him.

She saw his jaw tighten and the muscles in his shoulders turn to stone. "There's something I need to tell you. Something I should have told you earlier."

Her stomach lurched, and she placed a hand on it to somehow steady it. "Is Jack okay? Did someone follow them? Are there more dead people? Did you kill the loan shark? Are the police after me?" The words came tumbling out, all of her fears piling one on top of the other.

He shook his head slowly as though she mystified him. "Woman, calm down. This has nothing to do with anything but what's going on between you and me."

"Don't call me woman and don't tell me to calm down. Seriously, Callum, hasn't anyone told you that's the worst thing to say to a person when you want them to calm down? It just makes me want to scream." As she lectured him, his words registered and she felt pain around her heart. Most likely the beginnings of full-blown cardiac arrest. "Wait a minute. Are you married? Do you have a family somewhere else?"

"What? No."

"Are you sick? Did you come here to die?" Oh my goodness, that had to be it. Why else would he walk away from everything and hide in Arness?

"No."

She opened her mouth to ask if he was about to go on a dangerous mission from which he might never return—it was the next thing that occurred to her, but, given time, she was sure there would be plenty more.

"No." He strode right up to her and put his hands on her shoulders. "Enough. Don't say another word. Just listen to what I have to say."

"I can't. There are so many terrible things going through my mind."

He covered her mouth with a palm while his other hand cupped the back of her neck. His face went completely blank as he distanced himself from what he was about to say. Isobel almost threw her milk at him to get him to hurry up.

"I have prosthetic legs," he said at last, his voice devoid of emotion.

Callum stared down at Isobel and waited for her reaction, at the same time dreading what it would be. He knew as soon as the words left his mouth that there was no going back to the way she looked at him before he'd told her. She'd seen him as a hero. As almost invincible. He hadn't wanted to give that up, to see pity and disgust in her eyes instead of hope. He had been tempted to let the topic lie. To distance himself from her and never let her know about his legs. To have the memory of how she'd once looked at him to keep him going in the years to come. But he couldn't. He wasn't that man. He'd been a coward long enough.

Isobel blinked at him with her impossibly large eyes, then said something against his hand.

"Sorry." He dropped his hands, folded his arms and put some distance between them.

"What did you say?" She clutched at her glass of milk.

Twice. He had to say it twice. "I have prosthetic legs."

She studied his face for a minute before looking down at his jeans and then back up to his face. "I don't understand."

"My legs were blown off in Afghanistan. I lost both, above the knees. Everything from my thigh down is manmade." He hated saying it. Hated that he had to confess being less than a complete man. Hated that he was waiting to witness the dismay that would hit her. The dismay she'd try to hide. To be polite. To be caring.

"And?" she said, looking confused.

Callum reeled. "What do you mean, and?"

"Is that it?" She put her milk on the counter beside her. "Nobody's dead? Jack's fine? We're fine? In as much as two people can be who don't want a relationship with each other but keep having sex."

Callum felt a strange bubbling sensation in his stomach. It took him a minute to realise that it was the beginnings of hope.

"Woman, I just told you that I have metal legs. I have stumps where my knees should be. I have scars. It's ugly and it's a liability because I don't have the same mobility I had before I lost them. Isn't that enough for you? Bloody hell, woman, you had sex with half a man."

There was a heartbeat of silence and then Isobel burst out laughing.

"What the hell?" Callum really wished he still had scotch in the house, because he needed it. Never mind that he had lost his legs—obviously Isobel had lost her mind.

He watched as Isobel held on to the counter as she laughed hard. At last, she wiped her eyes and looked at him. "I'm sorry, I'm not laughing at you losing your legs. I'm laughing because I thought it was something serious. Not that you didn't go through something terribly serious. I can only imagine how traumatic and painful it must have been. I guess I mean I was expecting you to tell me about something life-threatening that affected us right now. Not something that happened in the past. And, before you say anything, a wife would have been life-threatening, because I would have killed you."

Callum didn't know how to react. He wanted to shake some sense into her or kiss her until she was panting. Or run hard and fast in the opposite direction. Or claim her as his, right then and there.

"I don't think you understand what I'm telling you," he said. "I don't have any legs."

She looked down and pointed at his jeans. "Yes you do. You just don't have skin-and-bone legs."

"Doesn't it bother you that you had sex with half a man?" Seriously, she needed a keeper, or a good psychiatrist.

Her smile was wide and her eyes sparkled. "Really, it's more like four-fifths of a man."

He raked his hands into his hair. "Why aren't you shouting at me for keeping this from you?"

"Callum, we've been intimate for three whole days. You don't know everything about me either. Neither one of us is perfect. I've had two kids, I live on junk food—most of the time. I have stretch marks and cellulite and flab. My boobs are saggy and my hips are too big."

"Are you seriously comparing your cellulite to my missing feet?"

Isobel giggled as she held up a hand. "I'm sorry. I don't mean to laugh, but that's a really funny sentence." She giggled again, and Callum felt the strange sensation of laughter inside.

"I don't think you're taking this seriously enough," he said. "I don't think you realise what it looks like, or what it means. I'm reliant on plastic legs. I spend a chunk of my time in a wheelchair. I don't have the same mobility as most people. Hell, without my legs, I can't even stand."

She started laughing so hard that she had to hold on to the counter to stay upright.

"I mean my prosthetic legs," he snapped.

She kept on laughing. Callum threw up his hands and waited for the little nutcase to calm down. But as he did, he felt a warmth flooding through him as her weird reaction undid some of the hardened anxiety that sat like a lump inside him.

"Sorry, sorry. I'm sorry." She worked to calm herself but couldn't stop grinning. "Carry on." She motioned for him to continue.

Callum stood watching her and shaking his head. In all the scenarios he'd imagined when he told her about his legs, laughter hadn't been one of them. Actually, now that he thought about it, the main reaction he'd expected was disgust and anger. He hadn't considered anything past that.

"I'm sorry, Callum, I have a sick sense of humour. I didn't mean to make you feel self-conscious about your limb loss." She was so earnest that he found himself falling into her beautiful eyes.

Strangely enough, her odd reaction had made him feel less self-conscious than he'd felt for a long time. "Limb loss?"

"I don't know what to call it. Is it a disability? An injury? A maiming? What's the right term? 'Disability' sounds kind of wrong when you're obviously very able." Her eyes went wide and her lips made a little oh shape. "Oh my goodness, that's how you broke that guy's wrist with one kick. You have bionic legs. It's like a superpower."

Callum shook his head. She was completely insane. And if he wasn't mistaken, her attention had taken a turn south. Towards a much hotter zone. Her eyes were skimming over his bare chest as she bit her bottom lip.

"You were so amazing during that fight," she said before she licked her lips.

"Isobel, focus. We're talking about my legs."

"Show me."

Callum almost took a step back. "What?"

"Show me the legs."

He couldn't move, couldn't think. The heat in her eyes was completely at odds with what she was asking. It made no sense.

"You don't want to see them."

"I do." She nodded. "I want to see you naked." Her cheeks flushed a beautiful shade of pink.

Callum ran a hand through his hair. "I think you have the wrong idea here. There's nothing sexy about this. You might think my mechanical legs give me superpowers or something, but the reality is that they are pieces of metal where flesh should be."

Her face turned suspiciously innocent. "Are you scared?"

"No." He said it far too fast, and she gave him a knowing smile.

"Chicken."

He growled, wrapped his hand around her wrist and strode towards his bedroom, dragging her behind him.

"I don't know why I bother with you," he said as he swung the door shut.

"Because I'm easy?"

He knew she was joking, but he also knew what the folk in town said about her. And he didn't like any of it. He grasped her chin and made her look at him. "Never say that again. You are a passionate and sensual woman. You lose yourself in the moment. You are not easy. Never that. Okay?"

Her eyes filled and she nodded before stepping back. She cleared her throat and signalled at his jeans.

"Strip." Her smile was devilish. "If you dare."

CHAPTER 21

Elle was dreaming. A firm, soft touch lifted her hands above her head and secured them with fur-lined cuffs. She smiled in her dream. This was new. He'd never used handcuffs before. And neither had she. Elle liked new experiences. Even if they only happened in her dreams.

"Did you miss me, gorgeous?"

"Mmm." She shifted on the bed, feeling the cool sheets against her suddenly hot and sensitive skin. "Where have you been?"

In her dreams, he often talked of new and exotic places, keeping her guessing about where he was, exactly the way he did in real life.

"You figured out who I am yet?" She felt his breath against her hair and realised he was sitting on the bed beside her.

"Nearly." She sounded sultry and needy. Something she would never have let him see outside of her dream. "It's only a matter of time."

"Time, huh?"

She felt fingertips trail down her cheek to her lips, and her eyes opened, seeking out the face she'd seen ever so briefly in Peru, but couldn't get out of her mind. "David," she whispered.

Only this time, the room was dark in her dream and she could barely make him out in the shadows. She blinked to get a better look and realised her eyes weren't only open in her dream. All at once, she was staring into the dark of her borrowed bedroom, looking up at the man she'd been trying to identify for months. She blinked several times, trying to figure out what was reality and what wasn't.

"You're really here, aren't you?" She sounded sleepy and slightly disorientated.

"Yeah." That nondescript accent of his seemed to roll more than she remembered. Southern US? Was there a hint in there? "Cute nightwear." She heard, rather than saw, a smile in his voice.

All at once, Elle was very much awake and more than aware that she had been sleeping in her Wonder Woman vest and underpants. She jerked up, but her arms held her back. Her eyes shot to her wrists, and damn if he hadn't actually handcuffed her. Only they weren't the fur-lined leather cuffs from her dream. These ones were fluffy and, if she wasn't mistaken in the dark, pink.

"Release me," she said with false sweetness, "so that I can kill you."

He barked out a laugh and sat back, looking down at her. "I like having you all tied up. It's the only way a woman like you would ever be at my mercy."

"This isn't funny. I'm going to scream, and you'll get your backside shot full of holes by my teammates."

"Go ahead." He spread his arms wide and smiled.

Elle scissored her legs under the blankets, hoping to free them and kick the smile off his face. All he did was lean over her and use his weight to pin her down.

"What are you doing here?" she demanded.

"Mostly I'm listening to you moan my name in your sleep. Makes a man wonder, gorgeous." He brushed her hair from her face. "Makes him wonder what it would feel like to hear those moans in reality. Makes him wonder if hearing you scream his name would be even better."

She felt her heart pick up speed and resisted the urge to wet her lips. No doubt he would only take it as an invite. "I'm really hoping you don't mean scream in pain."

"I would never cause you pain," David said. "Unless you begged me, and even then, it'd only be the kind of pain that leads to pleasure."

Why that made her insides melt, she didn't know. All she knew was that this man was dangerous. Not only to the world at large, but to her personally.

"What do you want?" She hated that her sultry voice gave away more than she'd like him to know. But then, the man had witnessed her very audible dreams about him. He'd become her obsession. Months of trying to crack the mystery surrounding who he really was and whom he worked for. He'd thrown down the gauntlet when he'd given her his DNA, and she'd been like a woman possessed ever since.

"I was in the neighbourhood and thought I'd drop in." His fingers played with her hair as he spoke. He sounded almost wistful.

"Last I heard, you were on a suicide mission in South America."

He shrugged, bringing her attention to his broad shoulders under his dark suede bomber jacket. "I get around. It's what you've been up to that's much more interesting."

"And what would that be?"

"You've been hacking into systems you really shouldn't be in, Miss Elle." He ran his thumb back and forth over her bottom lips. "Naughty, naughty, naughty."

Elle couldn't contain the shiver that went through her at his touch, and she knew he noticed.

"Is this about me trying to identify the body?"

She felt him stiffen slightly before he forced himself to relax again. "No, this isn't about a body. This is about your hunt for my identity. You've been looking in places you shouldn't be, and you've attracted the attention of people you really don't want to notice you."

"Well, you shouldn't have given me your DNA if you didn't want me to look for you." Bloody men. And they called women the contrary sex.

His smile was pure enticement. "That's true. It was a moment of weakness." He sounded almost bewildered, which made her think he wasn't the sort of man who ever had those moments. "I need you to stop looking."

Yeah, right, she'd get straight on that. "Of course."

Even in the darkness, she saw his eyes harden. "I'm serious, Elle. You need to stop."

"I understand." She'd stop when she knew everything there was to know about him. He'd unwittingly tapped into her greatest weakness—he was a puzzle she had to solve, a mystery she couldn't leave hanging. There was no way she could let the issue drop without having an aneurysm. It would go against her genetic code to do so.

He let out a sigh. "You aren't going to do what I tell you, are you?"

For a second, she thought about lying, but that didn't sit well with her. The game they had going was only going to be won fairly if she didn't cheat. "Yeah, I'm going to keep looking. And I'm going to find out exactly who you are."

"It's a mistake." His voice was soft—gentle, even.

"Won't be my first." And it probably wouldn't be her last, either. She had a gift for getting into situations she really shouldn't get into.

"Are you sure you want to do that? I'm not the only one with secrets that are best left hidden."

Now her heart was racing for a different reason. She told herself there was no way he could know her secrets. She'd hidden them herself, with the help of Harry. And there wasn't a hacker in the world better than her boss Harry Boyle.

"I'm sure." She tried to infuse the words with confidence, when really, she felt a little uncertain.

"Well, don't say I didn't warn you." Before she realised what he meant to do, he leaned forward and his lips met hers.

As kisses went, it was as chaste as a Jane Austen romance scene. But it was far more than that. The sensation of his warm, firm lips against hers. His ocean scent filling her senses. The softness of his lips as he rubbed them against hers. It was a kiss that she felt straight to her toes, one she'd bring up in every dream she had from then until eternity. Because it was a kiss that cemented her obsession and her future.

He sat back far too soon, staring into her eyes. For once, the man seemed shaken. "You are so…unexpected."

Elle felt dazed by his fleeting touch. She just watched him as he watched her back.

"I have to go." His words broke the moment, and he stood, leaving her reeling without him. "The key to the cuffs is on the dresser. Think about what I said. You're swimming with the sharks here, Elle, and you're doing it without the cage."

"I've always hated metaphors."

With a grin, he turned and walked out of her room as silently as he'd come in. Elle gave him plenty of time before she called for Megan. As much as she would have liked to see him dodge their bullets, she didn't like the idea of anyone other than her going up against the man. He was her puzzle. No one else's.

And she was seriously going to make him pay for leaving her secured in fluffy pink cuffs.

CHAPTER 22

Callum rested his hand on the button of his jeans. This was it. There was no going back. If he stripped, he was leaving more than his body bare before her. He was baring his soul. His team hadn't even seen him without his prosthetics until everything had gone to hell on their last mission together. He'd made an art form out of pretending that he was normal, that he was still whole. And now, here he was, standing in front of a woman who somehow managed to get through every barrier he put up, and he was about to make himself more vulnerable than he'd been in his life. More vulnerable than when he'd been in hospital relying on people to give him some semblance of his life back.

Isobel's eyes softened. "We don't need to do this, Callum. I'm in a weird mood. I shouldn't have pushed you." She turned and put her hand on the doorknob.

"No. It's time." He popped the button on his jeans.

Isobel turned back, leaned against the door and watched him as he unzipped his jeans. Her eyes turned molten as her gaze skimmed over his chest, lingering in the region of his tattoos, then back to his jeans. Her tiny pink tongue peeked out to wet her lips and her cheeks flushed. Callum almost groaned. She was turning something that should have been cold and awkward into something utterly erotic. He could feel himself becoming hard just from watching her watch him.

"You wear underpants," she said huskily. "Before I found out in person, I thought you'd go commando." Dark eyes looked up at him. "I spent a lot of time wondering about your underwear choices over these past few months."

She was killing him. Callum slipped his thumbs into the waistband of his jeans before remembering he needed to take his shoes off first. "Shoes," he said, and fought the embarrassment that followed. He felt like a teenager alone with a girl for the first time.

"Let me."

Before he could protest, Isobel was kneeling at his feet and untying his sneakers. Callum gritted his teeth and steeled himself for her reaction to his feet. His plastic feet. Isobel tapped his thigh to get him to lift his leg so she could remove his shoe. And then she stilled, with the shoe still in her hands.

Callum felt panic rise. It was fine to say something was okay, but the reality of coming face to face with it was something else.

"You wear socks?" Isobel grinned up at him. "In case your feet get cold?"

A wave of relief rushed through him, making him feel almost faint.

"Woman, you have a sick sense of humour." He was relieved his voice didn't shake.

"I know." She seemed proud. "All my sisters do. Family funerals are a riot."

She made quick work of removing the other shoe, and then his socks, putting them in a neat pile at her side.

Callum focused intently on everything she did, and held his breath for her first reaction to his skin-coloured plastic feet.

She poked at them. "I'm a little disappointed. I was expecting something out of a sci-fi movie. These look like something you'd take off a mannequin."

Callum couldn't fight a smile. "They're shells. They cover the sci-fi part of the foot, which is metal. You wear these so your feet look more normal and so your shoes fit."

"Oh." She poked them again. "So these rubbery bits come off?"

"Aye. But I'm not doing that right now." Bloody hell, he had enough to get through without dismantling his prosthetic legs so she could satisfy her curiosity.

She sat back on her heels and looked up at him. "I'm ready. You can take everything else off now."

Even as anxious as he was, Callum couldn't help but be amused at the sultry way she looked at him.

"You want to move back a bit, give me some room?" He hooked his thumbs in his jeans, and she wriggled back about three inches.

"I'm good here. Get on with it."

With a shake of his head, Callum lowered his jeans. She frowned at him, and he stopped with them at mid-thigh. The tops of the cups his stumps fitted into were visible, and he wondered if she'd had enough already.

"What about the underpants? Shouldn't you take them off too?" the little vixen said.

"I don't need to take off my underwear to show you my legs."

"Oh." She batted her eyelashes at him. "It won't be as much fun if you don't."

"This isn't about fun, woman. It's about showing you that I'm part man, part machine."

"I've always had a thing for sexy cyborgs. Take everything off, Callum. I want to see all of you. Please, pretty please?"

He shook his head. "You are dangerous." But he tugged at his underpants, being careful to lift them over his cock, and took them down with his jeans.

She gasped at the sight of him and licked her lips. Callum groaned. This was not going at all the way he'd envisioned it would. He looked behind him, ready to sit down and pull his jeans off the rest of the way.

"I'll do it," Isobel said eagerly.

Before he could stop her, she shifted forward and reached for his jeans. He was only inches from her luscious mouth. This was agony. Pure agony. How was he supposed to deal with her reaction to his legs when he was that close to heaven?

"Mmm," she said, her eyes firmly on his hard length, rather than his titanium legs. She tugged one jean leg over his foot and leaned in to get the other one. Callum put a hand on her shoulder for balance. As she yanked his other jean leg down to his foot, she licked the head of his cock.

"Isobel." He groaned, and his hand tightened on her shoulder.

She licked him a couple more times before helping him to get his jeans off, and then she sat back on her heels to study him. Callum was breathing hard. His cock pointed out towards her. He could barely think of anything else. Right then, the most important thing in the world was getting inside her.

Her eyes scanned up his body slowly, from his fake feet, over the black carbonite and titanium legs, up his scarred thighs, over his abdomen and tattoos, to his face.

"You are breath-taking," she whispered. "I don't think I've seen anyone more masculine in my life." She ran her hands up his legs, over the cool metal, until she reached the heat of his thigh. "You're all power and strength. So many muscles…" Her fingers mapped each indentation on his stomach. There was awe in her face. Absolute awe and raw desire.

Although Callum didn't move an inch, he felt the world shift beneath him. The foundations he stood on rearranged themselves and became stronger. He was suddenly standing on a very different planet. Because of Isobel. Because of how she looked at him. Because of how she made him feel. A rightness settled deep inside of him. And he knew. He knew that no matter what happened, no matter what they had to face, he was *not* giving up Isobel Sinclair. Not ever. She didn't know it yet. But she was his.

Beautiful eyes blazed up at him. "I have a lot of questions about these bionic legs of yours. But first…"

She leaned into him and took the head of his cock into her mouth. Callum spread his legs wide and gave her access, delighting in the way one hand wrapped around his girth while the other gripped his backside. She sucked hard and made him moan with desperation. His whole body felt as though it was on fire. He was desperate for her, desperate to spill himself inside of her, to claim her as his own. The hot, wet heat of her mouth, along with the sight of her on her knees in front of him, giving this to him, was almost more than he could bear. He was tempted to ride this wave of pleasure to its end, but he wanted one thing more. He wanted her under him.

"Stop," he growled, and tightened his hold on her hair.

She released him with a pop. "Don't want to." Her tongue swirled around him.

"Woman, you are driving me nuts."

She actually smiled. "Good."

Callum let go of her hair and reached down to lift her to her feet. Her eyes were heavy-lidded and her hands went straight to his chest. She moulded her fingers to his pecs and let out a tiny sigh of contentment.

"Is it wrong that I really, really like you being naked when I'm still dressed? It feels naughty."

"Naughty?" He couldn't stop the chuckle, even though his skin was past sensitive and he was desperate with the need to get inside of her. "Like a teenager?"

"Like a woman who is losing her mind over a man."

He liked the sound of that a whole lot. There was only one thing he'd change. "Over *her* man."

Her eyes shot to his, and for a second he thought he saw panic. He wasn't going to let that happen. He liked having Isobel all sensual and needy. He clasped her nape and slammed his mouth down onto hers, kissing her with a desperation that bordered on obsession. She melted against him, wrapping her arms around his shoulders to keep upright. Callum tugged at his old T-shirt and tried to get it over her head.

She shook her head and stepped back, her fingers still kneading his chest.

"I don't want to get naked." Her husky voice was an aphrodisiac in itself, and it took a second for Callum to realise what she'd said.

He cupped her cheek. It should be illegal to have skin that smooth. "Why not, darlin'?" He kept his tone soft, letting her know that her answer mattered. That she mattered.

She pulled her bottom lip between her teeth, and for a second he thought she wouldn't answer. "I know you think you're damaged goods or something, but you aren't. You're a freaking Michelangelo sculpture. Seriously. There isn't an ounce of fat on you. Everywhere I look there's toned, carved muscle." She looked up at him nervously. "I'm flabby. I have cellulite. And stretch marks."

Callum blinked, trying to understand. "Isobel, I don't have any legs." Was she seriously self-conscious? With him?

She nodded at him, ever so serious. "You do. You have these kick-arse cyborg legs. You look like the Terminator. The Arnie one, with lots of muscle and that intense stare that scares the poop out of people."

At the same time as her words astonished him, humbled him, they also made him want to laugh. "Poop? Kick-arse?" He shook his head. "There are some words you just shouldn't say. They don't sound right coming out of that gorgeous mouth of yours."

She slapped his chest and instantly spread her fingers to soothe the sting. "I'm being serious. You look like a master artist carved you out of marble. I look like a toddler made me out of Play-Doh."

He had to laugh. It rumbled out of him and astonished him at the same time. He never, in a million years, thought he'd be in the position of laughing while he bared his broken body and soul to a woman who mattered to him.

"You are a nut. I already saw you when you were in the shower."

"Yeah, but you didn't get a close-up look, and it only lasted a few seconds."

"I can't believe we're arguing about this. Get undressed and I'll make you feel good. I promise." He injected the words with heavy sensuality, and watched as her eyes darkened and she swayed towards him.

"How about we do one thing at a time? Tonight, I got to see your bionic legs. Tomorrow, maybe you'll take them off and let me see you without them. Then, in a month or two, if we're still together…" She suddenly looked uncertain. "Are we together?"

"Bloody hell, woman, aye, we're together." What the hell

was she thinking? That he'd let a one-night stand see him like this?

Instead of looking reassured, she frowned. "I'm not sure I can handle that. I don't exactly have a good track record with relationships."

"Neither do I." He swallowed hard. "My wife walked out on me when I came home injured. She said it was because we'd grown apart and not because I didn't have legs anymore. But her timing said something else. I think she liked the prestige, and the freedom, of being married to an SAS soldier who was away a lot of the time. The reality of dealing with an injured veteran who was home permanently was too much for her. You're not the only one with a past full of broken relationships."

Isobel's eyes hardened. "Don't take this as an insult, but your ex was a bitch."

Callum barked out a laugh that surprised him. "You can talk. Yours is still messing with your life." That took the humour out of the situation. He planned to deal with this problem for Isobel just as soon as he had a minute to spare. She wouldn't be paying off her ex-husband's loan and she wouldn't be acting as a punching bag, or sex slave, for any man.

"You look scary." She traced the design of his Celtic knot tattoo.

"I am scary, darlin'. Make no mistake about that."

"Not to me." She seemed very confident of that, and he liked it.

"Never to you." He pressed a kiss to her temple. "Now get undressed."

"I don't want to. Really. How about I just take off my knickers and bend over?"

"And they say romance is dead." He started to laugh again.

It'd been years since he'd laughed this much, if ever. It was a gift. One of many this incredible woman had given him.

"I'm serious here." She pouted at him. "You aren't taking me seriously."

She opened her mouth to protest some more, but Callum silenced her with a kiss. From his limited experience with Isobel, once she let the need take her away, she wouldn't give a damn about her cellulite. Crazy woman. She was beautiful. Possibly a little on the blind side if she thought he was a work of art, but she was still a miracle to him.

Isobel knew she was pathetic, but there was no way she was stripping in front of a man who could model for a romance book cover. Nope. Not happening. Never.

She knew what she looked like. Her skin was so pasty white it was practically blue. There were white stripes on her belly—her very soft, rounded belly. Her hips didn't gently curve out from her waist, they lurched out, like two skin-coloured saddlebags. The only time she experienced a thigh gap was when she spread her legs. And she could store a pencil under her saggy boobs—she'd tried after she'd seen it mentioned in a sitcom. If there was any muscle definition on her body, she had yet to find it. And then there was her cellulite. It looked like someone had taken a cheese grater to her backside.

There was no way she'd stack up compared to Callum. He might be missing his feet, but the rest of him was perfection.

"New plan," Callum said with a glint in his eye. "I'll do the undressing. You just hang on for the ride."

Yeah, that wasn't going to happen, and she opened her mouth to tell him so. She never got a chance, because Callum had apparently tired of talking and jumped straight to kissing. Which was a problem, because when Callum kissed her, the only thought in her head was *more.*

The kiss was deep and hard and long. His hands threaded in her hair, holding her, keeping her in place. Isobel felt like she was spiralling up into the atmosphere. Her feet were no longer on the ground. And the only thing keeping her from floating away entirely was Callum's hold.

His hands slid down over her shoulders and back, pressing her into him. She felt every single inch of his firm frame. And she desperately needed more. A moan of delight escaped when his hands slipped under the hem of her shirt and she could feel his fingers on her skin. They weren't soft. They were the hands of a man who worked. And the rasp of that roughness against her skin was deeply erotic.

"Off," he said against her lips, and she vaguely registered he meant her shirt.

"I don't want to be naked."

"We'll leave your socks on."

That suddenly seemed like a really good compromise. Isobel lifted her arms for him to whisk the shirt away and toss it onto the floor. A second later, her breasts pressed against that miraculous chest of his. Her sensitive nipples registered the rasp of the smattering of hair across his pecs. It was delicious.

"Can't get enough of you," he growled, and then strong arms lifted her.

His lips were on her throat. His tongue laved at her skin. His teeth nipped little stinging bites. Isobel grasped his hair and held him to her. She felt the soft sheets at her back. Felt Callum's weight come down on top of her. She heard a drawer open and close, but Callum's weight never shifted from her. She hoped it never would. She was lost, delirious with his touch.

Hands on her breasts, kneading, caressing, teasing. His

lips followed. She spread her legs and lifted her hips. Cold metal against her thighs was one more layer of sensation that made up the maelstrom that engulfed her.

Her fingers dug into muscles with very little give. Each flex beneath her touch drove her higher. She wanted to touch every single inch of him. Taste him. Nibble at him. His tongue made swirls on her stomach.

"Love these marks. They're your tattoos." He kissed along the stretch marks she bore from her pregnancies.

She heard ripping and realised her underwear was gone. He dipped his head lower, spreading her legs wider and kissing her most intimate of places, lapping at her with his tongue, teasing her with his teeth, driving her out of her mind with need.

"Callum, now," she demanded, tugging at his shoulders, trying to make him come up over her. Make him cover her. Make him fill her.

"Not yet." He continued teasing her most sensitive spot.

Isobel panted, desperate for him. "Callum. In me. Now!"

He chuckled, a darkly wicked sound that made her even hungrier for him.

"Not yet."

"If you don't get inside me now, I'm going to scream."

Her muscles were tight. Her toes were tingling. She needed him now.

"You're going to scream anyway." He sucked her clit and flicked his tongue over it.

Everything stopped. Froze. Suspended in the atmosphere. And then she was plummeting. Gasping for air. Feeling the rush of the earth coming straight at her.

She vaguely recognised the sound of plastic ripping and knew Callum had remembered to protect them. Then the thought was gone, because Callum was leaning into her.

Cool metal rubbed against her thighs. Warm muscle

settled over her. He licked up her throat and she felt the head of his erection press into her. Too slow. Far too slow. She fought against her heavy muscles to wrap her legs around him, pulling him to her in one desperate jerk. They moaned as one as they slammed together.

"Woman, you need to learn patience."

Isobel licked at his chest and tested the firmness with her teeth. He filled her, stretching her in a way that only he could. She never wanted it to end. She wanted to be locked with him forever.

"Vixen," he whispered against her ear, making her shiver.

And then he was moving. Long, slow, powerful thrusts that made her lose all coherent thought. This time, they flew together

CHAPTER 23

"I feel stupid lying here with only woolly socks on," Isobel said.

"You're the one who wanted to keep some clothes on. Now you're officially partially clothed. And, for the record, your stretch marks turn me on nearly as much as all those gorgeous curves of yours." Callum stroked Isobel's arm.

"You're old and your eyesight is obviously fading."

He grinned at the ceiling. "There is that, but I'd have to be completely blind not to notice how stunning you are."

"Idiot," she grumbled.

She lay with her cheek on his chest, playing with the hair. She had one leg thrown over his prosthetics, as though they were real limbs.

"You said earlier that we're together now?"

Callum honestly didn't know what answer she wanted to hear, so he went with the truth. "Aye. We're together."

She stilled before resuming the circles she was drawing on his chest. "I don't think I can do another relationship."

He completely understood. With her experience, there was no way she could trust that he would be there for her.

Even marriage hadn't been a guarantee for her. The only way to prove he was different from the losers she'd known before was to show her. And that would take time.

For a minute, he was shocked to find himself thinking about a future with Isobel. About permanence. About living his life with what he had now instead of lamenting what he'd lost. She'd given him that. His miracle.

"One day at a time," he said, and kissed her hair. "We've got enough to think about without planning a future. Let's see how things go first."

He felt her tense, and she looked up at him. "Callum, are you saying you want a future with me because you think I might be pregnant?"

"No. I'm saying it because you're you." He looked down at her. "It's early days, but Isobel, you've got to know that you've given me more than I ever expected to have. If this is all I ever get, then it's still a treasure worth having."

Her eyes filled with tears and she pressed her cheek back against him.

"What's it like—having prosthetic legs, I mean?"

The question would normally have sent him into a rage. Instead, he gave it serious consideration. "I'm getting more used to it now. These new legs have an amazing range of mobility. There are moments when I can even forget they aren't my natural legs. I can run in them, twist around, walk backwards, go upstairs, cycle, even swim. The prosthetics I had before this were much more basic."

"These sound like a real godsend."

He could hear the smile in her voice. "Aye. They are. But it's still different to having your own legs. You have to think about everything you would normally have taken for granted. Like in the morning, you'd swing your legs over the edge of the bed and walk to the bathroom. You wouldn't even think about it. Now, I need to decide if I'm going to put on my legs first, or get there in my chair." He stroked her thick hair and felt himself settle. "My body temperature has gone up—that's another thing that's different now. I rarely wear anything more than a shirt since the bomb."

"Why's that? The body temperature thing." She pressed an absent-minded kiss to his chest, which made him smile.

"Less surface area to disperse the heat."

"I would never have thought of that."

"The other thing I struggle with is not feeling connected to the ground. Before, my feet would be there, feeling the texture and terrain, sending continuous messages to my brain about where I was standing. Messages I didn't even register that I was receiving. Now, the ground seems far away most days."

"Like you're on stilts? Kind of."

"Aye, kind of."

She shifted to lie on her stomach, putting her chin on his chest. She humbled him with her beauty. He couldn't remember ever seeing a more beautiful woman. Inside and out, Isobel Sinclair was stunning.

"It must have been so painful. I can't even imagine what you've been through." There was compassion, rather than pity, in her eyes.

"It still is painful. Some days I go insane from the sensation of pins and needles in my lower leg or my foot. Phantom pains. On some level, my brain doesn't realise they're gone." He swallowed his pride and gave her the rest. "The worst part for me was feeling incapable. Having to rely on other people and pieces of equipment to get me up and going. Feeling like I wasn't a real man anymore."

Her smile was sexy as hell. "Oh, baby, trust me. You are *all* man."

He chuckled. "You're a nut, you know that? I'm pouring my heart out here and you're thinking about sex. Again."

"I admit nothing. But if you'd like to start over, I wouldn't say no." She batted her eyelashes at him.

"Give me a minute to recover. As you pointed out, I'm an old man."

"True." She glanced down his body to his legs. "Will you let me see you with them off?"

He hesitated. "It isn't pretty."

"Cry me a river, Mr Universe. You have more muscles than are probably legal."

With a shake of his head, he moved her aside and sat up. "You asked for it."

She lay on her side and watched as he released the suction valve on each of the cups holding his residual legs. Without looking at her, he slipped the prosthetics off and put them on the floor beside the bed. He sat there, waiting for her verdict.

His head jerked up when he felt a smooth hand run over the stump on his left leg.

"Badges of courage," she whispered as she traced a deep and ugly scar that ran up his thigh. "So much courage."

He looked around at her and saw only understanding in her face.

"You need to kiss me now," he said roughly.

She made a production of rolling her eyes. "Honestly, you are so demanding. Lie back and I'll force myself to give you what you need. But I want you to remember that this is a huge effort for me."

"I appreciate it." He lay back on the bed, expecting her to lean into him.

But, as usual, Isobel didn't do what he expected. Instead, she climbed on top of him and straddled his hips.

"Where are the condoms?" she said as she ran her hands up his chest. "I've decided to sacrifice myself for the cause."

"In the drawer. Want to let me in on what the cause is?"

"Why, I'm surprised you don't already know." She reached

into the drawer, the movement making her grind down on him and earning her a groan. "I'm sacrificing myself to bolster the male ego." She bit the pack and ripped it open. "Apparently, even though you have more muscles than Jason Momoa, you still need your ego to be stroked."

"Trust me, that isn't the part that needs stroking."

She handed him the condom. "Show me," she whispered.

And he did.

Twice.

Not bad for an old guy.

CHAPTER 24

"Elle," Callum barked, and Isobel wondered if that was his normal voice for talking to his team. "Why are you wearing fluffy pink handcuffs for bracelets?"

Isobel looked over at the computer expert, who was sitting at the dining table in front of her laptop, and sure enough, her wrists were ringed with novelty cuffs. They clashed with her blue hair and bright yellow sundress.

"Because the bas—" She glanced at Sophie, who was playing on the floor. "The…uh…moron took the key, that's why. Dimitri cut off the chain, but we can't get the bracelet part off. None of our keys work, and the nearest locksmith who could do the job is in Glasgow."

Megan started to laugh, and Callum cut her off with a look.

"You want to tell me which moron we're talking about?" Callum folded his arms over his grey Henley and glared at his team, which they all seemed really pleased about. Isobel couldn't help wondering if they were all a little insane, because if Callum gave her that look, she'd run for the hills.

"David. He's the ba—moron who did this," Elle said

grumpily. "He paid me a visit last night. Told me to stop hacking government databases and then he left."

"He left her cuffed to the bed, she means." Megan grinned.

Isobel spilled some coffee grounds. "There was a strange man in the house? How did he get past all of your security? I thought nobody could get in." She'd felt safe in the basement. In Callum's arms. In fact, she'd felt so safe down there that she'd spent most of the day hanging out in the basement with Sophie. She'd only surfaced an hour ago to make dinner for the team—her way of saying thank you.

His eyes softened when he looked at her. "You are safe. David worked with us."

"Plus, he's like a super spy," Megan said. "Think James Bond and the guy Tom Cruise plays in *Mission: Impossible*. He can get in anywhere. But he's a good guy, we think, so we're not too worried that he broke in."

"Not helping," Callum said.

"He's no super spy," Elle muttered. "He's an irritating pain in my backside, that's what he is."

"Why am I hearing about this now?" Callum arched an eyebrow at them. "Nobody thought that telling me about this when it happened was a good idea?"

Dimitri cleared his throat, and it was obvious he desperately wanted to smile. "Um, I tried to, boss. You were kind of occupied. Both times I tried."

"Way to go, Callum." Megan held up a hand for a high five, and he just glared at her.

The front door banged open and Ryan and Jack strode in.

"I need food," Ryan said. "Jack ate all the snacks in the car."

"I'm a growing boy." Jack flashed a grin at his mother.

"We haven't had anything since dinner, which we charged to Rachel's room." Ryan looked pleased with himself.

"She'll make you pay for that," Megan said. "And dinner was, what? An hour ago?"

Ryan shrugged and headed straight for the pantry. "An hour is a long time for my stomach."

"Clam." Sophie was fed up playing and had decided to harass Callum instead. He looked down at her and seemed a little bewildered at her sparkly purple clothes.

"Unicorns?" he muttered with a shake of his head when he saw the pattern covering her jeans.

Sophie was undeterred by his attitude. She lifted her arms in the air. "Up."

Without hesitation, he bent and picked her up. But Sophie wasn't satisfied sitting in his arms. She shouted, "Up," again and climbed onto his shoulders, managing to kick him in the face and yank handfuls of hair as she went. Callum frowned, but he was gentle with Sophie, patiently letting her climb all over him. Once she'd settled on his shoulders, Callum held her feet to steady her, as he very obviously ignored the smiles his team were desperately trying to hide.

Isobel felt a warm rush in the region of her heart and glanced at Jack, who was sitting at the table eating a bag of crisps. The sight of utter wonder on his face as he looked at Callum made Isobel tear up. With a sniff, she went back to making the coffee.

"Nice handcuffs," Ryan said as he sat down. He put a bag of cookies on the table in front of him and pulled them closer when Jack reached for them. "Mine."

"David," Elle said. "A gift from his visit last night."

"Kinky visit." Ryan looked at Isobel. "Can I say kinky with the kids in the room?"

"Who you calling a kid?" Jack snatched the bag of cookies from Ryan, making him lunge after it.

"Will you act your age for five bloody minutes?" Callum snapped at Ryan. "David is the least of our problems. Lake came up blank on our guy being a government operative. Nobody's missing an undercover agent. There are no rumours or whispers coming from any of his contacts, and he has some heavyweight contacts."

"Does that mean dead dude was a bad dude?" Jack said with sugar around his mouth.

"Aye." Callum frowned at Jack. "Have some orange juice with all that sugar. Get a bloody vitamin into you."

Megan made a suspicious coughing sound and appeared overly innocent when Callum glared at her.

"Here you go." Isobel put a glass of juice in front of Jack, who downed it in one long swallow.

"Where's the gear you picked up from Jack's friend?" Callum asked Ryan.

"We just got here. Can't a man have some food first?" He dumped a black leather sports bag in the middle of the table.

"You look at this already?" Callum asked Ryan.

"A glance. We were in a hurry. But I saw enough to worry," Ryan said as Dimitri upended the contents of the bag onto the table.

Callum turned to stone as he surveyed the contents of the bag. Isobel came to stand beside him.

"What are these things?" She pointed at some black devices that looked like headphones, but weren't. She knew—they'd tried to get them to work.

"Throat microphones." Callum picked up one of the four sets. "Used by the military, law enforcement, mercenaries. The sensors are placed against the throat and they can pick up even the quietest whisper. It's the way a team can communicate without making noise."

"Oh." Isobel stepped closer to him, wanting to feel the reassurance of his heat and strength.

Elle held up a strip of plastic with things welded onto it and wires jutting out. "This looks like it's part of a communications system. Might be related to the piece you found at the pawnbroker."

"These are detonators." Dimitri picked up one of the long metal rods with wire connections on one end.

"Like for bombs?" Isobel wrapped a hand around Callum's forearm and held on tight.

He tugged his arm away from her, and for a second she felt a surge of pain at the rejection, then he wrapped his arm around her waist and pulled her into his side. Right there. In front of everyone. She tried not to blush, but it was hard, and she wasn't sure she succeeded. Callum, meanwhile, ignored everyone else and carried on poking through the pile of odds and ends.

"Can you get prints off these, Elle?" Callum said.

Elle shook her head. "I'll try, but I wouldn't hold your breath."

Dimitri shoved some wires over to look underneath, and stilled. "Is that what I think it is, Elle?"

Isobel leaned in to see what he was talking about. There was a tiny glass cylinder, with wires and metal inside it, stuck to the back of some tape that was around one of the wires.

"Yes." Elle sounded awestruck. "That's an embedded version of an RFID chip."

"Dumb it down for the blondes in the room," Megan said, and tossed her long hair.

"It's a radio frequency identification chip." Elle looked up at them. "You all have them. They're in your credit cards. They store a small amount of information, like your bank details or the code to unlock a door. You know those cards they give you in hotels instead of keys? Those use RFID. That's what this is, only instead of flat and sealed into a card, it's in a tiny glass tube and can be implanted under the skin. I'm surprised it's still in one piece."

"I think the wires and the tape protected it." Dimitri

reached into his pocket, produced a Swiss army knife, pulled out the scissors and cut the piece of tape with the glass on it, off the messy heap of wires. He passed it to Elle. "I don't think they knew that was there." He looked at Callum. "You thinking what I'm thinking?"

"That this crew are all implanted with these things and that's why they were so desperate to get the body back?" Callum stared at the chip, looking grim. "And why they took the guy I dealt with at Isobel's house."

"I've heard whispers about covert groups using these implants," Elle said. "If no one knows you have them, then they're a great way to keep information secure."

"Yeah," Ryan said. "No way for the enemy to get hold of your access key unless they cut off your hand and wave it at the lock."

"And they'd have to know the implant was there in the first place," Elle said. "It's not the kind of thing you'd look for in a standard autopsy either. A tiny chip like this, implanted in the web between your thumb and forefinger would be pretty hard to find."

"I would still want to pick up a team member's body if I could, just to make sure the tech stayed secret," Dimitri said.

"I don't get it," Isobel said. "If these chips are top secret and they were so worried someone would find it in the body, why leave him on the beach in the first place?"

"I don't think they intended to be gone that long. I think they were planning on coming back for him," Callum said. "But you moved the body before they could get it."

She shook her head. "That's an awful big risk to take."

"Was it? You said yourself, no one goes into that cove."

"I agree with Callum's theory," Elle said as she typed. "I checked all the photos of the beach. There was one set of prints other than the Sinclair sisters' and the body. You saw two people get off the boat. It stands to reason that only one of them made it out of the cove."

"So," Dimitri said, "two people, carry something heavy off the boat. There's an argument. It gets out of hand. One of them kills the other and has a choice: deal with the body right then, or get his cargo where it needs to be while it's still dark." He looked at Callum. "I would have taken the cargo and come back for the body."

"But his plan goes to hell, because Isobel moved it while he was gone." Callum looked back at her. "How soon after seeing them get off the boat did you go down into the cove?"

"I called my sisters as soon as I saw them with what I thought was a body, and we went down to the cove a few minutes after we heard their car leave," Isobel said.

"And you were down there how long?"

"Twenty minutes, maybe."

Callum looked back at Dimitri. "Not enough time for him to deliver his cargo and get back to the body before Isobel took it."

"They must have been freaking out when they discovered the body was gone," Ryan said. "If the cops had taken it, it would have been autopsied by now."

Callum nodded. "And there was a chance they'd have found the chip. Elle, can you get the information stored on that thing?"

"If there's any information on there, I can get it," Elle said. "It isn't exactly hard. You can buy an RFID reader from a local tech store. It's just a case of finding the right one. But first, I can try my phone. It has tech in it that activates a passive RFID chip and transfers the information to the phone."

"Does that happen with bank cards too?" Megan said. "Because my account increased dramatically when I married

Dimitri, and I don't want to lose any of it. It's the best thing I got out of this relationship."

"That's my girl," Dimitri said with a grin. "Always making me feel loved."

She blew him a kiss.

"Yes, you can steal people's bank information with a decent phone and a little know-how." Elle dug out a piece of futuristic technology that doubled as a phone, and Jack actually whined at the sight of it.

"One day, I'm going to get one of those," he said with the wistfulness only a teenager could pull off over a phone.

"What the hell for?" Callum demanded.

"To text. To surf the net. To play games and take pictures. To look cool. What else?"

"When I was your age, a phone was for talking to people."

"Dude, when you were my age, dinosaurs roamed Scotland."

"I'm only forty-two, you cheeky wee arse."

"Ancient," Jack coughed into his hand, and grinned at Callum.

"Dinosaurs!" Sophie shouted. "I like dinosaurs." She smacked the top of Callum's head for emphasis.

Elle pressed the phone against the chip and swiped across the screen. A few seconds later, it beeped. "Got it. Let me send it to my laptop and we can see what it is." She tapped at her phone screen, then sat back at her keyboard, her fingers flying. Which looked very strange with the fluffy cuffs around her wrists.

"Right," she said. "We've got a couple of things on here, but not much. Remember that RFID chips only hold about two kilobytes of data. Which is nothing. It's enough to store your name, bank account number, the code to your door, that sort of thing, but not enough to store massive amounts of information. Basically, these chips point the way to something else. The one in your bank card sends the reader to your bank, that sort of thing." She leaned into the screen. "We have a bank account number, an IP address, and a code for something. No name."

"Where's the bank account located?" Dimitri said.

"Caymans, by the looks of it."

"Can you hack the account, see who it belongs to?" Megan asked.

"I doubt it. The security is multi-layered. I could try, but there's no knowing how long it would take and whether I'd be arrested before I got in."

"I don't get it," Megan said. "You hack governments all the time. Isn't a bank easier?"

"No. Banks are way harder."

"I thought you could do everything," Megan said with a pout. "You've shattered my illusions."

"Delusions, more like," Callum muttered. "Where does the IP address take you?"

"Checking that out now," Elle said.

Everyone in the room seemed tense, expectant, waiting for the information they'd been chasing to be revealed.

"It's dark web," Elle muttered. "This will take a few minutes."

Isobel looked at Callum, ready to ask what Elle meant. Callum felt her move and looked down at her. "The dark web is an area of the internet where information is exchanged anonymously. It's where you can buy and sell anything. If it's illegal, it's on the dark web."

"Oh." She spied Sophie's grinning face peering over Callum's head and couldn't help but smile at her. Her fingers were tight in Callum's hair, but he didn't say a word. "She's hurting you. Let me take her down."

"Darlin', she's three. There's no way she can hurt me. Leave her be. She's happy."

And that was when it happened. Isobel felt the bottom fall out of her stomach, and her head felt light. And she knew.

She was falling in love with Callum McKay.

She felt him still. "What is it?" He searched her face, looking for answers, and Isobel looked away, afraid that she gave away too much.

"N-nothing." She felt her cheeks burn.

"You're lying." It was barely a whisper, but she heard the steel in it.

"I'll tell you later. I promise. Okay?" She looked back at him and saw the worry there. "I promise," she said again as she leaned into him.

"Oh," Elle said. "That isn't good." Her fingers flew and she leaned into the screen. "That isn't good at all." She suddenly switched the laptop off, turned it over and removed the battery and the hard drive. She looked at Callum. "They backtraced me."

"Oh crap," Ryan said, and immediately lost interest in his food.

Suddenly, Ryan and Dimitri were running.

"I'll get weapons," Dimitri called. "Megan, check the windows and doors."

"On it," Megan shouted, and ran.

"They know our location?" Callum asked Elle.

"They were too fast, Callum," she said. "I'm sorry. I should have expected it after the way they'd wiped their operative's background. They have someone on their team who's really good."

"And they know we were looking into them? Here?" Callum said.

Elle was obviously shaken. "Yes."

"Callum." Isobel's voice shook. She couldn't help it. She felt like her whole body wanted to shake and keep on shaking until she disappeared entirely. "What's happening?"

He held her. "There's a team in the area. The ones who blew up your house. The ones who saw my face. They now know we're onto them and they know where we are."

"The police…"

"By the time they get here, it could be too late. And the local police force isn't equipped to deal with something like this. They won't be armed."

Isobel looked at Jack, who was paying close attention to every word Callum said. He looked so much older than his years. And he looked ready to fight. Her gaze shot to Sophie, who was tugging at Callum's hair and watching everyone with that intense expression she got. She knew something serious was happening, she just didn't know what.

Callum let go of Isobel's waist and stepped back. He put a hand on her shoulder and looked her in the eye. "The police might not know how to handle this, but we do. Dimitri, Ryan and I are ex-military. Elle and Megan have been in situations like this before now and have had training in handling weapons. You have to trust us. We will keep you safe."

Isobel nodded, just as a light above the door started flashing.

"The perimeter has been breached." Callum lifted Sophie from his shoulders and handed her to Isobel. "Get downstairs. Now. Jack, Elle. Move it. Downstairs."

They turned and ran.

CHAPTER 25

They didn't have comm devices, so there was no way for Callum to keep in touch with his team. They were working blind, and he didn't know what each of them was dealing with. The team had brought a few weapons with them and Callum had a couple stashed in his house, but it was nowhere near what they would need if they were under a full-scale assault.

His phone buzzed as he ran down the stairs, and his heart surged. Phone. Text. It was better than nothing. He pulled it out. Dimitri.

Three in front.

His phone buzzed again. It was Ryan.

Two back.

Five men.

Callum's mind was racing as he hurried the women and kids into the basement. The room wouldn't protect them for long. It wasn't a proper panic room; it was an old guy's project that Callum had tinkered with because he'd been at a loose end for months.

His phone vibrated. He looked at the screen. Megan.

Two big-ass cars coming down the drive.

"Who the hell are these people?" Callum muttered.

Elle pulled him aside as they rushed into the underground room.

"I got some information before the backtrace shut me down." She looked visibly shaken, which didn't bode well for what she had to say. It took a lot to shake Elle. "I saw the ACAB Militia logo."

Callum actually felt sick. His eyes shot to Isobel, who was terrified and desperately trying to hold it together for her kids. Jack was scared but clearly determined to help. He'd deliberately positioned himself between his little family and the doorway. Callum felt a surge of pride for the boy. His eyes went to the tiny three-year-old in Isobel's arms. Sophie's little thumb was in her mouth as she watched Callum intently. The trust he saw when they looked at him, changed something within him. His life clarified. He'd found his purpose again. It was standing in front of him, and he would do everything within his power to save them and give them the secure life they needed.

"It's going to be okay," he told them. "I'll make sure of it."

"What's the ACAB Militia?" Isobel asked.

Callum's jaw clenched as he quickly decided how much he should tell her. His memory brought up an image of the letters tattooed on the dead guy's knuckles. He'd thought it was the more common use of the acronym. He hadn't even considered other possibilities. If he had, they wouldn't have been in this position. He'd have taken Isobel and her kids far from Arness and called in every resource he could get his hands on to protect them.

But he'd been careless. And now, they were stuck in a makeshift bomb shelter with one of the most dangerous groups on the planet bearing down on them. And Isobel deserved the truth.

"It stands for Anarchy, Chaos, Annihilation and Brotherhood. They're a group of mercenaries, disenfranchised gang members and self-taught military. They're guns for hire. Terrorists without a country or a home. They take jobs that cause as much trouble as possible, and they only care about the money."

"Oh." Her eyes clouded with tears, and she blinked fast. "Okay. Thanks."

Callum touched the keypad on the gun safe beside the door at the bottom of the stairs. There were two handguns inside. Not enough to defend them for long. He took one out, inserted the clip and checked the gun. He did the same with the other one before looking at Elle.

"You still practising at the range?" After the Peru mission, he'd made it mandatory for everyone in the London office to know how to use a weapon.

"Yes. I can even hit what I'm aiming at now. Mostly."

That was good enough. It had to be. He handed her his spare gun. It looked completely out of place in her hand. Blue hair, yellow dress, pink handcuffs, purple Doc Marten boots —and a Beretta. Callum ran a hand over his face and hoped they wouldn't all die.

Jack put his arm around his mother's shoulders, his serious gaze on Callum. "What can I do?"

"Protect them. You still have the stun gun I gave you?"

Jack nodded, but it was clear he knew it wouldn't be enough against the team coming for them.

"Elle." Callum turned to his blue-haired tech. "You need to get hold of Lake. Tell him he needs to call in everything he has, and get it here fast. Tell him we don't know what we're dealing with, but let him know who it is."

She nodded, pulled out her phone and looked at the screen. "No signal. Hundreds of pounds on a state-of-the-art phone and it won't work in a bloody basement in Scotland."

Callum pointed at the wall. "Landline. Old school."

She rushed for the phone, her eyes wide when she looked back at him. "Dead."

They'd cut the line. That knowledge rippled through the room, ratcheting the tension up as it went. Isobel started to shiver, and Sophie made a little whimpering noise as she picked up on her mother's distress.

Callum tossed his phone to Elle. "Mine works on the stairs. You call. I'll cover you." He looked at Jack. "Get your mum and Sophie into the middle bedroom. Guard the door and stay there until I come for you."

Jack nodded and turned towards the room.

"What about you?" Isobel grasped his arm.

"I need to deal with this."

"Be careful." Her bottom lip trembled, and it was too much to take.

Callum clasped the back of her head and pulled her in for a quick and deep kiss.

"Wanna kiss too," Sophie demanded when he pulled back from her mother.

"This is too gross," Jack said, but there was amusement in his eyes.

Callum kissed Sophie's cheek. "Be a good girl for your mum. Jack, watch over them."

Jack nodded, and they ran for the room Callum had been sleeping in. The room he'd been hiding in for the past few months. Well, he was done hiding from life. He wanted to live large and live well, with the woman and kids who'd stolen his heart.

"Let's get going." He held his gun tight in his hand.

When Callum nodded, Elle turned the lock and they headed up the stairs, coming to a stop behind the door that led into the kitchen. There was an eerie silence, the sort of ominous silence that occurs right before a storm broke.

Callum gestured towards the wooden door separating them from the room beyond. Unlike the one downstairs, this one wasn't reinforced. He held a finger to his lips.

Elle nodded and, instead of calling, texted. The reply was instantaneous, the vibration loud in the stairwell. Elle replied and Callum stayed alert, straining for sounds that would tell him what was happening. Elle turned the phone so he could read Lake's reply.

Nearest armed response unit is in Glasgow.

Callum felt sweat break out on his lower back. That was three hours away by road. The phone buzzed again. Texts coming in fast.

Police mobilised. Coming in by air. One hour.

My team one hour later.

Active military regiment in Irvine. They are mobilising. 40-50 mins.

Stay alive.

The phone stopped buzzing. Callum looked at Elle's pale face.

"They aren't going to get here in time, are they?" she whispered.

No. They weren't.

Callum handed the phone to Elle because she was faster with it. "Text everyone," he whispered. "Tell them to retreat to the basement. Tell them help is an hour away. We'll defend the basement until it gets here."

Elle nodded and typed furiously on the tiny screen. She nodded when the message had been sent, and Callum inclined his head, indicating for her to go back downstairs. He kept himself between the upstairs door and Elle as they hurried downward. Behind him, he heard a short, sharp whistle, a warning his team were coming in, and then the door opened. Callum looked up to see Megan hurry through it. Dimitri followed, his gun pointed back into the kitchen, covering his wife.

"Ryan?" Callum mouthed at Dimitri.

He held up a hand to signal he'd be there in one minute. Ryan was obviously up to something, and Callum hoped to hell he knew what he was doing.

They hurried down the stairs. A gunshot rang out above them. Elle stumbled. Another gunshot. And then a massive explosion rocked the house, sending the four of them tumbling down to the door below.

The blast boomed through the basement, making the floor shift and the walls shake. Sophie started to cry, and Isobel held her tightly, shushing her.

"It's okay, baby. It's only a big bang. It's okay." She looked at Jack, who was facing the door, stun gun in his hand. "Jack?"

"I don't know what it was." His lips were a thin grim line, but his hands were steady.

"I should be the one standing guard," Isobel said.

"Then you should have taken kung fu classes instead of eating cake with the three witches." He smiled at her, trying to calm them all. Her boy, who wanted so badly to be a man.

"Okay, I agree, you have more skills."

"And more muscle." Jack's attention was back on the bedroom door. "I don't hear anything." He cast a worried glance over his shoulder at her sitting on the bed, Sophie curled in her lap. "Should I check?"

"And do what?"

"Medical help if someone needs it?"

"Callum told us not to leave this room."

"What if he's hurt?"

Isobel had to swallow back the bile that burned her throat. "He won't be." *He can't be.*

"He isn't Superman," Jack said, but he didn't sound convinced, and Isobel realised that Callum had become exactly that to all of them—their larger-than-life hero.

"He has bionic legs." It was the only thing Isobel could think to say. She wanted to reassure her kids, let them know that Callum did have superpowers.

"What?" Jack frowned at her.

"His legs." She rocked Sophie, keeping her voice calm and soft. "He lost them in Afghanistan and was fitted with prosthetics. They look like something the Terminator would have, all black metal and computer parts. They give him extra strength and power." That much was true—she'd seen how Callum had used them to destroy the man he'd fought at her house. "And he has all that training. He was SAS. Aren't they the elite of the armed forces?"

Jack nodded, hope in his eyes. "Yeah. So he doesn't have anything left of his real legs?"

"Nothing from the thigh down."

"No way." Jack looked as awed as she'd felt when she found out.

"I know. He really is Superman. Only he can't fly. I think." For all she knew, those high-tech legs had booster rockets built in.

Sophie took her thumb out of her mouth. "Wanna see Clam's legs."

Isobel kissed her hair. "I'll make sure he shows you once this is over."

There was a thud outside the door, and the three of them stilled. Isobel's hold on Sophie tightened, and she had to make herself relax before she hurt her daughter. She looked at Jack, who had to be as nervous as she was, but seemed to be a whole lot better at hiding it.

"I'm going to see who it is." Jack whispered.

"No!" Isobel felt sick. "Stay here."

"We're safe in the basement." Jack didn't sound so sure. "It could be someone who needs help."

"No." She shook her head adamantly. "Stay in here."

"I'll just sneak a look." He reached for the door handle.

A scream stuck in Isobel's throat. She couldn't get to him to stop him because Sophie was in her arms. "Jack!"

"It's okay, I have this." He held up the stun gun and opened the door a crack.

Isobel's whole body broke out in a sweat.

Callum! she silently shouted for him.

Jack put his eye to the crack.

It felt like time slowed down completely as she watched her son.

Sophie whimpered and Isobel stroked her hair.

"It's—"

The door crashed open, throwing Jack back into the room. He landed in a sprawl on the floor. And a man Isobel had never seen before filled the doorway.

"Where is chip?" His accent was heavy and difficult to understand. Eastern European, Isobel thought, but she had no idea which country.

Sophie started to wail as Jack jumped to his feet and aimed the stun gun at the man. With a sneer, the man lunged at her son. Isobel hadn't even noticed the knife in the man's hand until it was thrust at her son's gut.

"No!" she screamed, and rushed at them.

Jack froze, a look of utter disbelief on his face. The useless stun gun fell from his hand. A second later, Jack crumpled to the floor after it.

"No!" Isobel landed on her knees beside him, Sophie still in her arms. "Jack!" She reached for him, but the man grabbed her hair, stopping her.

Complete and utter panic paralysed Isobel. Jack lay sprawled on the floor, his head and shoulders propped up by the end of the bed. His hands covered the bleeding wound in his abdomen and his eyes were wide with shock. Sophie was wailing as she clung to Isobel. The tip of a bloody knife was pressed against Isobel's cheek. She couldn't breathe. Couldn't move. All she could do was sit there, frozen in horror.

"Mum?" Jack said

She hadn't heard that uncertain, shaky voice since he was a toddler, and it jerked her back into action. "It's going to be okay, Jack. It's going to be okay."

Sophie screamed, a siren that wouldn't stop. Isobel patted her back and tried to shield her with her body.

The hand in her hair tightened. "I ask one more time. Where is chip?"

Two more men came into the room, both armed with handguns. One leaned against the wall, watching with clear amusement. The other stood over Jack.

"What's taking so long?" The man beside Jack looked down at him and then across to Isobel and Sophie. Calmly, he lifted his arm and pointed the gun at Jack's head. "The wound is bad, but he might still live. If I put a bullet in his head, he won't. Answer the question or I pull the trigger. And then I'll get Arno over there to carve up the little girl."

Isobel could barely see through the tears streaming from her eyes so fast. "I don't know where it is. I don't."

"He's going to kill us anyway." Jack winced as he tried to look up at the man pointing a gun at him. "We know who they are."

"Do you?" The man seemed amused, but his eyes were blank and hard. "Who exactly am I, boy?"

"Jack, please," Isobel said, hoping he would stop talking. She wanted the men's attention on her, not on her children. Her babies.

Jack lifted his chin, his brow covered in sweat from the pain of his injury, but still he was defiant. Blood oozed over his hands and onto his jeans. Isobel sobbed. She was watching her son die while a monster held her in place.

"Jack, concentrate on staying alive." She looked up at the man with the gun. He seemed to be the leader. "Please, let me help him. I'll tell you everything I know. I promise. Please, just leave my kids alone." She was barely able to talk. She needed to get to her son. She needed to shield her daughter. She struggled against the hold on her hair, hoping he'd lose his grip and free her. He only tightened it.

"You'll tell me everything anyway." The man pointing the gun at Jack laughed, a cold, dark sound devoid of hope.

"Where is chip?" The guy behind her shook her hard.

Sophie screamed and screamed. There was no calming her, even if Isobel were able.

"I don't know where the chip is. I don't. It was on the table upstairs. The one in the kitchen. That's all I know."

"Who accessed it?" The man holding her hair yanked it to make her look up at him.

"The computer woman. Elle. I don't know anything else. I only just met her." *God forgive me for giving Elle's name to them.*

"Is woman still in house?"

"I think so. I don't know." She shifted her eyes to look at Jack. He was losing colour fast. There was a grey tinge to his skin that terrified her. And so much blood, everywhere, seeping into his clothes and down onto the rug.

"Mumma!" Sophie wailed.

Isobel swallowed the bile that burned her throat. "Leave my children alone. Don't hurt them. I'll tell you everything you want to know. Please, just don't hurt them."

"That depends on whether I get an answer to my question or not," the guy with the gun pointed at Jack said. "Just who do you think we are?"

A gunshot exploded through the room. Isobel screamed. The hold on her hair loosened and the man who'd been restraining her fell to the floor. Isobel flung herself away from him, reaching for Jack, desperate to get to him but terrified to let go of Sophie. She couldn't see the wound. But Jack had to have been shot—she'd heard it. The guy had to have pulled the trigger. *Oh God!* Her son had been shot. She reached for Jack, frantic. Sophie wailed, shaking so hard that Isobel thought she might vomit.

Oh God, my children. Save my children.

"I'll tell you who you are. You're the fucker who has ten seconds to put down his weapon or I'll put a bullet through your head as well."

Isobel's eyes shot to the door. She blinked hard. The silhouette was massive. Powerful. Confident. Deadly.

Callum!

"Superman," Jack whispered.

CHAPTER 26

They'd come in through the stupid tunnel his grandfather had insisted on digging. The tunnel he'd fought with the local council about because it came out on council-owned land beside the road. The tunnel that was recorded in council documents and was easy enough to find. The tunnel Callum should have filled the minute he'd moved in.

Callum aimed his gun steadily at the arsehole threatening his family, his finger on the trigger. The only thing stopping him from pulling it was the fact that his gun was inches from Jack's head. And the other guy in the room was pointing his weapon at Isobel.

"Well, if it isn't the famous Callum McKay," the arsehole near Jack sneered. "There's a lot of talk about you in Kintyre. They say you eat children for breakfast."

"No, I only eat wannabe mercenaries who threaten my family."

Callum saw Jack's eyes go wide. He'd deal with the boy later. Explain that he meant every word. They were *his* family. Jack was *his* son. Sophie was *his* daughter. And Isobel was definitely *his* woman. He wouldn't accept anything else.

"This *wannabe mercenary* is going to put a bullet in your kneecap for pissing him off."

Callum almost laughed. His knees were made of carbon and titanium. For the first time since an IED took his legs, Callum was grateful for the replacement.

"You'll be dead before you try," he said.

A flicker of movement drew his eye, and he caught sight of Jack's fingers slowly curling around the stun gun on the floor beside him. A million thoughts ran through Callum's head, but only one mattered. He had a chance to save his family. To get them all out of there alive.

"You think I should have Arno shoot the woman first?" the arsehole said. "Or the kid? At least it would shut her the fuck up."

Callum heard Isobel trying to calm Sophie. It was a wasted effort; both mother and child were far too traumatised for it to work.

Jack shifted the stun gun, gently touching it to the gunman's leg. Nobody except Callum was looking at the boy. Nobody saw what he did. Callum caught Jack's eye and nodded. The boy nodded back.

Callum felt resolve settle within him, the calm before the battle.

"Go ahead, take your best shot," he told the guy with the gun. "See if you can hit me before I hit you."

"Callum!" Isobel screamed.

"Fucking SAS think they're the kings of the world." The guy swung his gun towards Callum and pulled the trigger.

It all happened at once. The gunman shot at his leg. He felt the impact of the bullet hitting the metal, but all it did was shake his balance. Callum aimed at the guy pointing his gun at Isobel. He had one shot. One chance to take him out. And he took it. He hit Arno in the centre of his forehead and watched him fall. There was the unmistakable sound of electricity sizzling as Jack dealt with the other guy. The gunman spasmed and hit the floor hard. Callum turned his gun on the electrocuted man and pulled the trigger. Targets down.

"Callum!" Isobel's scream went right through him. "Jack, honey, look at me. Callum, help him!"

Callum came to his knees beside Jack, lifting his shirt to look at the damage. The knife wound was deep and bleeding profusely.

Ryan ran into the room and stopped dead. "What do you need?"

"Medical kit, kitchen."

Ryan ran, while Callum applied pressure to the wound. "What blood type is he?"

Isobel's eyes were glazed, showing signs of shock. Sophie was busy weeping into her mother, but she wasn't screaming anymore.

"Isobel, blood type?"

"O—he's O positive."

"Good, that's good."

Ryan rushed back into the room, kicked the dead guy out of the way and knelt beside Callum. "What we got?"

"Knife wound to the abdomen. He's lost a lot of blood. We need to transfuse. Who's O positive?"

Ryan, Megan and Elle all said, "I am," at the same time.

"Elle, you're up," Callum said. "The rest of you have better combat skills. Megan, come over here and put pressure on this wound."

She hurried to his side and took over applying pressure. Callum raked through the medical kit, grateful that his military training meant he kept more on hand than most people.

"Ryan, can you put a line in Elle, while I insert an IV in Jack?"

"No problem." Ryan grabbed what he needed and turned to Elle.

Callum ripped open the pack of sterile needles and started searching Jack's arm for an suitable vein.

"Did you mean it?" Jack's voice was a weakened rasp.

Callum didn't even need to ask what he meant. "Every. Single. Word."

"Never had a dad," Jack whispered.

Callum found the vein and inserted the needle. He looked at Jack, making sure he met his eyes. "You have one now, if you want me."

With a smile on his face, Jack lost consciousness. Isobel sobbed, bringing Callum's attention to her. There were tear tracks on her face, her hair was tangled and there was blood all over her. She held Sophie against her with one arm. The other hand held Jack's. Sophie had stopped crying, but was still whimpering. There was nothing Callum could do about that right now.

"He's going to be okay," Callum said to Isobel. "I promise you. We'll keep him alive until we can get to a hospital. I've dealt with a lot worse than this during combat."

She sniffed and nodded, but her eyes stayed on Jack.

"The door to the kitchen is barricaded," Dimitri said. "I'm going to do the tunnel now."

"Take these bodies and dump them in the tunnel first." Callum didn't want them lying there for Sophie and Isobel to look at. Plus, it would make whoever came down the tunnel after these guys think twice.

Dimitri picked up the nearest body, slung it over his shoulder and headed for the tunnel entrance.

They heard a massive crash and the sound of cracking wood.

"That will be the door to the kitchen," Ryan said as he finished with Elle. "Sit on the bed."

They were going the old-fashioned route and using gravity to get the blood from Elle into Jack. It wasn't perfect, but it might keep him alive. *No. It* will *keep him alive.* There were no other options.

There was a loud bang that made Isobel jump and hold Sophie closer.

"They're trying to get through the downstairs door, but they won't." Callum kept his tone matter-of-fact, hoping to ease her worry. "It's steel-plated. I put it in myself." He'd been having what passed as fun for him at the time, keeping his hands and brain busy while fortifying his grandfather's bunker. Now he wished he'd finished the job instead of messing with his grandfather's woodturning equipment.

Dimitri came back and carted away another body. There was another thud at the door.

Callum took a pressure dressing out of the med kit and moved Megan aside to fix it to Jack. There was internal damage and he needed a surgeon. The best Callum could do was stem the blood flow until they got to one.

"I don't think the knife hit anything important," he told Isobel. "The biggest problem is the loss of blood. Megan, get Elle orange juice from the fridge. She needs to stay hydrated."

Megan rushed away. She came back a few seconds later with clean hands and a bottle of juice. Ryan hauled the last body out of the room, and Callum heard Dimitri telling Ryan to barricade the door to the tunnel.

Another thud shook the steel-plated door, but it didn't give. It wouldn't give.

"Megan, keep pressure on here while I talk to Ryan and Dimitri." For once, his trainee didn't object to being left out of the loop. She knelt beside Jack and took over applying pressure to his gut.

Callum crouched in front of Isobel, reluctant to touch her because his hands were covered in Jack's blood.

"Isobel, sweetheart?"

She looked up at him, but she was struggling to fight the

effects of shock. Callum stood, pulled the blanket from the bed and wrapped it around her and Sophie.

"We're going to get out of this," Callum said as he crouched in front of them again.

Isobel's lip trembled as one huge tear rolled down her cheek. "Will Jack live?" she whispered.

"Aye." There was no way that boy would be allowed to do anything else. Not on Callum's watch. "I need to go deal with this situation. I want you to keep Sophie warm. I'll send in more orange juice for both of you, and you have to drink it. You need the sugar to help you cope with the adrenalin. Do you hear me, Isobel?"

She nodded, her attention straying back to Jack.

"Watch her," Callum ordered Megan and Elle before he strode from the room.

As he left, he heard Elle murmur encouragement to Isobel, and he was almost overwhelmed with appreciation. Walking wasn't as smooth as it had been before someone shot at him. His knee joint had suffered some damage. He could still move, but there was a stiffness that hadn't been there before.

"I'm getting really pissed off with people shooting my prosthetic legs," he told Dimitri as he came into the kitchen.

"You still able to function?" Dimitri said.

"Aye, I think it's just dented." Callum washed his hands in the kitchen sink, watching Jack's blood drain away and hating every second of it. "What are we dealing with?"

The two men had stacked every piece of furniture they could find against both doors. The team attacking them were still trying to get through the steel-plated door. The thuds and shouting were almost continuous. It was only a matter of time before they tried the tunnel entrance.

"There are at least seven men outside. All armed to the teeth," Ryan said. "As we came downstairs, two SUVs turned up. So there's more guys than the seven—sorry, ten, including the three you dealt with—that we know about."

"Weapons?" Callum dried off his hands, keeping an eye on the door to the room where Isobel and the kids were.

Dimitri held up his handgun. "I didn't fire, so I still have a full clip."

"I fired, but I still have most of my clip left." Ryan gave him a smile. "I took out the gas canister beside the building you use for woodturning. I got two guys coming out of their SUV."

"That was the blast," Callum said. "I've got half a clip, a spare gun Elle's holding and a box of bullets. But that's it. I wasn't exactly planning on waging a war out here."

"How long until the cavalry arrives?" Dimitri said.

Callum looked at his watch. "Forty minutes, maybe more."

There was nothing to say. They knew that forty minutes when under siege by a group like the ACAB Militia was a very long time to try to stay alive. Another thud against the door emphasised the point.

"How secure are we down here?" Ryan asked.

Callum cocked a thumb at the door leading up to the kitchen. "That's reinforced steel. The tunnel is narrow, so the chances of them using it to rush us are slim, but at some point they're going to figure out that the best way to get to us is to go through the floor of the house."

"Are there any parts that are concrete?"

"The section above the bathroom. That's the securest room down here. It's also the smallest. The walls aren't reinforced though, so if the militia get in here, they could break through the walls to get into the bathroom. Or just fire at them until the bullets make their way through."

"What if we put the women and kids in the bathroom,

pad the walls and barricade the door, then we go hunting," Ryan said. "We can go out through the tunnel."

"They used the tunnel to come in. They're probably watching the entrance. Plus, it's too narrow in there to defend ourselves coming out."

"We're stuck down here, aren't we?" Ryan said.

"Aye." Callum looked around. "But we aren't helpless. They're going to get in. It's a matter of time. We need to move the women and kids to the bathroom and then position ourselves so we can take out as many as possible once they get in here."

A large blast rocked the building. Sophie screamed and Isobel cooed at her. Callum could hear the fear in her voice.

"Let's move them," Callum said.

The men jogged towards the rest of their team. Megan looked up at them as they entered the room. "How long have we got?" she said.

"Ten minutes, maybe more," Callum said. If they were lucky. "We're moving everyone into the bathroom."

"No." Isobel held her son's hand tightly. "We can't move him. What if it makes him worse?"

Callum crouched in front of her and stroked her hair. "We have to. We have to keep you safe. There's a good chance these guys are going to get in here, and we need you in the securest room we have."

"Clam." Sophie's red face turned to him. "I'm scared."

He reached out and lifted her from her mother. "I know, baby, but we're going to get through this, okay? I need you to be a brave girl and help your mum and Jack. You can do that, can't you?"

She didn't look sure, but she nodded before wrapping her arms around his neck. Callum stood, turning to see Dimitri take the door off the closet. They would use it as a stretcher to get Jack into the bathroom.

"Come on, Isobel." Callum held out his hand. "Let the guys take Jack into the other room. We'll grab some bedding and make it comfortable for him."

Isobel didn't look certain, but she put her hand in his and let him tug her to her feet. Callum wrapped his free arm around her waist and pulled her into his body. Her bloodstained hands curled in his shirt.

"I'm scared too," she whispered.

"I know, sweetheart, but we're going to get through this." He kissed her hair, hating that the arsehole had used it to hurt her. "Trust me."

"I do."

He pressed his forehead to hers. "You're it for me, Izzy." Her hands tightened and she pressed closer to him. Callum leaned back. "Let's go."

They hurried to the bathroom, where the closet door was placed on top of the bath with Jack on it. He was still unconscious.

"Wash your hands," Callum said gently to Isobel as the rest of the team went to gather materials to barricade the room. Callum put the toilet lid down and sat Sophie on it, wrapping the blanket Megan handed him around her.

Once he'd settled Sophie, Callum unhooked Elle from Jack and attached a bag of saline solution to the line in her place. It wasn't as good as blood, but it would help.

"Why do you have that in the house?" Elle said as she put a Band-Aid on her arm. "It isn't exactly standard first aid stuff."

Callum almost smiled. "Hangover cure. From my days when hitting a bottle seemed preferable to dealing with life."

"Nutter." She shook her head.

Using cupboard doors and mattresses, Ryan and Callum padded the walls between the bathroom and the rest of the basement. Isobel sat on the toilet lid with Sophie in her arms, watching everything with wide eyes. Dimitri nodded at Callum, and Callum crouched in front of the woman who'd come to mean everything to him in such a short time.

"No matter what you hear," he said, "stay in this room. Do you understand?"

She nodded and tears started falling again. "Come back to me."

"You know I will." He cupped her cheek and pressed a kiss to her soft, soft lips. "Look after your mum, Sophie." He pressed a kiss to her head before turning to look down at Jack. He was grey, but still breathing. And Callum planned to keep it that way. He looked at the two women he was trusting to act as the last line of defence for Isobel and the kids. "Put the mattress and boards in front of the door once we're out. Stay in the corners, low to the ground. If anything starts coming through the walls, get as many of you as possible inside the bath. Jack will cope with the move if you have to do it." He looked at the gun in Megan's hand. "Shoot anything that comes through the door. If it's us, we'll let you know. We have about a half-hour to get through before backup arrives. Do whatever you have to do to stay alive." He glanced at Isobel, Sophie and Jack. He was coming back to them. It was his promise to himself.

Elle put her hand on his arm. "We'll protect them."

Callum nodded and walked out of the room.

"Kill as many as you can," Megan called cheerily after him.

CHAPTER 27

Silence had never been so oppressive. Waiting had never felt so torturous. Sophie had fallen asleep in Isobel's arms, exhausted from all the emotion and trauma she'd been forced to deal with. Jack was lying on the wooden door, on top of the bath. A tube ran from his arm to the bag of fluids hanging from the shower curtain rail above him. The dressing on his abdomen was getting redder by the minute, but the blood wasn't pouring out of him anymore.

"I wish I was out there," Megan said softly.

She sat on the floor facing the door, her back to the bath and her legs stretched out in front of her.

"You do?" Isobel couldn't comprehend such a thing. She wanted to be as far away from the guns and violence as possible.

"I'm only a trainee badass. I'm not allowed to play with the big boys until I graduate." Megan thought about it for a minute. "I need to ask someone how long this traineeship is. That was never specified."

Elle snorted a strained laugh. She was sitting Buddha style in the corner beside the door. "The answer is that it will never end. There's no way they'll trust you enough to let you out of the trainee programme."

"I'm beginning to think that there is no trainee programme," Megan said with a frown. "I suspect they just labelled me a trainee because I wouldn't go away."

"And because you were a loose cannon who needed to learn how to play with others."

Megan shrugged. "That too. I still wish I was out there, though. I really want to shoot these bastards." She looked at Sophie and winced. "She's asleep, right? My sister Claire has twin babies, and she's always telling me to watch my language around them."

"She's asleep," Isobel confirmed, and her eyes strayed to Jack again.

"This isn't your fault," Elle said.

Isobel turned to look at her. "I know. I did feel responsible, because I was the one who found the bag and sold its contents, and the one who moved the body. But then I realised I wasn't the one using the cove for illegal activity. And I didn't slit that man's throat. And I didn't blow up my house. And I didn't come here and stab my son. This isn't on me. It's on them."

"Well said," Megan said. "Let's hope the boys shoot them all."

They sat in silence again, straining to hear the slightest sound that would let them know what was happening. There was nothing. Isobel was so tense that she thought she might have a heart attack from the stress of it all.

"Twenty minutes to go," Elle said. "Someone should come to help us soon."

"The thumping stopped," Megan said. "I think the morons eventually figured out that they couldn't get through the door."

"I wish Callum wasn't out there," Isobel said before she

could stop herself. She knew he was more than capable and used to dealing with combat, but he was out there. Cornered. Waiting for an attack.

"This is what they do," Elle said. "I'm the computer person. I'm normally in an office, behind a desk. But these guys thrive on this stuff. They don't react like normal people. When you and I have gunmen bearing down on us, we freak out, we scream, we cry. These guys get calm, efficient. All their training kicks in and they block out everything except the fight in front of them. They were made to function like this. We don't understand it, but they are the best at what they do."

"Plus," Megan said, "if Dimitri gets shot, I've told him no nooky for at least six months. It's important to reinforce their motivation. Like puppies. They need training."

The blonde seemed completely serious, and Isobel caught Elle's eyes and saw that she too was caught between amusement and bewilderment. Isobel thought Megan would fit right in with the men on the other side of the door. There was a certain bloody-thirsty attitude about her.

"I hope you get to graduate to full-fledged badass soon," Isobel said. "You look like you'd really enjoy shooting people." Elle smothered a laugh, and Isobel flushed. "That didn't come out how I intended."

Megan grinned. "It sounded totally fine to me."

"Eighteen minutes," Elle said.

"I wish Callum was in here," Isobel said again. "Sorry."

"You're crazy about him, aren't you?" Elle said.

Isobel looked at her son and then at her sleeping daughter. "He's the best man I've ever met."

"But grumpy, right?" Megan said. "I mean, terrifyingly grumpy. Don't you think?"

Elle leaned forward and smacked Megan's leg. "He isn't grumpy with her."

"Oh, you're right." Megan looked at Isobel. "So when this is over, you totally have to come to London and hang out with Callum all the time. Sex obviously improves his disposition, and we could use a lighter atmosphere around the office."

Elle groaned. "You look at the two of us and you'd think the one with the blue hair must be the strange one. But you'd be wrong."

"What?" Megan said. "What did I say? She doesn't have a house. It blew up. She obviously loves Callum, and Callum loves her. Callum has a house. A big house. Where else is she going to go? And if Callum gets sex out of the deal, and we get a mellow boss, who loses here?"

Isobel found herself smiling and shaking her head. "I don't know what I'm going to do. I have a tendency to rush into relationships, and it never goes well. I've only known Callum a few days."

"Yeah," Megan said. "But they were intense days. And intense days should be measured like dog years. Emotionally, you've known him about a decade."

"Please come to London," Elle said. "I could use someone normal to talk to."

Isobel smiled. "He hasn't asked me." She wasn't sure she wanted to go, but there still hadn't been a conversation.

"Maybe you should ask him," Megan said. "Girl power and all that."

That wasn't going to happen. Isobel reached forward and held Jack's hand. He was still breathing normally, and that was good. She knew the women were trying to keep her mind off things and keep her calm. She appreciated it, she did, but it didn't change the fact that she was barricaded in a bathroom with her seriously injured son and her traumatised daughter.

"Fifteen minutes," Elle said. "Why does time slow down when you want it to pass?"

"Horrible things always slow down time," Megan said. "Like childbirth. Claire said her labour lasted almost four months. Grunt said it felt like longer."

"Grunt?" Isobel said.

"My monosyllabic brother-in-law. Built like a mountain. Looks like King Kong. Talks in grunts."

"Oh." Isobel looked at the door, wishing she could see through it to the rooms beyond. Was Callum even still out there? Had he gone out to fight the men upstairs? Would they hear it down here if he had?

"Fourteen minutes," Elle said.

"Stop counting. You're making it worse," Megan said.

And then an explosion rocked them. Isobel dove for the space on the floor between the toilet and the bath, holding Jack's hand and keeping Sophie pressed tightly to her. Sophie woke and started crying. Another explosion. Shouting. Another explosion, smaller this time.

And then the gunfire started.

They came through in three areas. A blast took out a section of the ceiling above the kitchen area, another the ceiling in one of the bedrooms and a third came from the tunnel. Callum was positioned behind the kitchen counter and fired up into the hole above him. Shots came back, but it was hard to tell if he hit anything.

He heard Dimitri rushing into the bedroom, and more shots were fired.

"We're going to die," Ryan said as he crouched beside Callum and fired at the tunnel. "And we're running out of ammo."

They heard a grunt from the bedroom, and a man came

flying out into the living area, followed by Dimitri. He launched himself at the militia guy, taking him out with a kick to the head. He grabbed the guy's ammunition belt, tossed his gun to Callum and strode back into the bedroom. A few seconds later, there was another explosion.

Ryan fired into the hole that had been blown through the tunnel barricade. "Building that barricade was a waste of bloody time."

Dimitri came running back in and headed straight for the kitchen. "Cover me."

Callum aimed into the hole above the kitchen and fired rapidly. Dimitri ran to a spot under it and lobbed a grenade through the hole.

The explosion brought down more of the ceiling. There was a scream. A gunshot. Silence.

"They're killing their wounded," Ryan said.

At the other end of the room, the rubble shifted and the muzzle of an automatic weapon poked through the debris blocking the tunnel entrance.

"Take cover!" Callum ordered.

The men dove for the floor as bullets sprayed the room.

They heard a thud, and someone landed on the floor beside Ryan. Ryan was on his feet in a second, knocking the gun away from the militia guy and kneeing him in the stomach. Ryan shoved him back into the living area and followed.

"Dimitri, the automatic," Callum called.

"On it."

Callum aimed for the hole in the ceiling and pulled the trigger as soon as he saw something. There was a grunt, and a man fell into the basement, landing in front of Callum. He was dead. Callum helped himself to his gun. Ammo wasn't going to be a problem after all.

Ryan was fighting hard with the other militia man.

"Get it done," Callum said.

Dimitri had snuck up beside the hole into the tunnel. The automatic weapon poked through again.

"Down!" Dimitri shouted as he lunged at the gun, shoving the muzzle upwards so that it sprayed the ceiling. His other hand thrust his gun into the space the automatic had poked through, and fired several shots. He yanked the automatic from the dead man's grip, turned it and fired into the tunnel.

Ryan took the guy he was fighting to the ground, yanked his knife from his belt and twisted it into the man's side.

"What took you so long?" Callum asked.

"Dickhead was hard to kill." Ryan got to his feet, taking the dead man's weapon with him.

There was a thud, and Callum turned in time to see a grenade land about a foot from him.

"Fire in the hole!"

He threw himself over the kitchen counter just as the blast went off.

Two more men dropped through the hole in the ceiling following the blast. Callum rolled to his back and shot at them. Another blast rocked the house above them. A militia guy ran into the living area from the bedroom. He aimed at Dimitri. Ryan was on him instantly, taking the man down. Gunfire rang out in the house above them. There was shouting. Running.

Dimitri covered the tunnel while Ryan covered the hole in the bedroom ceiling. Callum got into a better position to fire at anything he saw through the gap that used to be the floor of his kitchen upstairs.

More gunfire. This time farther away.

"I think our boys are here," Ryan said.

There was a noise from above.

"Don't shoot," someone called. "This is the Strathclyde armed response unit. Put down your guns."

Callum wasn't taking any chances. "This is Callum

McKay of Benson Security. I'd rather you show yourself first, and then I'll put down my gun."

"Callum," someone he recognised called. "It's clear up here." Lake Benson peered through the gap in the ceiling. "Casualties?"

"One. Jack Sinclair. Sixteen years old. Stab wound to the abdomen."

Lake stood back and spoke to someone else. Ryan and Dimitri came into the room, guns in hand. Dimitri held out a hand to help Callum to his feet. His right leg didn't work properly and the knee wouldn't bend.

"That's seventy thousand pounds down the drain," Callum said.

"Seriously," Ryan said, "you don't have insurance?"

"I don't think gunfire is covered."

Lake's face appeared again. "Get the door unblocked. The stairs are still functional. We have an ambulance on its way, ten minutes out. We'll get the boy to Campbeltown hospital."

Ryan and Dimitri started clearing rubbish from the door as Callum limped to the bathroom.

"Megan, don't shoot," Callum shouted. "It's safe to come out. Do you hear me?"

"About time," Megan shouted back.

He leaned against the wall, listening to the women clear the door. It flew open with a bang, and Isobel rushed out to him. She launched herself at him, and he caught her. Elle followed with Sophie, who watched everything with wide, red-rimmed eyes. Callum wrapped his arms around Isobel. She pressed her face to him and sobbed.

"It's okay. It's over." He stroked her hair and held out an arm for Sophie. His heart turned over when she held her arms out and leaned towards him. He gathered her to him. "It's okay," he told them. "I've got you now."

Ryan opened the steel-plated door, and Lake walked in.

As usual, the Englishman looked like he'd been to the country club instead of in a gunfight.

"About time you got here," Callum said.

Lake's mouth twitched into his approximation of a smile. "We managed to hitch a copter ride from Glasgow, otherwise you'd still be waiting for your rescue."

"Rescue." Callum scoffed. "We were handling it."

"Yeah," Ryan said. "We didn't need no rescue."

Lake's lip twitched again as he signalled to two members of his team, whom Callum hadn't met, and they rushed into the bathroom. "We'll get the boy upstairs. The ambulance should be here any minute."

Isobel pulled back from him and made to rush into the bathroom after Lake's men. Callum held her in place. "Let them get him out. We'll go with them."

"Be careful going up the stairs," Lake said. "You're missing some of the steps. And your house is rubble."

"Figures." Callum didn't care. He was holding the woman he loved, and that was all that mattered.

"Does this mean you're coming back to Benson Security?" Lake said as the men carried Jack past him on the closet door.

"Arsehole, you never let me go."

Lake gave him a real smile and followed Jack up the stairs. Callum looked down at Isobel, whose worried eyes were on her son.

"He's safe."

"I know. He's safe now." She turned to him. "But only because of you."

"Don't forget the rest of us," Ryan grumbled.

"All of you," Isobel said with a hiccup.

"You need help getting up the stairs?" Ryan asked, and the rest of his team stilled.

There was a time when even insinuating that Callum needed help would have gotten a man shot.

"Aye," Callum said. "Dimitri, take Sophie. Isobel, you follow them up. Ryan has to help me because my leg is stuffed."

She peeled herself from him reluctantly. Callum understood; he had to force himself to let her go. As he watched her disappear into the stairwell, Ryan came up and swung an arm around his waist.

"Lean on me, boss," he said.

With a growl, Callum put his arm around Ryan's shoulder, and they started towards the door.

"Does this new attitude mean I can start making leg jokes?" Ryan said.

"No."

"Are you sure? It seems to me that your argument for keeping me quiet is moot." Ryan grinned. "In fact, some might say you don't have a leg to stand on."

"When we get out of here, I'm going to shoot you."

"Well, we'd better *hop* to it, then."

"Moron."

Ryan just laughed.

CHAPTER 28

Jack had been in Glasgow's Royal Infirmary hospital for three days. They'd had to operate on him to fix the internal damage caused by the knife. Isobel had been assured that nothing major had been hit and he would make a full recovery. He'd always have a scar, but it would be small. Sometimes, when she was alone and no one was looking, she had to hold on to the nearest wall to stop herself passing out at the thought of her son having a knife scar.

Callum had gone with her to the hospital, making sure that she and Sophie were looked over and given the all clear. They were physically fine, although Isobel expected there would be many nightmares in her future. She looked up from Jack's bedside in the small private room Callum had finagled for them, to see him stride in. The fix for his leg had been simple—all it needed was a part swapped out—and Isobel had been relieved about that.

"How's he doing?" Callum put a plastic bag on the end of the bed and glanced at the kid's bed that had been set up in the corner for Sophie. He smiled when he saw she was cuddling the hippo he'd given her to keep the giraffe company.

"Good." Isobel smoothed back Jack's hair. It needed a cut. Something else to add to the list of things she had to do when they eventually got out of the hospital.

"I cleared everything up with the police," he said. "They don't plan on charging you with anything."

Part of the tension coiled inside her released. "That's great."

He nodded. "They're over the moon about the information we were able to give them on the ACAB Militia. They're tracing money from that account in the Caymans and they've found several threads to follow from that dark web address. The militia site had been closed down, but there's still enough to go on."

There was an awkward silence as the two feet between them seemed to stretch to miles. Isobel badly wanted him to close the gap and hold her, to tell her things would be fine, in that convincing voice of his. At the same time, she knew she had to stand alone and figure things out for herself. She'd made so many mistakes, and she was terrified of rushing into yet another.

"I saw on the news that the police had foiled an attack on the Scottish Parliament," she said.

"Aye, that's what they were planning." He looked around awkwardly. "That was your doing, Isobel. If you hadn't been so nosy, they would never have found out about the planned militia attack. In fact, they would never have known who was behind it. That's how the militia work. Someone else always takes the credit for their work. That's what they're being paid for."

There was another uncomfortable silence. "I'm sorry about your granddad's house," she said at last.

"I was only hiding there. It's time to rejoin civilisation." His eyes captured hers. "What are you going to do?"

She looked up at him. So tall and strong and indestructible. "I don't know."

She still had the three thousand he'd gotten for her. It was enough to start again.

He cleared his throat. "I want you to come to London with me. The three of you."

Isobel's breath left her in a rush. Part of her wanted to run to him, screaming yes at the top of her lungs. She fought that part of her under control and made the sensible choice. The painful choice.

"I don't think I can."

His head jerked back slightly before his jaw clenched. "You want to tell me why? We have something between us. Something important. The kind of thing that only happens once, maybe twice, in a lifetime."

"I don't trust what I feel. I've made so many mistakes. Twice I thought I loved a man, and twice I was used and cast aside. I can't keep risking myself or my kids."

"And you think I'd use you and cast you aside?" The vein in his corner of his jaw throbbed harder.

"No, I don't, but I don't know if what I feel for you is real. We had an intense week together. But it was still only a week. Do you really want me in your life knowing that reality will be far different from what we experienced? Everyday life with two kids is boring and repetitive and stressful. You really want that?"

"Aye." There was no hesitation.

Isobel blinked back tears. It seemed that all she did these days was cry. She couldn't do it any longer. She had to be strong. For her kids. For herself.

"I can never repay you for what you've done for my family," Isobel said, wanting to give him something. Wanting him to know how important he was to her, even if she couldn't go any further along the road he wanted her to.

"I don't want your thanks, or your repayment. You don't owe me anything." He took a step towards her. "I want you and the kids to live with me. I want a lifetime with you. I want to wake up in the morning and have you as the first thing I see. I want to teach Jack how to be a man and scare off every boy that dares sniff around Sophie. I want to be the man you lean on when you need it. I want a life with you."

Isobel sniffed, feeling her throat close up. "I can't. Not right now. I need time."

He nodded, taking a step back again. "I love you, Isobel Sinclair. Take what time you need to figure out what I already know, that you love me too." He strode towards the door. "Let me know if there's a baby."

And then he was gone.

Isobel sank back into the chair beside Jack's bed and put her face in her hands. Silent sobs racked her until she felt like she was going to die. A soft hand settled on her shoulder, and she looked up to see her sisters. Each face filled with love and sympathy.

"Oh, Izzy," Donna said. "What have you gone and done?"

"I sent him away." Isobel threw herself into Agnes' arms and felt her other sisters pat her back.

"Why on earth would you do that?" Agnes asked, but there was no censure in her voice, only sympathy.

"The Sinclair curse!" Isobel wailed. "I don't know what's real anymore. I can't tell if he's a good man or if I just want him to be. I can't think straight. I need time to figure out what's happening and if this whole thing is real. I can't make another mistake just because I fall fast and hard. I can't do that to my kids."

"You're scared," Donna said. "We all are. But you have more reason to be than the rest of us. You saw Dad make

Mum's life a misery for years, then you got pregnant and Darren ran out on you, then your marriage failed. Of course you don't trust that Callum is real. It's okay, we understand."

"Take all the time you need, honey," Agnes said. "If he loves you, he'll wait for you."

"I can't make another mistake," Isobel said as she clung to her sisters.

"We understand," Donna said.

"I don't," Mairi said. "The guy almost died protecting you. He saved Jack's life. He took you in and strong-armed the pawnbroker for you. What makes you think he's anything like the losers you've chosen before? *This* is the Sinclair curse. It isn't that we choose badly, it's that we can't recognise a good man when one bites us on the backside."

"Mairi!" Donna said. "Have some sympathy. Isobel has been through hell this past week."

Isobel sat back and looked up at her sisters. Donna and Agnes were sympathetic and annoyed with Mairi. Mairi was annoyed with Isobel.

Isobel faced her youngest sister. "Did I screw up?"

The sisters looked at each other.

"Maybe a little," Donna said.

"What do I do now?" Isobel asked. "Do you want me to run after him?"

"No," Mairi said firmly. "Take your time. Sort yourself out. And then go get him. Otherwise he won't know you mean it when you do."

"Where is this coming from?" Agnes said. "None of this sounds like you."

Mairi waved a hand. "Cosmo."

There was a pause before the sisters burst out laughing. Isobel smiled through her tears and her eyes strayed to Jack. He was awake and staring at her.

"Jack," she whispered, and reached for him. "You okay, baby?"

"Yeah." He licked his lips, and she reached for the glass of water beside his bed and put the straw against his lips. He sipped while Isobel and her sisters stared at him. All of them kept a hand on him somewhere, as though touch was the only way to assure themselves that he was still alive.

"You're going to be fine," Isobel told him.

"I know." He motioned for her to take away the straw. "Where's Callum?"

"He's gone back to London, I think." Isobel forced a smile.

Jack frowned. "That doesn't sound like him. What did you do?"

"See?" Mairi said. "Even the kid knows Callum is a good guy."

"Do you think that?" Isobel asked him.

"Mum, he took a bullet for you. He had a chance to run away and he didn't. He didn't run. He's the only one who hasn't run from us." His eyes drifted closed.

"I'll sort this out," Isobel said, but Jack was already asleep. She looked up at her sisters. "I just need some time."

There was nothing in Arness to go back to. Callum's grandfather's house was a crime scene, and the police had promised to call once he was allowed back in to see what was salvageable. Callum didn't care. There wasn't anything in the house that he was that attached to. Everything that meant anything to him was in the hospital behind him.

The strange thing was that he understood Isobel. She'd been damaged and didn't trust what was staring her in the face. She said she needed time, and he'd give it to her. But he wasn't going away. She'd learn that he wasn't like the guys she'd known before. He didn't run when things got tough.

And he didn't walk away from the woman he loved. Not ever. So he'd give her time, and then, if she didn't come calling, he'd go looking for her.

In the meantime, he had some things he needed to settle. He pointed his car towards Glasgow's East End and pressed the phone app on the dash while he did it.

"What is it?" Betty demanded.

"You owe me money, old woman." Callum negotiated Glasgow's city centre traffic as he talked.

Betty cackled. "You heard about your porn movie, then. No, wait, they call them sex tapes now. All the B-list celebrities have them because they think showing their bits on the internet will make them more money."

Callum let out a sigh and wondered yet again how he was going to pay Lake back for bringing Betty into his life.

"You'd better not have made any copies," he said.

"Now, would I do that?"

"Bloody right you would."

Her cackle was like nails on a blackboard.

"This is your only warning; I want all copies destroyed by the end of the week or I'm coming to see you." He turned into a narrow street, flanked by tall red sandstone tenements. Young men loitering on the corner stared at him. Graffiti covered the boarded-up windows of the ground-floor spaces that used to be shops. It was a dump.

"And you'll do what? I'm eighty-nine. Threats of violence don't work on me, son. You'll need to do better than that."

"I wasn't planning violence. I was planning on taking care of you. I hear there's a really nice nursing home in Aberdeen that you might like. I'm willing to pay for you to move in there and live out the rest of your life in comfort. Sure, it's far away from Invertary and they lock the residents in at night, but you'd be happy there. Okay, maybe not happy, but definitely contained. I have the paperwork all drawn up that says I'm your son and I have power of attorney over your health, seeing as you're suffering from dementia and all."

"You'd never get away with it."

"Try me." He hung up as he pulled the car up in front of the last close in the tenement.

There was a crowd of young men hanging around outside the entrance to the flats. They all looked undernourished and beady-eyed. Callum got out of the car. He'd worn his shoulder holster for this occasion, and made a show of putting his gun in it. Guns weren't a common sight on Scotland's streets, not even in areas like this, and Callum knew if the young men were armed, it would be with knives.

He strode towards them, making his way right through the middle of their group.

"The car stays in one piece," he said.

"Or what?" A young punk stood in front of him. Callum grabbed him by the nape and smashed his face into the wall of the building. He heard his nose break and then the howl of pain and disbelief. Callum kept on walking without saying a word, confident his message had been heard.

The close was remarkably clean, considering the state of the street outside the building. Callum made his way up the concrete steps to the top floor, passing doors that remained firmly closed. When he turned into the last flight of stairs, he wasn't surprised to find two men waiting for him. They were bigger and more muscled than the boys downstairs. One wore knuckle dusters; the other held a knife.

"Either of you boys called Ray?" Callum asked.

They shared a look. "No. Who are you?"

"I'm here to see Eddie."

"Eddie's no' takin' meetin's." The one with the knife pointed to the stairs. "Get oot of here while ye still can."

Callum didn't bother arguing. He jabbed the guy with the knife in the throat, disarmed him and threw his knife into the stairwell. The man fell to his knees, choking. The other guy threw a punch. Callum ducked, grabbed his arm and used his forward momentum to propel him down the stairs. He didn't turn to see what state he was in. Instead, Callum strode forward, lifted his foot and kicked in the door to Eddie's flat.

Inside, a woman screamed. Callum ignored it and headed down the hallway. A short, nasty-looking guy with heavy rings on all of his fingers and a gun in his hand stepped into the doorway at the end of the hall.

"Who the fuck are you?"

"Ray?" Callum asked, striding towards him.

"Ray, who is it?" someone shouted from inside the room.

Callum nodded. "Then you're Ray."

This was the man who'd hit Isobel and threatened to rape her. Callum saw Ray lift the gun. He wasn't fast enough. Callum grabbed the arm with the gun, bent back Ray's hand and released the gun into his own hand. Ray tried to head-butt him, but Callum sidestepped it, pressed Ray's gun to his thigh and pulled the trigger.

Ray squealed like a pig and crumpled to the floor. Callum pointed the gun into the room, aiming it at the two men sitting on the leather chairs with glasses of whisky in their hands.

"Don't move," he ordered them.

Then, keeping the gun pointed in their direction, he looked down at Ray. "You like to hit women, Ray? You liked hitting my woman."

"Fuck off," Ray said as he held his thigh.

"Wrong answer." Callum pointed the gun at him. "Hands up above your head, flat on the floor, or I put a bullet in the other leg."

Ray cursed, his face turning red, but he put his hands on the floor. Callum didn't hesitate—using the strength of his prosthetic leg, he stamped on both hands, satisfied when he heard the crunch of bones.

"That should stop you punching women." He looked down at the sobbing Ray, who held his hands against his chest. "But if I ever hear that you've done it again, I'll come back and smash the rest of you. Are we clear?"

Ray only whined, and Callum took that as a yes. He stepped over Ray and into the room. "Which one of you two is Eddie?"

There was silence.

"Should I just shoot both of you?"

"Him, it's him." One of the guys pointed at the other.

"Johnny, you fucking coward," Eddie said before looking back at Callum. "Who are you and what do you want?"

"Well, that's easy, Eddie." Callum pointed the gun at Eddie's head. "I'm Isobel Sinclair's man, and I want to put a bullet where your brain should be."

There was the unmistakable stench of urine, and a wet patch appeared on the front of Johnny's trousers.

"I'll keep away from her," Eddie said, tripping over his words.

"Now, why don't I believe you?" Callum stepped closer. "You told her to pay you with sex."

"It was a joke." The weasel started to sweat.

Callum looked at Johnny. "Does he normally ask for sex?"

Johnny nodded, and Eddie's face turned into a mask of pure menace that promised retribution. In Eddie's tiny pond, he was the one to fear. But Callum wasn't a local fish. Callum was a shark.

He lifted his foot and slammed it into Eddie's crotch, using all the force of his bionic leg. A high-pitched whine escaped Eddie, he grasped what was left of his dick and keeled over, landing in a heap on the floor. Callum wiped Ray's gun and pressed it into Eddie's hand. With Eddie's finger on the trigger, Callum pointed at the man's foot and shot. The scream was piercing.

Callum looked at Johnny. "If you want to live, leave now."

He ran, dropping the glass of whisky onto the carpet as he did so.

Callum pulled out his phone. "I'd like to report gunshots," he said to the police, and rattled off the address before hitting the end button. He leaned into Eddie. "This is your last warning. Go near any of the Sinclair sisters again and I will cut off your dick and staple it to your door. And, if the cops ask, I was never here. Ray kicked you, you shot him and then, being a stupid bastard, you shot yourself. I don't know how Ray's hands got smashed. You can make that part up."

He turned from the writhing man, stepped over Ray and left the apartment. Nobody stopped him on the way to his car, and he was pleased to see it was still in one piece. As he opened the door, he heard sirens. The cops could sift through Eddie's paperwork and deal with him and his henchman. Callum knew that there was enough evidence lying around Eddie's flat to put him away for a very long time. His source in Eddie's team had made sure there would be.

Callum put the car in gear and pointed it south.

It was time to go back to work.

It was time to head home to London.

CHAPTER 29

Isobel had never been to London before. She'd never been anywhere. The farthest she'd travelled was Glasgow. It'd been three miserable weeks since she'd let Callum walk out of the hospital. Three weeks to think about her life and what she wanted to do with it. Three weeks of camping in Agnes and Mairi's living room while the police went over the debris of her home. Three. Long. Miserable. Weeks.

And now she stood in front of Benson Security's London office, their very grand London office, and wondered what the heck she was doing. There hadn't been a single word from him. Nothing. Of course, she hadn't contacted Callum either, but still, the fact he hadn't even been in touch to find out if there was a baby or not worried her. Did it mean she'd missed her chance and he didn't want her anymore? She wouldn't blame him. She came with a lot of baggage.

"Hello?" The speaker on the wall came to life, making her jump. "Hello, miss, are you planning to stand out there all day or do you have some business with Benson Security?"

The voice was female and polite, but it still made Isobel

rub her clammy palms on her jeans. "Um, I was hoping to see Callum. Callum McKay."

"Do you have an appointment?"

"No." Should she have made one? "I can come back if he's busy." *Maybe.*

She wasn't sure she'd have the guts to go through this again. In fact, the only reason she was there this time was because she had backup. Her sisters and the kids had come with her to London. They were at the zoo while she went to talk to Callum, and would be there to pick up the pieces after she'd learned that this was all a mistake.

"What's your name?"

She cleared her throat, wondering if she should give up and walk away. "Isobel Sinclair."

"Oh my goodness! You're Callum's woman. Come in, come in." There was a buzzing sound and the door popped open.

Hesitantly, Isobel let herself into the building. The reception area had obviously been remodelled, and was more open than she would have expected. There were massive plants everywhere, a comfortable waiting area with beautifully upholstered seating that matched the colour scheme and a grand staircase that led upstairs. Dominating the space was a large reception desk, painted lilac, with the company logo in the centre of it, and behind that was an office. A woman peeked out of the office door, but didn't come any closer.

"Hi," the woman said shyly. "I'm Julia. The office manager. Sorry about the intercom. Our receptionist moved to Scotland and I don't like to man the desk."

"Hi," Isobel said, and awkwardly came to stand in front of the reception desk. "Is Callum in?"

Julia nodded and said to her shoes, "I've sent for Joe. He'll take you up to him. Callum's in a team meeting in the conference room. I'd take you, but Callum's been shouting a lot lately. A lot more, I mean."

"Oh." Isobel glanced behind her and wondered if she should sprint for the door.

"Don't scare Callum's woman, babe," a handsome man said as he came down the stairs. He looked Italian and sounded American, and his eyes melted at the sight of Julia. He held out a hand to Isobel. "Joe Barone, Julia's fiancé. You have no idea how glad we are to see you. Callum has been like a bear with a sore paw for weeks." Joe studied her. "Please tell me you're here to stay?"

"Joe!" Julia said. "That's between Isobel and Callum."

"Babe, he's driving us nuts. He needs his woman."

"So I've been told," Isobel said wryly.

She'd had daily phone calls from different members of Callum's team, extoling his virtues and begging her to take him back. She'd explained that she'd never kicked him out, she only needed time to think, but nobody paid any attention to her protests. She'd even had a scary old woman called Betty call her and tell her to get her backside to London and give Callum some nooky to calm him down. Isobel shook her head at the memory.

Joe's eyes sparkled with amusement. "Been getting some hassle from the crew, then?"

"And someone called Betty."

"Ouch. You attracted Satan's attention. That's not good."

Isobel wasn't sure what to say to that, so she said nothing.

"Come on, I'll take you up to him." He started for the stairs.

"Good luck," Julia called before disappearing back into her office.

"You aren't going to break his heart, are you?" Joe said as they went up the stairs. "If that's why you're here, it's probably best if you just leave. I don't want Callum losing his mind. He has the access code for the armoury in the basement, and I don't fancy trying to disarm a pissed-off Scot."

"As your fiancée would say, that's between Callum and me. But I'll try to keep him away from weapons."

"That's not the answer I was hoping for." Joe led her down a corridor towards what sounded like a riot. "Tempers are fraying. Especially Callum's."

As they approached the door, with the brass plate declaring it the conference room, Isobel could make out voices.

"I don't care if you think it isn't your job," Callum shouted. "Suck it up and get on with it."

Isobel shivered at the sound of the voice she'd missed so much these past weeks. It didn't even matter to her that he sounded like he was about to go on a rampage.

"I am not your employee," someone else said. "I'm your partner. I don't take orders from you or anyone else."

Ah, it was Rachel. Isobel cast a glance at Joe, and he shrugged. "Welcome to Benson Security, or as we fondly call it, hell."

"You're part of this team," Callum roared. "I'm in charge of this team. You need to pull your weight."

"And you need to get laid before we kill you," Rachel shouted. "For the love of Gucci, call the woman and tell her you're sorry. Do whatever it takes to get her back. Buy her things. Give her money. Promise her a pony. Just get her back before it's too late for all of us."

There was a roar of approval at Rachel's statement.

"For the last time," Callum barked, "we didn't split up. She needs time to think."

"About what?" Rachel asked.

"How the hell am I supposed to know? Can anyone really tell what a woman is thinking? She's had some bad experiences. She needed to think. I'm giving her time because I'm a bloody modern man! If I wasn't, I'd have thrown her over my shoulder and locked her up until she got over this crap."

"You're a modern man?" someone asked.

"Damn straight. I'm sensitive," Callum shouted.

Isobel started to giggle and covered her mouth. With a shake of his head, Joe put his hand on the door.

"You can see why we need you," he said as he pushed the door open. "Hey, Mr Modern Man, you've got a visitor."

Isobel followed him into the room and found everyone seated around a large table. Well, everyone except Callum and Rachel, who were standing at one end, glaring at each other. As soon as they all saw her, there was a cheer.

"About time!" Elle shouted.

Isobel blushed, and then her eyes caught Callum's. Everything else faded away. His jaw clenched, his eyes narrowed and then he was stalking towards her.

"Everybody out," Megan shouted, and people rushed past Isobel without even stopping to say hello.

Isobel froze, like prey in the sight of a large, hungry cat. Callum came right up to her, slammed the conference door shut, slipped his hands under her arms and lifted her. Her back slammed against the wall and his mouth was on hers. All before she'd even managed to take a breath.

SHE WAS HERE.

Nothing else mattered except the fact Isobel had walked into his office on her own two feet. She'd come looking for him and he didn't care why, because no matter her excuses, he wasn't letting her go this time. He threaded his fingers through her hair and clasped the back of her head as his mouth came down on hers.

Bliss.

Cinnamon-chocolate bliss. Isobel. Nothing tasted like

Isobel. Nothing slaked his hunger the way she did. Nothing felt as good in his arms as Isobel. He'd been lost without her. Trying to work his way back into his life while he felt like he really was only half a man. His better half was missing. She was in Scotland, trying to find herself. And he'd run out of patience waiting for her. He'd planned to give her until the weekend and then deal with the situation the only way he knew how—kidnapping.

She wrapped her arms around his neck and held on. He felt her legs curl around his hips as he pressed her against the wall. It felt right. Perfect. He felt complete for the first time in weeks. And he needed more. He needed to be inside her. Joined to her. Part of her.

She ripped her mouth from his and he moved to her throat, teasing the sensitive skin he found there.

"I came here to talk," she said breathlessly.

"Then talk." He just didn't plan on stopping while she did it.

Her fingers tightened in his hair, and she tugged his face up out of the crook of her neck.

"Callum, I need to talk." She didn't look like she needed to talk. She looked like she needed him.

"The only thing I want to hear is you telling me that you're here for good. Have you decided to give us a chance, Isobel?" Man, she was beautiful.

Her green eyes softened. "Yes," she said, and Callum wanted to roar.

A cheer went up from the hallway.

"Bog off!" he shouted at his team, but he'd lost the edge of anger that had been riding him for weeks. "Perverts," he muttered before taking her mouth in a kiss that was punishing and desperate.

Damn, he needed to get inside her. She pulled her lips from his again.

"That means taking us all on. Jack and Sophie too." She looked at him, anxiety in her eyes.

"I spent the past three weeks decorating bedrooms for Sophie and Jack. One is bubble-gum pink and covered in glitter. The other is full of video games and workout gear." He kissed her nose. "You're mine, Isobel Sinclair. And those kids are mine. Never worry about that."

The depth of emotion he saw in her eyes humbled him. His woman. His. And he was never letting her go.

"I'm not pregnant," she whispered against his mouth.

Disappointment washed over him. "Do you want to be? Because I want to be inside you right this minute."

She smiled at him and melted his heart. "Let's get settled first."

Aye, he liked the sound of that. "I don't have a condom here." Which meant he had to drag Isobel through the building, past his grinning team, and out the back door to his house at the end of the garden—all the while sporting a hard-on from hell.

She put her hand in the pocket of the denim jacket she wore and pulled out a little foil packet. "I came prepared, for a change."

He grabbed the condom and kissed her hard.

"It was Mairi, wasn't it?" He put her on her feet and started pulling off her jeans.

"Yeah," Isobel said with a giggle, because they both knew her chances of remembering were slim to none.

Callum stripped her of her jeans, shoes and underwear in record time before sheathing himself and lifting her again. When he had her pressed between his chest and the wall, the way he liked it, he stroked her hair. "I promise you foreplay the next time."

"You keep saying that," she whispered against his mouth, "but it never happens."

"I'll work on it." He reached between them and lined himself up with paradise.

They groaned as he slid into her wet heat. Muscles tensed as he fought for control, Callum rested his forehead on Isobel's. They stood like that, joined, together, complete.

"Never leave me again," Callum whispered.

"Silly man, I didn't leave you this time. I just needed to sort out my head."

"Are you done with that?"

"Yeah." She clenched around him, and they both moaned. "I fell in love with you in Arness." Isobel confessed.

Callum felt a warm glow spread throughout his body. "I'll always love you, Isobel Sinclair, and I'm going to spend a lifetime showing you that you made the right choice this time."

"Are you saying I broke the Sinclair curse?" She smiled, teasing him.

"Aye, that's exactly what I'm saying. Now give me your mouth, woman. I need to taste you."

And Isobel did just that.

READ THE FIRST CHAPTER OF CAN'T TIE ME DOWN

It was an idyllic summer's day on Scotland's Kintyre peninsula. The sun was shining. The sky was blue. Gentle waves lapped at the shore beside the village of Arness. The Atlantic was calm, and through the morning haze, you could just about make out the coast of Ireland. The old gray stone buildings dotted around the village were postcard perfect, and there was purple heather growing on the bluff above the sea. Even the fields seemed greener than usual. Mairi Sinclair half expected a couple of Disney-style bluebirds to flutter past her bedroom window, carrying a sheet to hang on the line. It was perfect, until someone pounded on her front door.

"You need to get your bum out of bed and answer that," Agnes, Mairi's roommate and sister, snapped from the bathroom. "I'm getting ready for work."

And there went her chance at a lazy day in bed.

Reluctantly, Mairi threw back the bedcovers, just as there was another round of loud and impatient thumping at the front door.

"I'm coming," Mairi shouted, with quite a bit of irritation.

She threw on a pair of jeans, and a t-shirt with a photo of Princess Leia holding a blaster and the words Don't Mess With a Princess and ran, barefoot, for the door.

And that was when Mairi realized there was no way to salvage her potentially perfect day.

Because at eight thirty on a Saturday morning, she opened her front door to find Captain Kirk smiling at her—a five-foot-four Pakistani Captain Kirk.

"You are surprised." He beamed. "This is good."

Mairi blinked several times, but no, he was still there. "Amir?"

"Who else would it be on this fine Scottish morning?" He tugged at the hem of his gold captain's uniform.

"Amir? In Scotland? At my house?"

He opened his mouth to say something else, but Mairi needed a minute. She held up her hand. "Just a sec." And shut the door.

"Who was that?" One of Mairi's three older sisters, Agnes, was dressed for a shift working reception at a hotel in Campbeltown. She wore a navy pantsuit, black heels and a crisp white shirt. Her golden blonde hair was in a neat French knot, and her makeup was minimal. She looked every inch the hotel manager she aspired to be, and no doubt would be, once she'd passed her final exams. "Mairi, pay attention. Who's at the door?"

"Amir." Mairi wondered if more coffee would help her brain cope with finding one of her online boyfriends on her doorstep.

"Amir who?" Agnes headed for the kitchen alcove in their living area.

"He's an online boyfriend."

Agnes stopped dead and turned slowly toward her. "One of your geeks is here? In person?"

Mairi nodded.

"How does he know your address? I thought the agency you work with said those details would never get out. I thought all those guys were supposed to stay firmly online."

"Yeah." There was nothing else to say.

When she'd been a little girl, Mairi hadn't dreamed of growing up to become a fake online girlfriend to a bunch of socially inept men. Nope, she'd dreamed of castles and princess gowns and white knights. She nearly burst out laughing at the thought. It was so far from the truth it was almost hysterical. In all of Mairi's childhood dreams, she'd been the knight. And she hadn't been concerned with saving any foppish princes, either. No, Mairi had wanted to travel the world, seeking adventure and fighting dragons. Instead, she was stuck in Arness, sharing a tiny flat with her grumpy-arsed sister and dealing with an unwelcome Captain Kirk wannabe. This was not the happy ending she'd hoped for.

"Why is your online boyfriend here?" Agnes demanded, jarring Mairi out of her maudlin thoughts. "How did he get your address?"

"I don't know." And she didn't like it. There was a reason this job was perfect for her: it meant she got to keep men at arm's length. No chance of getting in too deep. No chance of falling in love and getting her heart broken by trusting the wrong man again.

"Well, ask him!" Agnes did that toe-tapping thing that Mairi hated, which was even more intimidating when she was dressed in her power suit.

With a scowl at her sister, Mairi turned and opened the door, to find a beaming Amir, exactly where she'd left him.

"Amir, how did you get my address?" And why the hell did you fly all the way from Pakistan to visit me? Didn't he realize their relationship was fake? He paid her weekly—that should have been a giant clue.

He looked slightly confused for a second, before the smile

appeared again. "This is a test, beautiful Mairi. I can answer this most easy of questions. You yourself posted the address on your website page. Now, I have something of the utmost importance to ask you." He rooted around in his trouser pocket.

"Just a minute." Mairi shut the door and looked at her sister. "He says I put the address on my page."

Agnes pointed at the laptop sitting on their tiny dining table, and Mairi headed toward it. A few keystrokes later, and she was looking at a notice she had definitely not posted.

I'm tired of being single. As much as I've enjoyed being a girlfriend to all of you, I now want more. I want marriage and a family. I want my own happily ever after. The only problem is that I've managed to fall a little bit in love with all of my wonderful boyfriends. So, I'm giving you a challenge—a quest. Whoever gets to Arness, Scotland, first and wins my heart in person will win my hand in marriage. So, scale the walls of my castle, woo me with your knightly skills, and save this fair maiden from a life of loneliness and heartache. May the best man win!

It was followed by her street address, and a link to a Facebook page called Mairi's Wedding Challenge, where supposedly she was going to give updates as things progressed. The message ended with a Photoshopped image of her as Rapunzel, leaning out of a tower and gazing wistfully into the distance, presumably for her prince.

"I'm going to vomit." Mairi bent over and put her head between her knees.

"Get up." Agnes smacked the back of her head. "Get on that site and delete the post. Write something that tells all those sad sacks you talk to that this is a mistake."

There was a sharp rap at the door. "Mairi, my love?" Amir called.

Mairi swallowed hard and brought up the login page for

the Girlfriend site. She typed furiously. Three times. And then panicked. "I'm locked out. I'm emailing the owner." She opened her emails and typed. The answer was instantaneous. "Oh no." Mairi moaned.

"What?" Agnes peered over her shoulder.

"They've been hacked." Mairi resisted the urge to thump her head on the table. It wouldn't help anyway. "They're locked out of their own site and can't change the message either."

"Mairi, my little Scottish flower, open the door. I have something important to ask you." Amir's voice floated into the room.

"You need to deal with that." Agnes pointed at the door. "Now."

"Fine." Dragging her feet, Mairi went to their front door and opened it.

No Amir. A throat cleared. She looked down. He was on one knee, holding out a ring box.

"Mairi, my love," he said solemnly, "I must be asking you the most serious of questions. I wish for you to be my wife. Together we will explore strange new worlds and seek out new life and new civilizations. I wish to boldly go where no man has gone before. I wish to be your husband."

Mairi shut the door and leaned back against it.

"This isn't good," she said to her sister.

"You think?" Agnes glared at her.

"Mairi," Amir called, "is that a yes?"

* * *

"Heads up, there's a Wookiee coming this way."

Keir jerked up at his fellow mechanic's words and hit his head on the underside of the car hood. "What the hell are you talking about now?" he asked his fifty-two-year-old second-career apprentice.

Hamish pointed, and Keir looked through the open garage doors. Sure enough, there was a guy in a huge hairy costume, sauntering across what passed for the main street in Arness. Keir stepped back from the car, grabbed a rag and wiped the oil off his hands.

"Can I help you with something?" he asked the Wookiee.

"Argharghah!" the Wookiee said.

There was a split second where Keir wondered if he'd inhaled too many petrol fumes and this was the result. Then a short guy wearing jeans, and a t-shirt that said, Physicists Do It at the Speed of Light, ran across the road to join the Wookiee.

"Ignore him," the short guy said. "He likes to think he's being authentic. He won't talk anything but Wookiee while he's in his Chewbacca costume. He's a Star Wars purist."

The big, furry guy opened his mouth and warbled.

"No." The little guy frowned, "I'm not going to translate for you. Every man for himself." He turned back to Keir. "We're looking for Mairi Sinclair. The woman in the shop told us she lives over here, in the apartment upstairs. Do we get there through the garage, or is there another entrance?"

Keir put down the rag, folded his arms over his black tank, making sure they noted his muscles and tattoos, and stepped into their space.

"What do you want with Mairi?" The Wookiee opened his mouth to answer, and Keir held up a hand. "In English."

"She's going to be my wife," the little guy said with pride. The Wookiee roared with what was clearly a protest. The other guy scowled up at him. "How are you going to propose? She doesn't speak Wookiee. You shot yourself in the foot wearing that costume. It's not my fault I'm going to win."

Keir uncrossed his arms and pressed his fingers to his temples. "Win? What the hell are you two talking about?"

The smaller guy dug into his pocket and came out with a phone. He flicked at the screen before turning it to Keir. He found himself looking at a website called Girlfriends for Hire. And there was a photo of Mairi, smiling out at him from a fake medieval tower and telling him that she specialized in online relationships with geeks. Geeks? Keir shook his head and kept reading. Under her photo was an updated message to her "men." One that obviously hadn't been written by Mairi. For a start, it said she wanted to get married. If this was the real deal, he'd eat an oily rag and wash it down with antifreeze.

"Mairi wants a husband," the little guy said. "She challenged her online boyfriends to woo her." He looked up at the Wookiee. "Do people still say woo?"

The Wookiee shook his head and made some noise.

"Wait a minute," Keir said, as the words sank in. "Why the hell would you want a girlfriend who only exists online?"

"Hiring an online girlfriend is a sensible alternative to being alone forever." The little guy sounded like he actually believed what he was saying. "Most of us work in male-dominated industries, like tech or research. Or we live in isolated areas. We don't have a lot of time to meet women, and most of us don't have a clue what to do with them when we do. That's how we ended up on the Girlfriend site. For a small weekly fee, you get to interact with a woman who helps you learn how to, well, interact with women. It gives you confidence. Practice. That sort of thing. It's all aboveboard. Strictly no nudity." He looked so disappointed about the lack of nudity that Keir almost laughed.

The Wookiee started gesturing and making Wookiee noises.

"Yeah," the little guy said, "and it means we can get people off our backs about relationships. My parents totally stopped setting me up with random women once they'd Skyped with Mairi."

Keir stared at the two of them for a minute, letting the explanation sink in. A campervan rolled past the garage and came to a stop outside the village shop. Two more guys got out. One wore jeans, and a black t-shirt, and looked normal; the other wore a short-sleeved checked shirt, with a clashing tie. There were pens in his shirt pocket. It didn't take a PhD in logic to figure out Keir was looking at yet another "boyfriend."

"How many of you are there?" Keir asked.

The short guy checked with the Wookiee. "About thirty, we think. Mairi capped the number because she wanted to spend quality time with each of us."

More likely, she capped the number because that was the most her fluffy little brain could cope with. "And you all know each other?"

They nodded in unison, before the little guy said, "She specializes in geeks. And being geeks, we formed an online forum to talk about her. Kind of like a boyfriend support group, or a Mairi fan club."

"You don't care that she's fake-dating all of you?" Keir said.

"We're smart guys. We knew it was a business deal. And then she changed everything with her declaration. Now, the boyfriends are at war, and the forum has been disbanded until one of us wins her heart for real."

"You're serious. This isn't some kind of nerdy cosplay event? You really want to marry Mairi?" Keir glanced around, wondering if someone was going to jump out and shout "punk'd" at him.

"Dude, have you seen Mairi? She's hot, and she's a fangirl."

"Fangirl?"

He received a look of derision. "She can geek with the best of them. She knows the names of all the Star Trek TOS episodes, and she understands the wrongness of Jar Jar Binks."

The Wookiee said something, and the little guy nodded. "That's true. She doesn't know anything about anime. It's her one flaw."

Keir pinched the bridge of his nose. It was going to be a long, long day.

"I have a couple of questions," Hamish said from beside Keir. The older man folded his arms over the shirt and tie he insisted on wearing to work every day and frowned at the Wookiee. "In this internet message Mairi wrote, she told you to make your best effort to romance her. Do you really think dressing like a scabby bear and yawning your words is your A-game?" He turned to the little guy. "And for your information, doing it at the speed of light isn't something you should advertise, son."

Keir groaned.

"What am I going to do?" Mairi said. "I need a plan. And a rope ladder. Amir's blocked our entrance, and I can't use the stairs down into the garage or I'll have to deal with Keir. If I had a rope ladder, I could go out the bedroom window and make a run for it."

"You're acting like you really are Rapunzel," Agnes said. "Get a grip. You can't run. You need to get online and sort this mess out before the rest of your fake boyfriends turn up." She stalked to the living room window, which overlooked the Arness main street. "Oh, this can't be good."

"What can't?" Mairi rushed to her side, and together they

peeked out from behind the ancient net curtains that had come with the flat. There was a Wookiee standing in the middle of the road, staring up at their windows. "Crap, that's Jonas."

He waved, and she waved back. It was all a bit surreal. As she watched, two men came out of the village shop and climbed into a campervan. Twin men. "Oh no." Mairi groaned. "That's the Dawson twins." She watched as they maneuvered the van into the parking lot behind the shop.

"You're the girlfriend of twins?"

"Fake girlfriend!" Mairi frowned at her sister. "Why can't anyone remember the fake part?"

"But brothers? Is that even legal?"

"It doesn't matter if it's legal or not. It's fake!" Mairi stomped away from the window. "And to be fair, only one of them is a geek. The other one just talks to me for a laugh. He has plenty of real girlfriends."

"Oh, well then, that makes it okay." Agnes perched on the edge of their wobbly dining table. "As long as it's fake."

That was it. Mairi'd had enough. She stood in front of her sister, hands on hips, and glared. "You're being judgmental? Really? When my job helps pay for your study?"

"You're right. I'm sorry." Agnes didn't look even slightly contrite. "But twins?"

"Get a grip. It's fake. It's all fake. I don't even like bloody Star Trek!"

"Mairi," Amir called. "I am still waiting for your most glorious of answers."

Mairi stared at the ceiling while she counted to ten. The rope ladder idea was still looking pretty good. She could climb out the window, hitch a lift to Campbeltown and then catch a bus to London. Surely her sister Isobel would put her up for a week or two until this blew over?

"I know what you're thinking," Agnes said. "You can't

dump this on Isobel's doorstep. She needs time to get used to living with Callum. She deserves to be happy. She's spent her life sorting out other people's messes. You need to deal with this on your own."

Mairi sighed. Unfortunately, Agnes was right. Although… Isobel was living with a guy who was a partner in an international security company. A security company with a genius hacker on board. Mairi perked right up.

"I could call Isobel, though, and ask her to get someone to look into who hacked my web page."

Agnes frowned as she thought about it. "Don't you think that's a bit presumptuous? Asking favors from Callum's business when Isobel's relationship with him is so new."

"It's their honeymoon phase. This is exactly the time to get her to ask him for a favor. Right now, he'd do anything to get her to drop her pants. Not that it takes much." Their eldest sister was a bit loose with her favors. Unlike Mairi, who was nursing a born-again hymen.

"You could offer to pay," Agnes said.

They looked at each other and burst into hysterical laughter. Offer was all they could do. Every penny the sisters made had either gone into Agnes' degree or had been used to help Isobel pay off her ex-husband's debt.

"I'm calling Isobel," Mairi said, when she'd calmed down a little. "I have to do something. If she can get someone to undo the mess the hacker's made, and get me back on my web page, that would be great. I need to tell everyone that I don't want a husband. I can't let these guys turn up expecting me to marry one of them. I have thirty online boyfriends—what if they all turn up? What if they camp here forever? You can't underestimate the stubbornness of a geeky man. They'll view this like an online game and keep playing until one of them gets the highest score. Me!"

"Calm down," Agnes said helpfully.

"Calm down?" Mairi glared at her sister. "This is a crisis situation. These guys don't think like you and me. They think like Gandalf and Luke Skywalker! You read the website message. They think they're on some freaking quest to vanquish evil and win the fair maiden. Before you know it, they'll be out there, dueling with lightsabers and mocking each other's costumes. Trust me. I need to deal with this now, before it gets a whole lot worse."

"Hey, gorgeous," a deep male voice said. "I hear you're looking for a husband."

Both women squealed and spun toward the voice. Keir was standing in the doorway that led down to the garage, grinning like an idiot.

"See what I mean?" Mairi shouted at her sister. "It just got worse!"

Get Can't Tie Me Down now and read the rest of the story!

ABOUT THE AUTHOR

I'm a Scot, living in New Zealand and married to a Dutch man. I write contemporary romance with a humorous bent – this is mainly due to the fact I have an odd sense of humour and can't keep it out of anything I do! If I wasn't a writer, I'd like to be Buffy the Vampire Slayer, or Indiana Jones. Unfortunately, both these roles have already been filled. Which may be a good thing as I have no fighting skills, wouldn't know a precious relic if it hit me in the face and have an aversion to blood. When I'm not living in my head, I'm a mother to two kids, several pet sheep, one dog, four cats, three alpacas, two miniature horses, eight guinea pigs and an escape artist chicken.

Printed in Great Britain
by Amazon